H. Sample

The Horse and Dog not as they Are but as They Should Be

Vol. 1

H. Sample

The Horse and Dog not as they Are but as They Should Be
Vol. 1

ISBN/EAN: 9783337715434

Printed in Europe, USA, Canada, Australia, Japan

Cover: Foto ©Andreas Hilbeck / pixelio.de

More available books at **www.hansebooks.com**

THE HORSE AND DOG

NOT AS THEY ARE
BUT AS THEY SHOULD BE.

OLD AND ERRONEOUS THEORIES RELATIVE TO
THE MANAGEMENT OF THE HORSE BROUGHT
FACE TO FACE WITH THE FACTS OF THE
NINETEENTH CENTURY.

BY

H. SAMPLE.

TOGETHER WITH AN ELABORATE AND SCIENTIFIC ESSAY ON
HORSE-SHOEING ; ALSO, THE ORDINARY DISEASES OF
HORSES AND DOGS, AND THEIR TREATMENT,
WITH MANY VALUABLE RECIPES ;

HOW TO TELL A HORSE'S AGE UP TO 21 YEARS, AND

A FULL EXPLANATION AS TO HOW HORSES AND DOGS
ARE TAUGHT NUMEROUS TRICKS.

105 Illustrations.

Address Eastern correspondence to H. SAMPLE, Upland, Delaware Co., Pa.
Address Pacific Coast correspondence to H. SAMPLE, San Francisco, Cal.
Correspondents desiring answers will enclose postage stamp.

INTRODUCTION.

In undertaking the production of this work the author fully understands the gigantic task he has shouldered. There is probably no subject so extensively written upon and so little understood as the one in hand. I think the public will bear me out in the assertion that there are more balky men than balky horses.

In consideration of the magnitude of the Horse interests of this country—the total valuation being seven hundred and seventy-one millions nine hundred thousand dollars, that valuation of the same number of Horses actually being one hundred per cent. less than it would have been had all engaged in training and using this useful favorite of all the domestic animals—understood thoroughly the arts of training, shoeing and using the animal as they should. I feel positive that in this treatise I can convince every unprejudiced mind that much that has been written upon this subject by able authors is erroneous, and is not sustained by the practical experience of intelligent men of modern times, who will not take mere assertions as truth, unless it is sustained by the developments of careful and intelligent scientific and practical observation.

Having devoted eighteen years of my best days in teaching the proper methods of educating the Horse, and in a field that extends from the frozen and lakey regions to the Gulf of Mexico, and from the Atlantic to the Pacific Coast, I feel confident that the knowledge collected will be of great service to the Horse world. In connection with the training of the

Horse, I will give my full and complete system of telling the Horse's age, from the time of foaling up to the age of twenty-one years—a system that has given general satisfaction to the horse-men of the day—together with a complete description, in plain language, of the symptoms of the diseases of the Horse and the most modern and specific remedies for their treatment. An elaborate essay on horse-shoeing, that drew the first prize before the Scottish Society for the Prevention of Cruelty to Animals, will be added to my work. For the benefit and interest of dog-fanciers, I will give a chapter on the diseases, training and education of the dog. The author is still canvassing the entire country in introducing his new system of training the horse, and, at the same time, guarding against impairing their physical structure, or shortening their period of usefulness and profit. Should I succeed in this, I feel that I shall be a benefactor, and thereby secure my highest aim.   **H. SAMPLE.**

PRELIMINARY REMARKS.

The Horse is the noblest animal we have. He assists us in all the pursuits of life, guides the peaceful plow, and rushes into battle 'mid the roaring of cannon and the clashing of musketry. He is man's humble and obedient servant when properly trained and educated. While he is the most serviceable and useful, he is the most abused of any domestic animal, as the statistics of the societies for the prevention of cruelty to animals will prove. In the most of cases, the abuses that are practiced upon him arise from the fact that his natural laws and habits are not thoroughly understood by his manager.

Man is governed by education, while the Horse is governed by fixed laws and instincts. The general impression among men is, that the Horse is a very intelligent animal. Under this misapprehension they undertake to manage him from an intelligent standpoint. For instance, if the Horse stumbles or slips down the whip is applied as an instrument of correction ; if he should run away and smash up a valuable vehicle, he is taken by the bit, and in some instances the whip is used in an inhuman manner, as much as to say, "If you run away again I will kill you." If he balks in the street or road, the owner or driver, as the case may be, gets out of the buggy or wagon and rubs him on the head and neck, saying in horse language, "That is right, my little fellow, every time you stop I will rub and caress you." After waiting some time and getting his horse under way again, he jumps to his seat, and begins whipping the poor beast in the most cruel and inhuman way, saying to the horse, by his actions, "Every time you stop when I want you to go, I will caress you ; and when you go as I want you to, I will whip you." Most likely somebody is on the sidewalk laughing at him, and he, man-like, whips his horse to show that he is boss. The result is, the horse soon learns to stop to be treated kindly, and refuses to go, because he is whipped for going.

The same ignorance is displayed in the blacksmith shop. The horse or colt is led into the shop to be shod, and when the smith takes up his foot to prepare it for the shoe, a well-directed kick sends him half-way across the shop. The owner or groom, standing at the horse's head, rubs and pats his neck, saying to his understanding : "That's right, my little boy ; if he takes hold of your foot again, kick him clean out of the shop." The smith, in his anger, attempts to punish the horse as he deserves, but the owner refuses and says :

"This is my horse. He can kick you as much as he pleases, but you cannot punish him; he is *mine*. I will

take him to another shop and let him kick some other smith. He must be treated kindly, for this is my way of treating horses."

The proper way to do in a case of this kind would be to take the horse and put him through a regular course of instructions before taking him to the blacksmith shop, handling his foot and leg in every conceivable manner. If he kicks, punish him; and if he stands quiet and submits, treat him with kindness, patting and caressing him; thus showing to the horse what you want him to do. We will speak more fully upon this subject under its proper heading.

Another very erroneous idea exists not only in this country, but throughout the civilized world, and that is, when the horse is approached by the owner or groom he must use the word "Whoa!" when the horse is already standing perfectly still. If he goes to put the harness on—"Whoa!" if he goes to take the harness off—"Whoa!" if he goes to hitch him up—"Whoa!" and if he goes to unhitch him—"Whoa!"

In fact, when he mounts, dismounts, looks at his mouth to see how old he is, goes to him when he is hitched and standing perfectly still, or approaches him for any purpose whatever, the word "whoa" is invariably used. It is used so often that it becomes a habit so strong that a man seldom approaches the horse without using it. If a little boy should happen to go up to a horse without speaking to him, his father would take him to task, and tell him never to go to a horse without speaking to him. The little fellow will naturally say:

"Well, father, what shall I say?"

The father instructs him to say "whoa." The boy grows up thinking he has had a good teacher, who understands the horse, hence he practises what he has been taught, and in this way the word "whoa" becomes almost a household word. I say this teaching is all wrong. Some one will ask the question:

"What will you say? He will kick if you approach him without speaking."

Anything to give the horse warning of your presence will do, such as, "I'm coming, Billy, or Kitty," or any other word that you may choose to use. But never, under any circumstances, say "whoa" to your horse except he is in motion and you want him to stop. If the writer understands this word, it means "stop," and nothing more.

THE HORSE'S EYE.

Next we will call the attention of the reader to the Horse's eye. It is generally understood by horsemen that if the horse is approached, while in the stall, on the near side, he will stand quiet; whereas, if you go on the off side he will squeeze you up against the stall or kick you; demonstrating that he understands you on one side better than he does on the other, especially if he is of a high-strung, nervous temperament.

A horse that is trained to carry the rider in a circus ring, in coming out of the dressing room he will invariably turn to the right with the ring-master on his near side. He will notice every movement of the ring-master's whip and perform every requirement with accuracy and promptness. If the same horse is taken back into the dressing-room and then brought out again into the arena and turned to the left, he will be just as awkward, when looking at the ring-master with the off eye, as though he had never been trained at all.

A colt that is trained to run around a ring at the end of a halter, with the trainer on the near side, for some time it will be a difficult task to make him turn and go the other way, with the trainer on the off side.

This can be illustrated in another way. The Indian's horse is always mounted from the off side, and in traveling among the Indians we find it a difficult matter to mount their horses from the near side, which is the custom with the white man.

The same thing is true of the cow that is accustomed to being milked on the off side. If she is approached on the near side, and an attempt is made to milk her, she will start off or kick the bucket over.

The same thing is true of the ox that is trained to work gentle and quiet with the driver on the near side. Now let the driver go on the off side and his commands will not be obeyed, but the ox will be as green and stupid as though he had not been trained at all, thus proving conclusively to the writer's mind that if we want these animals trained to understand us on either side, we must educate both eyes.

This peculiarity of the horse I first discovered in performing with my educated horse, "Tom," some eighteen years ago. One day I accidentally got on his off side and commanded him to perform a trick that he had performed a thousand times while I was on his near side, but to my

great astonishment he refused to do it. After vain endeav-
ors to force him to perform the trick, I gave up and
returned to his near side, and at the first command he performed the trick as promptly as usual. If the reader is
still skeptical on this subject, we would advise him to make
the following experiment: Take any horse that is very much
afraid of a top-buggy, and hitch him to it, putting on a bridle
with only one blind, so that he can look back and see the
top of the buggy with one eye only. Work on him, hitched
in this way, until he is considered perfectly gentle and quiet;
then cut the other blind off of the bridle, letting him look
at the top with the eye that has been covered, and he will
at once become frightened at the top of the buggy, and attempt to run away.

This is not so in the human. When man sees an object
with one eye only, on looking at the object with the other
eye he will say, " that is the same," and if a boy is taught
a lesson at school with one eye closed, when he sees the same
lesson with the eye that was closed, he will understand it
to be the same lesson. If we want the horse to understand
a lesson with both eyes we must educate both eyes. In
conclusion on this point, I will state for the benefit of the
reader, that the optic nerve crosses or connects between the
eyes and the lobes of the brain in the human, while in the
horse, it goes directly from the near eye to the near lobe of
the brain, and from the off eye to the off lobe of the brain,
therefore making no connection between the eyes and the
lobes of the brain.

Another false idea prevails in regard to the Horse's eye,
that it magnifies objects to seven times their real size.
Hence, a man will appear seven times as large to the Horse
as he really is, and this gives man the power to control him.
If this was so, when the Horse was eating corn off the ear,
or going to bite an apple that was two inches in diameter,

he would open his mouth fourteen inches to receive it. Another case in point: let a horse see an opening in the stable a foot wide and he will imagine it seven times as large as it really is, and will attempt to walk through it. We might enumerate scores of instances that supporters of this theory might advance in support of their argument, but think the above sufficient to illustrate to the reader that the theory is incorrect.

Then again, some people will say there is great controlling power in the eye of man. In fact, while I was traveling through the Blue Grass Regions of Kentucky, a very prominent stock-raiser and physician, and a gentleman who was highly educated, in conversation with me one day in Lexington, stated that he could plainly see how I had such control and power over the horse. I had just been teaching a class of gentlemen my art of managing horses, and as an experiment for the class, I had a very high-strung, nervous horse, that was very much afraid of an umbrella, and I was swinging it all around his head, and he (the horse) stood perfectly quiet and gentle, and I remarked to this gentleman:

"How do you think I got the control of this skittish animal? If your ideas are correct I will own up before all these gentlemen." The doctor replied:

"When you took hold of that horse you kept your eye right on him, and he saw in your eye that you were determined and not afraid of him. There is great power in man's eye."

In fact, there are hundreds of people who believe the Horse, Lion, and the Elephant are controlled by this wonderful power in man's eye. For instance, they claim that the Lion-tamer, on entering the Lion's den, fastens his gaze on the Lion's eyes, by which means he controls the treacherous brute. I admit that the Lion-tamer does keep his eye on the Lion, but in the same manner that two men in combat eye each other narrowly to anticipate any offensive move on the part of the adversary. The Lion-tamer knows too well the nature of the animal before him, and for this reason he keeps his eyes constantly on the Lion to frustrate, with his club or whip—which he invariably has vith him—any offensive move on the Lion's part. If the reader of this book is of the opinion that those animals are controlled by the eye of man, let him, the first opportunity that offers, visit a menagerie and ask permission of the keeper of the Lion's den to enter the cage and try the experiment, and after having tried the experiment, I feel satisfied that he will become thoroughly convinced that his is a false idea. We know exactly how the Lion and the Elephant are tamed and trained, and what cruelties and harsh measures are resorted to in their education, thereby proving to the satisfaction of the author that the eye is not the controlling power.

THE FIVE SENSES OF THE HORSE.

The Horse has five senses—like the human being—feeling, seeing, hearing, tasting and smelling. The strongest of these five is the sense of feeling, and the part he feels with is the nose or tip end of the upper lip. This is what he examines all his food with, and in fact everything that he wants to understand, and by this means he can understand the nature and character of it better than by any other one of the senses. For instance, if a horse is afraid of a buffalo robe, or an umbrella, blanket or anything of that kind, when you throw it down in a small lot and turn the horse in, he may see the article or smell it; this alone will not suffice, until he goes up and touches it with his nose. After doing this a few times he will become satisfied that it is harmless and will not hurt him. Should a little breeze come up and move the umbrella, blanket or robe, it will frighten him some, because it operates on the sense of sight. We can familiarize the horse to any object with one of his senses, and that will not be sufficient for the others. We may have the horse educated to submit to any object touching him, on any part of the body, and if it should be moved quickly about him, thereby operating on the sense of sight, he will become frightened.

He may submit to the object being moved about him so long as it does not touch him, but if the object should touch him he is liable to kick or strike. Again, he might be educated to submit to have the object touch him or see it in all positions, without moving in the least, but should the same object make a noise, thereby operating on the sense of hearing, he will again become frightened. Therefore, if we want a horse to understand things thoroughly, we must educate all the senses.

An old gentleman once told me of a horse he owned that was perfectly gentle and quiet in "all harness," but would become uncontrollable on hearing a noise resembling the rattling of nails in a tin can. This bad habit he contracted as follows: The owner saddled him up and started for town, a distance of some four or five miles. When he got through his shopping and started for home, he re-mounted his horse, carrying in his hand a small tin bucket containing a few nails. Everything went along smoothly until the horse started into a trot. This caused the nails in the bucket to rattle and make an unusual noise, which operated on the sense of hearing, and the horse took fright and started to run away, thereby giving the old gentleman considerable trouble. He was finally compelled to throw away the bucket and nails in order to pacify the horse. Ever afterwards this horse would get frightened at anything on his back that would make a noise resembling that made by the can and nails.

We could relate numerous similar instances, where horses have become almost useless from being frightened at some particular object, such as a locomotive, steamboat, street car, load of hay or covered wagon, etc.

Another case in point: While traveling through Wisconsin, I visited a small village, and while there, sitting in the hotel, some gentleman came in, who had been to a funeral. In conversation with them I learned that the deceased, whose funeral they had attended, had been killed by his horses having ran away with him. I inquired into the particulars concerning his death, with this result:

On Decoration Day, when the military and citizens turned out to do honor and show their respect for the dead soldiers, by decorating their graves with beautiful flowers, the deceased, with his family, in a two-horse wagon, started for town. One of his daughters raised a parasol. The horse looked back and saw it. He took fright and ran away, throwing the deceased and his family out, killing him almost instantly and crippling several of the family.

While I was journeying through North Carolina, a very eminent physician was killed by his horse throwing him out of the buggy, when going down hill to the ferry-boat. The breeching-strap accidently broke. This, of course, let the crossbar of the shafts come up against him, and the touch frightened him and caused him to run away with the above result.

When passing through the State of Pennsylvania another accident of this kind was brought to my notice, that occurred in Reading. A lady's horse, that was considered perfectly quiet and gentle, took fright at the smell of a slaughter-house, ran away and almost killed the lady.

The examples of serious accidents I have given tend to

show the importance of educating the different senses of the horse so that such accidents may be prevented. The sense of sight should be first attended to, that the animal may become familiar with all objects that may come within his vision, and nothing will then frighten him, be it steamboats, cars, odd-looking objects or buffalo robe, etc.

Then again as to the sense of hearing : Accustom your horse to all sorts of sounds, that he may not be startled on hearing them, which might cause an unusual, awkward or sudden move on his part, perhaps straining or breaking some part of the harness or buggy.

The sense of feeling should be thoroughly educated, so that if the shaft-bolts drop out, thereby letting the shafts down on his heels, he would not become frightened at the touch, but understand that it would not hurt him.

Accustom your horse to everything that might tend to annoy any one of the senses. Then, and only then, can he be considered thoroughly trained to indifferently overlook all such annoyances as are likely to fall to the lot of any horse in constant use. I will speak at greater length on this subject further on.

In presenting this work to the public, I am well aware of the criticisms it will be obliged to undergo at the hands of horsemen and others. For, no matter how well a subject of the magnitude and importance of this one may be presented to the people, there will always be found those who will differ in their opinions, and are ready to severely criticise the ideas introduced.

I am well aware of the difficulties inventors and others devoted to progressive theories have encountered in their laudable efforts in the advancement of scientific principles. Professor Morse, in introducing the wonderful telegraphic system, had cold water thrown on his invention by men of learning and ability. By way of illustration : The gentlemen who were chosen from different parts of the United States to represent the people in the halls of Congress, in 1843, we would naturally suppose to be men of much learning, intelligence and integrity, who would represent the interests of the people to the best of their ability. But Professor Morse, in presenting his invention before Congress, met with severe criticism and opposition at the hands of those gentlemen, and it was not until 1844 that Congress granted him a small appropriation for the establishment of a line from Baltimore to Washington, a distance of only forty miles.

The result of this little experiment is that the whole civilized world has become one vast network of telegraph wires, and it is now considered one of the greatest inventions of the age.

We look back over the history of railroads, and see the first little road that was built in the United States, between Schenectady and Albany, New York, distant only sixteen miles, traveling at the rate of ten miles an hour, with a stationary engine on top of the hill to haul up and lower down the small train of cars. We see the engineer, who was imported from England, with his broad-brimmed hat and swallow-tailed coat, his barrel of wood and water on the tender of the locomotive, and we look on top of the car, and see the brakeman seated, with his foot on the brake, ready when the whistle blows " down brakes," looking more like a stage-driver in comparison with our brakeman of the present day. The small coaches, with seating capacity for six or eight persons, look small indeed when compared to our magnificent and commodious Pullman Palace sleeping, dining and parlor cars, accommodating fifty to sixty persons each, making up a train of a dozen cars or more—all drawn by a single monster locomotive that climbs the snow-capped Rocky Mountains with apparently little or no effort, bringing the

Atlantic and Pacific shores within a few days' travel of each other, thus binding and strengthening the bonds between our Eastern and Western people. When the first steamboat steamed up the Hudson River, it was looked upon as a miracle ; and, as the hundreds of spectators who lined the shores, gazed with awe and curiosity at the movements of the walking-beam of the craft, many of them concluded the end of all things was approaching.

We next call your attention to the wonderful invention of Mr. McCormick, to whom we are indebted for that very ingenious, useful and valuable piece of machinery, the reaper and self-binder. See with what opposition his machine met with—first, because it was an unheard-of thing ; and again, because the laborer saw how it would do the work of many men at comparatively a small cost. They even went so far as to intimidate the farmers who had purchased a mower, threatening to demolish it on sight. The reaper of that day was a heavy, cumbersome thing, necessitating the employment of four strong horses to haul it through the grain, whereas now they have so much improved, simplified and lightened, at the same time increased its usefulness, that two ordinary horses will walk through the fields of standing grain, cutting, binding and throwing the straw in rows, ready to be picked up by the farmer.

By these few instances mentioned, it will be readily seen by the reader that all new and progressive attempts at improvement have invariably met with the severest criticism, opposition and condemnation.

The author being aware that he is advancing many new, original and scientific ideas relating to horses, anticipates much criticism ; but is confident from his long and varied experience, that if the reader will properly consider and experiment with the methods recommended in this work, he will be ready to accord them the credit justly due their merit.

We are familiar with the various methods employed by the numerous horse-trainers throughout the United States and Europe. Such men as the justly celebrated Rarey, who went to Europe and tamed the vicious horse Cruiser, and afterwards brought him to the United States, exhibiting him on the stage in all the principal cities, creating no little excitement and curiosity by his many performances.

We also have a very high opinion of the widely known and highly esteemed horse-trainer R. H. Rockwell, who drove his educated horses, Star and Tiger, without lines, bits or bridle, through the streets of all the principal cities of the United States and Canada, attracting the attention and admiration of all persons who witnessed his wonderful performance.

We might mention numerous other inferior horse-trainers who have been traveling throughout the United States, teaching various methods and systems of training horses, and could give every strap rope and appliance used for the subjugation of the horse, from the days of Sullivan, the Irish Whisperer, down to the present day, but this would take up too much of the reader's time to no purpose.

The author will do away with all these patent bits, bridles and appliances, and show that the wildest and most vicious horse can be managed with a common, ordinary set of harness, such as is used ordinarily on the farm, in the livery stable, or by private individuals.

In examining the works of the celebrated gentlemen we have just mentioned, and various other writers on the subject of managing horses, I find their universal opinion to be that the horse is a very intelligent animal, and they have endeavored to manage and control him from an intelligent standpoint.

Now the writer will endeavor to prove that if the horse had half as much sense as is attributed to him, he would kick the heads off of more than one-half of the people who undertake to manage him. We will endeavor to prove before we get through that the horse is a machine to a certain extent, and is controlled and managed the same in the hands of a good horseman as the locomotive is controlled by a skillful locomotive engineer, with one exception, to manage and control the locomotive, we must have an artificial motive power, while the horse has been supplied by nature with motive power. In order to make a horse start, stop, turn to the right or left, in fact to go where and when we want him to, we must understand how to control him.

We put the bridle on, with the bit in his mouth, take hold of the lines, pulling to the right or left, according to the way we want him to go. And when the horse is trained and educated properly, he will obey every command, and he has not the intelligence to resist our control.

The horse is eight times stronger than man, and had he the intelligence to resist our commands, we could do nothing with him.

In order for a man to be able to manage a locomotive, he must be educated and taught how it should be done properly, and in accordance with the structure and purposes for which the machine was constructed. He must know how and when to start, stop, slacken or increase the speed; when to feed it with fuel and water, and how much to give it, otherwise serious results may follow.

The same remarks will apply to the intelligent handling of the horse. To fully control his every movement, and guide his footsteps, the man must first be taught the best methods of getting control of the animal—to learn his weak or strong points, that he may take advantage of them to impress certain things or acts on the horse's mind. He must learn the cause and effect of every movement of the horse, and the most likely impressions caused by certain methods of training.

The locomotive engineer thoroughly understands every part of his engine and the relation of each part to the others, and the effect of any effort on his part to guide and control it. So must the man be educated to understand the horse's natural laws that govern him, and devise means and adopt plans to overcome him and make him what he was intended to be—man's humble and obedient servant. While man has the power to manage and control this noble animal, he should not abuse it in the way and manner in which some cruel and unprincipled men do, by hitching him to loads too heavy for him to draw, and whipping and abusing him because he is unable to pull it—thus getting his horse balked—and driving him to death because he is willing to go; hitching him in the hot sun or in the cold and bleak winds—sometimes in severe storms without blanket or covering—while, perhaps, the owner or driver is snugly housed and warmly clad.

If the horse was intelligent he would not submit to this treatment, but would break his halter or bridle and seek a place of shelter.

In 1880 the writer was in Chicago, engaged in teaching his system of handling the Horse. His attention was called to one of the most cruel and outrageous performances that was ever permitted to go on in a civilized community. O'Leary, the celebrated pedestrian, and Jack Haverly, the well-known minstrel man, erected, on a large lot at Lake Front, an immense tent—the largest, perhaps, ever put up in Chicago—for the purpose of conducting a go-as-you-please race of horses against men, lasting six and a half long days and nights.

While the men were allowed to go as they pleased, resting when they felt so disposed, the poor, suffering dumb brutes were compelled to go as their masters dictated. One of the horses died before the conclusion of the race, and another died shortly afterwards. Their deaths were caused by the cruelties practiced on them with whip and spur, and by heartless driving beyond nature's limit. There were five or six horses entered in this race, and at the conclusion the poor animals were completely exhausted and broken down.

We have no objections to men walking themselves to death if they feel so disposed, but we have a very serious objection to the forcing of horses into these unnecessary and unprofitable exhibitions.

We will here take occasion to remark that, had these horses been possessed of one-half the sense, reasoning power and intelligence that is generally accorded them, they would most assuredly have rebelled against such brutal treatment as they experienced during this race, and demolished the canvas, dispersed the spectators who, by their presence, encouraged such brutality, and kicked the heads off the managers.

This outrageous performance was allowed to go on, undisturbed, under the eye of the Society for the Prevention of Cruelty to Animals.

We could relate instances without number, to sustain our argument on this point, that had the horse the intelligence credited to him he would never submit to the treatment he receives at the hands of many who are engaged in handling, driving and working him. We are convinced that the above will clearly illustrate our ideas to the careful reader.

A great many people mistake the natural instinct of the horse for intelligence.

Should night overtake a horse in the woods or thicket, at a place where he had never been before, his natural instincts will guide him home ; whereas, if an intelligent man be placed in the same predicament, the chances would be in favor of his wandering aimlessly about all night and perhaps all day, until he found some person to direct him on his way.

If a horse and man are on a sinking steamboat on the river, during a dark night, and both are obliged to seek safety, the horse will boldly strike out and swim to the nearest land, while the man may be a good swimmer, yet if he cannot see the shore, even if it be within easy reach of him, is as likely to swim into the middle of the channel as he is to go to the land.

A little pig placed in a sack, and taken in a buggy some five or six miles from home, if it should accidentally get loose will return, even if it has to swim rivers and cross ditches to do so.

A man with all his intelligence, if taken away from any place under the same circumstances and in a strange locality, could never return to the original starting point without receiving aid from some one or by the use of scientific instruments.

The bee, in wandering miles from its hive, gathering honey from flower to flower, on securing a goodly store of sweets, takes a direct course to its hive, or, as generally spoken of, makes "a bee-line for home."

Man with all his intelligence, education and scientific acquirements, even had he wings and was able to fly like the bee, could never find his way home in a direct line, as does the little busy bee. From this, we hold that man, with all his attainments and acquired knowledge, is unable to perform the mysterious feats that the horse, hog, bee, and we might mention hundreds of other animals, fowls, insects, etc., go through every day.

But we must not lose sight of our main subject, and will return to the education and training of the horse.

MANAGEMENT OF THE HORSE.

HOW TO BREAK A COLT PROPERLY.

The first important consideration in the management of a colt, is the proper selection of a yard, corral, or lot, clear of all obstacles that would be at all liable to injure him, and also to have a fence around the place of proper strength and heighth to prevent him from jumping out.

We would suggest that the yard or corral be some thirty-five or forty feet square, if convenient.

If the colt is domesticated and halter-broke, lead him into this lot or corral. Prepare yourself with a pole some ten or twelve feet long, from an inch to an inch and half in diameter, made of hickory, ash, or any hard, tough wood, sandpapered smooth.

If he is not halter-broken, drive him into the corral with other stock, then turn out all the others.

Take one end of the pole in both hands. Now proceed to handle the colt with the other end. This at first may scare or excite the colt very much—but get him in one corner of the corral. Then reach out your pole and touch the neck or withers as though it was your own hand. We can do this, knowing that if the colt should kick or strike, the trainer will be ten or twelve feet away from him, and will not get hurt.

Handle and touch him with this wooden hand until he becomes reconciled to the sense of touch. As the colt becomes more docile, the trainer can keep rubbing and touching him on the neck with the pole, and gradually approach closer and closer as the colt gets used to being touched.

If he should whirl and attempt to kick, handle him a little roughly with the end of the pole, and get him into the corner again, and proceed as before, rubbing him on top of the neck with the pole until he will allow you to approach close enough to enable you to place your hand on him, being careful not to reach out your hand too quickly for fear of frightening him by the sudden motion of the hand.

Remember all this time that the colt does not understand what you are going to do. When you succeed in getting your hand on him, rub him very gently and quietly until you can rub about the head and neck. Do this for some little time, then take a common five-ring leather halter, and place it on the colt's head quietly and easily.

Be careful, in placing the strap over his neck, to do it very gently, so that it will not strike his neck, causing him to jump and escape.

When the halter is on him, take hold of it and draw his head toward you slowly, rubbing the colt with the right hand along his side and back until you can get it back near the tail.

Be careful all the time that the colt does not whirl and kick at you. As soon as the colt will submit to this, catch him by the hair of the tail with your right hand, holding firmly to the halter with the left hand at the same time. This will bring him into a circling position, and cause him to move around. Give him a few quick swings around, holding firmly to the head and tail. This will soon make him dizzy; then slacken up a little on the tail and he will stop.

Then tie a single knot in the hair of the tail, draw it tight and hold the knot firmly in your right hand; divide the hair evenly between the knot and the end of the tail with the fingers of the left hand; slip the lead of the halter between the hair of the tail, and draw the head and tail together, or near enough to get his body in a circling position, making the halter fast to the tail with a half hitch, and let him go. [See cut No. 1.]

No. 1.

But be careful at first not to tie him up too tight, as this will cause him to whirl around very fast and make him fall down, which is unnecessary.

Use your judgment according to the horse you are operating on. If he is high-strung and of a nervous temperament, it will not be necessary to tie him as short as if he was of a dull, stupid disposition.

When the colt is fixed in this position—head and tail—his strength is divided against itself. The more he pulls with his head on the halter, the more he pulls his own tail. He will soon learn to stand hitched, and we are sure that a colt hitched in this way will never learn the bad habit of breaking the halter.

The philosophy of this system is to impress the colt at once with the fact that he cannot break loose.

He can lie down, walk about, run around, etc., still he is hitched and can't get loose.

The natural instinct of the colt is to pull upon anything that may be placed on his head or neck, and we take this method of putting pressure on the head.

The next duty of the trainer, after the horse has submitted to this treatment and has learned to stand perfectly still, is to take the pole used in the first instance, holding on to one end and handling the colt with the other. This may start him to going again. [See cut No. 2.]

No. 2.

We now want to operate on the sense of feeling, and by having this pole touch him while he is going around, he will soon find out that it will not hurt him, and will stop as before.

The object in view, in handling the colt with the pole, is to accustom him to being touched all over. If he should kick or strike, do not be alarmed, but keep the end or side of the pole touching him on some part of the body all the time. While he is going around, handle his front and hind legs with this pole, being careful at the same time not to hurt him.

It will take from three to five minutes to accustom the colt to being handled all over with the pole.

This will prepare the colt for the harness. Now, while

he is still under the influence of this whirling around, un-
fasten his head and tail and put on the harness as quick as
possible.

The colt will stand perfectly quiet for two reasons—first,
because he is dizzy from whirling around ; and, second, because he has been touched all over with the pole, and the
touch of the strap or harness will not frighten him.

I use a common set of harness, with a common jointed
bit. Have the bit as large as possible, so as not to cut and
scar the colt's mouth.

Put the harness on the colt and tie the traces into the
ring of the breeching, and instead of putting the lines
through the rings on the saddle, put them through the shaft
tugs and fasten them to the bit, using long lines, so as to be
out of range of the colt's heels—never using any check-rein
in breaking a colt.

Now you are ready to teach your colt to guide.

The lines should be placed in this manner, so as to give
us a leverage power on the side of the colt, to force him to

No. 3.

the right or left. Instead of attempting to make him go
straight ahead, first teach him to turn readily to the right or
left. (See cut No. 3.)

Instead of pulling on the lines slow and steady, pull with

a quick jerk on one line, turning the horse half way around, then reverse. This will teach him quickly that he must come around when you pull on the line. Then let him go straight ahead or around the corral. Every little while turn him around quick and short, forcing him to go the other way. When he turns easily and readily by a pull on the line, then he is ready to be taught to stop and start at your command.

While he is walking or trotting around the corral, say "Whoa!" Of course he will not understand what this means. Then pull up sharply and quickly on both lines. Repeat this until the colt will stop at the word "whoa." This will generally take from five to ten minutes.

Secondly, you want to teach your colt to start promptly as well as to stop; this you can do by touching him sharply on the heels with the whip. Always use common sense in the use of the whip and do not slash and welt him all over the body.. You had better have no whip at all than to use it injudiciously.

When you command a horse to move forward never repeat the command, and if he refuses to start promptly then touch him keenly on the heels with the whip.

Now, your colt is taught to turn to the right or left, and stop readily at the word of command. And when he does stop go up to his side quietly and gently, pat and rub him, showing to him that when he obeys your command you will treat him kindly, and if he refuses to obey, you will punish him by jerking the lines.

The next operation with the colt will be to get him accustomed to the sound or crack of the whip.

This you can do in a very few minutes by taking hold of the end of the lines in one hand, cracking and snapping the whip with the other. Allow me to say here, that your lines should be sewed together and not buckled, as the buckle will have a tendency to tear and cut your hands.

Every time the colt starts forward jerk sharply on the lines, and he will soon learn to stand quietly while the whip is being cracked about him.

Every time he stands quietly while you are cracking the whip, approach and caress him.

When this is accomplished and you can hold him with perfect ease, we have another lesson to impart to him.

Let your assistant take hold of the long pole and stand in the centre of the corral, while you drive the colt around him. Have your assistant touch him quickly on any part of the body with the end or side of the pole. (See cut No. 4.)

No. 4.

This will represent some break-down, and be very likely to frighten and startle the colt again.

Stop the colt as soon as possible, keeping your assistant still touching him lightly with the end of the pole. Start up your colt again, and repeat this until he submits to being touched with the pole.

While he is in motion, walking around the corral, touch

him lightly with the pole on the legs and belly, getting him accustomed to being touched all over.

This lesson is to prepare him for receiving the shafts, and he should be handled thoroughly with the pole in every place where the shafts and cross-bar would be likely to touch him, even in the case of an accident, as this treatment is really to guard against accidents that may occur at any time after he is hitched up.

Always be sure that you can hold your colt when he is excited or frightened.

Most any person can hold a colt that will not try to get away; but *you* want to be able to hold him when he is trying his best to get away.

After the colt has submitted to all of the above treatment and goes along kindly and gently, it would seem as though he was ready to be hitched up.

You will bear in mind, however, that thus far the colt's senses have been but partially educated. Now take an old tin can of any kind that will make a noise; tie it to the hair of his tail and allow it to drag behind him, so as to accustom him to the rattling of a wagon or any other noise likely to be made while he is on the road. (See cut No. 5.)

No. 5.

Drive him around on a walk at first, then in a trot. If he attempts to run away, stop him as quickly as possible, and bring him to a walk again.

Repeat this lesson until the colt has become familiar with the noise made by the tin can tied to his tail.

Always have the can tied far enough from his heels so it will not become tangled about his legs.

The next lesson to teach the colt will be that of becoming accustomed to the sig'.t of an umbrella, or anything likely to meet his gaze suddenly on the street and frighten him.

This can be done in a few minutes, by letting your assistant take an umbrella, opening it suddenly in front of him while you are driving him around the corral.

If he whirls and attempts to run away, straighten him up quickly with your lines and make him go past the umbrella.

Repeat this until he becomes accustomed to the sight of the umbrella. Then we have him educated to understand the sight, touch and sound.

This lesson will be sufficient for the first day.

If the colt, during this training, should get into a profuse perspiration before putting him away, it is essential that he should be "scraped out" and rubbed perfectly dry, and good care taken to prevent his catching cold.

The next day, take the colt into the corral and harness him, and commence to train where you left off, driving him around, testing him with the pole and can.

If he is easily handled and managed, after handling him a few minutes, he will be ready to hitch into the shafts or along-side of another horse, as the trainer may think best.

We always prefer hitching them in shafts first while in the training yard.

Where the colt is hitched to the cart as explained in another part of this book, you will see the breeching strap is not fastened, but hanging loose, as represented in cut No. 6. This is done so that the cross-bar of the shafts will touch him when he stops, in fact, when you put the colt in the shaft for the first time you should allow the cross-bars to

touch him, and if it seems to alarm him, he needs more training with the pole before he is hitched in to prepare him to
receive this unusual touch without becoming frightened.

No. 6.

A colt handled this way for one hour—say, half an hour
each day, will be better broken and safer than if handled in
a gentle, quiet, easy manner for six months.

We believe that it is necessary to test the colt in every
conceivable manner before risking our lives behind him in a
buggy or a wagon.

On the same principle, the boiler on a steamboat is tested
by the Government Inspector, by putting on a cold-water
pressure before getting up steam, to ascertain whether the
boiler has the requisite strength to resist the pressure
brought to bear on it by future use.

If it will stand the cold-water pressure, which is greater
than that produced by steam, the Inspector pronounces it
safe, and then, and not until then, will the owners be permitted to get up steam and run the vessel.

On the same principle, we consider it safer to " test the
colt " in every conceivable manner to guard against serious
accidents that are likely to occur every day with a colt that
is handled in the old-fashioned way.

When the trainer has hitched the colt up, and is driving him on the road, it will be necessary, for a few days, to watch his every movement closely.

If he should attempt to kick, run, or do anything that is objectionable to the trainer, punish him with the bit, and he will soon learn to act right, because he is punished only when he does wrong.

A colt will often kick, strike or bite as a means of protection to himself, and not because he is naturally vicious; and the trainer must remember that the colt was not made for the harness, but the harness was made for the colt.

There are a great many people under the impression that the colt was made for the saddle, harness and bridle. This is a mistaken idea. The saddle, harness and bridle were made for the colt, and when we put them on him, we violate the laws of nature, and as self-preservation is one of the laws of nature, the colt may kick or attempt to run, in order to protect himself.

In order to illustrate this, we will say :

If a fly should alight on the horse's neck he will shake his head to remove it ; if it alights on his breast he will put his mouth down to bite it off ; should it alight on the side of his body, he will put his head around to do the same thing ; if on his front leg, he will stamp his foot on the ground quickly ; if it alights on his rump, he will switch his tail and sometimes kick up ; if on the hind leg, he will kick with his hind foot to remove it.

If we take a pin and prick him lightly, he will do the same as he did to remove the fly.

So that should any other object touch him he is likely to do the same in order to protect himself. Hence the necessity of accustoming the colt to the sense of feeling, hearing and seeing, as directed in the preceding lesson.

The writer is of the opinion that every colt and horse, let

him be ever so gentle, should be drilled as directed in the above lesson.

While operating with a very bad kicking horse in Peru, Indiana, after driving him around in the cart a few minutes, standing upon the axle-tree and holding the kicking horse by the tail (see cut No. 7, p. 39), one of the members of my class, a well-known banker, said he did not believe his horse would stand to be driven that way. I invited him to bring his horse out the next day before the class, and I would try him. This horse was considered very quiet and gentle, but the banker wanted to have the pressure put on, so he brought him out the next day, and, after giving the horse a thorough training according to my method, the banker said :

"I always thought he was gentle, but now I know it."

A Pennsylvanian with whom I was personally acquainted, who was considered a good horseman, and who employed a careful, pains-taking young man, concluded to break his colt.

The farmer directed his man John to be very kind, easy and gentle with the colt, and not to let him step over the traces, nor to have the singletree touch him, for fear of frightening and causing him to run away.

John followed all the directions given concerning the management of the colt, never even allowing him to step over the traces, nor letting the singletree, or any portion of the harness, hang loosely and strike him. If John, while driving the colt, saw any unusual object on the roadside, he would take particular pains to drive out of sight of the object, for fear of the colt becoming frightened at the *sight* of it.

He would also take special care never to approach the railroad depot or flour mill, for fear the unusual noise and rattling of the cars and machinery would startle the colt, causing him to attempt to run for home, and perhaps breaking the cart.

In fact, John would never permit the colt to approach an object near enough to understand the nature of it, nor to have the harness or tugs touch him about the feet or between his legs, to prevent any liability of his kicking. Neither would he let him go near any place or object where he would *hear* any unusual noise.

Having handled and driven the colt in this gentle and careful, old-fashioned manner for about a year, the old gentleman considered him perfectly broken, and as being a kind and safe animal that had never yet kicked or ran away.

The following season he had another colt to break and John was given the task.

The first colt broken, being considered thoroughly trained, was given to a new hand to do plowing with.

This colt accidentally stepped over the tug, by which act the tug was forced against the inside of his legs, where as yet he had never been touched by any object.

The consequence of his being touched in this unhandled part, was that he got frightened, and, obeying the impulse of his nature, kicked out at the objectionable tug in self preservation, and started off at a run to free himself from his imaginary danger.

The old gentleman, on seeing the fleeing horse with fragments of the harness dangling about him, was naturally amazed to see the colt that during all the year in which he had been handled and driven by John, and had never shown a disposition to kick or run away, acting in such a manner.

He had been impressed with the idea that the colt was perfectly trained and gentle.

His next thought on seeing the frightened steed, was to

abuse ne unfortunate man who had been using him, and blaming him for the damage done, which he himself was really to blame for.

Had the colt been put through the preparatory course of training which I have suggested under the head of "How to Break a Colt Properly," he never would have become frightened and kicked himself free from the plow, injuring his limbs, learning a bad trick, and causing other damage.

Many would agree with the old gentleman in thinking it was the carelessness of his man, in letting the colt step over the trace, which caused this accident and all the trouble.

The writer will at once proceed to place the blame where it justly belongs—on the old gentleman.

He should have said to John :

"John, I *know* you are a good horseman ; take this colt out in the lot, put the harness on him, and accustom him to everything before you hitch him up—or, in other words, 'Sample-ize' him, by putting things between his legs, tying tin-cans to his tail, fire-crackers, or anything that would have a tendency to frighten him." We are fully satisfied, had this been done, the accident would never have occurred from the colt's simply stepping over the trace.

A RUNAWAY HORSE.

First find out, if possible, what caused him to run away ; and when the trainer has found out, take him into the lot or corral and tie him, head and tail, with the halter, and handle him with the pole, as directed in the lesson for training the colt. Whatever has been the cause of his running away will frighten him the most ; so that it will be necessary to operate more on this point than any of the others ; and when he submits to the sense of feeling, seeing and hearing, put the harness on as directed in the lesson on the colt, and handle him in the same manner as the colt was handled, until you can hold him by the lines with perfect ease, while the assistant is exciting him with the pole, umbrella, or any other object which would have a tendency to make him run away.

The trainer will remember that it will be necessary to get the mouth so that he can hold him with perfect ease before undertaking to excite him to resistance.

At this point we will state that there is no man who can hold a horse by main strength; hence the necessity of giving him thorough training with the lines and bit, as directed in the training of the colt's mouth.

Teach the horse to start and stop well, even under excitement, and repeat this lesson two or three times before hitching him up.

In ordinary cases this will take from thirty to forty minutes, to give the horse a good lesson—always being careful to take good care of your horse on concluding your lesson.

KICKING HORSES.

A kicking horse is one of the most dangerous horses we have, and in a very bad case is considered almost worthless.

While I was traveling through Richmond, Virginia, a very ugly kicking mare was brought to me, that had been traded from stable to stable until she was considered as worth very little money.

A gentleman—one of my scholars—asked me one day if I thought she could be broke, and I replied:

"Yes—certainly she can."

I think she was one of the worst mares I ever came across in my travels of over eighteen years.

I gave her a short lesson, lasting thirty minutes, every day for a week, and some of my scholars began to talk as though my plans would not work on her.

On the seventh day she gave up, and I told the owner to take her and hitch her up and drive her, which he did.

He drove her himself for about one week. I stayed in Richmond four weeks, and when I left there his man was driving her all over the city, delivering groceries.

Another bad kicker, in Virginia, I met at Woodstock, where I formed a class.

The subject furnished me to handle was a gray horse, fifteen years old, that the owner told me had been kicking all his life, and had been traded around from one horseman to another, until it was considered impossible to drive him in harness.

We commenced with this horse about four o'clock in the afternoon, before the class, and worked with him until six in the evening. Myself and assistant worked on him faithfully, using our best efforts, and some of the class went off with the impression, when we adjourned at six o'clock, that he could never be broken.

The owner of the horse, a hotel-keeper, and others who were deeply interested, turned out again the next morning to see us handle the horse.

When we commenced on him—after putting on the harness—every time we would touch him with the pole he would kick, and every time he would kick we would punish him with the bit, until finally, after a hard fight of two hours, resting occasionally to get our wind, he quit kicking, to the great astonishment of all present except myself and assistant.

We drove the horse, without breeching, to a two-wheeled cart, standing on the axle and holding the horse by the tail. [See cut No. 7.]

Every time we stopped him, the cross-bar of the shafts would bump up against him. This was in the fall of 1876, during the Presidential campaign.

I was advertised to perform at Stanton the next day, and had to leave Woodstock.

While in Stanton, I got a letter from the owner of the gray kicking horse of Woodstock, stating that he had driven the horse, with his family in the wagon, and if I would return to Woodstock he would give me a certificate that would carry me triumphantly through the valley.

I relate these two extreme cases for the purpose of encouraging the trainer, should he meet with such brutes as I have mentioned.

No matter how mean and obstinate they may be, you can conquer them by persevering in this treatment, and the

No. 7.

average kicking horse, by this treatment, can be controlled in from thirty to forty minutes.

We could mention hundreds of such cases, but have selected these two because they were the worst we have met in all of our travels.

The horses above mentioned should receive the same treatment as recommended for the breaking of the colt.

In fact, there is but one way to break a horse of any bad habit in harness, and that is to treat him kind and gently when he does all that we require of him, and punish him when he refuses.

BALKY HORSES.

The balky horse is the one that will try the horseman's skill, power, ability, and temper more than all the kicking, runaway, bucking, striking, biting, and shying horses, or any other kind of horse that we can think of.

There are several kinds of balky horses.

There are those that will not go in any harness, light or heavy.

Then, again, there are horses willing to go in a light vehicle, but will refuse to pull an ordinary load. There are some that are hard to start from the stable or lot, but will go along all day after they are started; there are horses willing to go straight ahead on a road, but if you wish to turn them to the right or left, they will stop—these we call "bridle balkers."

In fact, any horse is a balky horse when he refuses to go when and where we direct him to go. To break him and make him a true and valuable horse, we will begin with him the same as though he was a green colt, and put him through the same training and lessons as are directed in breaking the colt, always being careful to keep the point we gain in working with him, until we have the complete mastery over him on that point, never expecting him to pull all he is able to at the first lesson, but beginning with a light load, and gradually increasing it until he gains confidence in himself. Then he will pull all that any ordinary horse ought to pull.

The first point to be gained with a balky horse in giving him his lesson, is to teach him to start and stop, turn to the right or left, go forward or backward at the command of the trainer. This you want him to do before you hitch him to the cart. And when you do hitch him in, be careful not to have the cart too heavy. A two-wheel cart is the best.

The kind of cart I use in hitching the colt or horse, to the *first time,* is simply two wheels and an axle, without any seat, and a good pair of buggy or express-wagon shafts. This cart will be illustrated in Cut No. 7, page 39, showing the breaking of the colt.

We never use this cart except in the training-yard, and then for the purpose of getting the colt used to shafts and load.

We can teach the horse to pull by strapping one of the wheels to the shaft, after he goes well with the wheels loose. Sometimes we fasten both wheels in this way, and we can increase the weight as we feel disposed, by tying an empty sack to the axle, and throwing in a shovel or two of sand or dirt at a time, in proportion to the amount that the horse will draw. In this way, the wheels being locked, we can make as heavy a load as is necessary, by adding sand and dirt to the sack. Stop and start the horse often while hitched in this way, always encouraging him by kind treatment when he obeys promptly.

When you come to a hill, or any place where the horse refuses to go, after making a short effort to start him, should he still refuse, take him right out of the cart or vehicle, put the lines through the shaft-tugs and drive him up and down the hill and all around the place he refuses to pass with the cart.

By passing the lines through the shaft-tugs you are able to keep his head from you and his tail toward you, thus preventing him from turning around and twisting the lines out of your hands. Should you leave the lines through the rings of the saddle as they were when you were driving in the cart, he would perhaps whirl around and twist the lines around his body and out of your hands, and in some cases get away and give you considerable trouble.

While in Chambersburg, Penn., a very eminent physician brought a balky horse to me to have him broke. After giving the horse one lesson, my assistant was driving him on the road hitched to a buggy, and he stopped at the foot of a hill, refusing to go any further.

He took the horse out of the shafts and fixed the lines as directed above, and drove him up and down the hill several times. At this moment the doctor happened to come along and asked him what he was doing with the horse. He replied :

" I can manage the horse better than I can the horse and buggy, hence I leave the buggy on the roadside until I can get the horse to go without it. In other words, if the horse refuses to go when there is no buggy hitched to him, there is no use to hitch him to it. Always break your horse first and the buggy afterwards, and never undertake to break the horse and buggy at the same time."

In conclusion, we would say that this is the simplest and most lasting way to manage a balky horse.

We could give various methods for starting the horse as laid down by other trainers, but to start a horse when he is "balked," or to make him pull at one time, will not make him start or pull at all times.

We must be able to teach the horse that he is what he was intended to be, man's willing and obedient servant at all times and places and under all circumstances.

In a figurative way of expressing it, we must make him believe that we can put him through a knot-hole, and when we get him through the plank, show him by our actions that we are not only his master, but also his best friend.

HOW TO BREAK A BAD HALTER-PULLER.

Of all the objectionable tricks and bad habits the horse is subject to, one of the worst is that of pulling back or " halter-breaking," and has, perhaps, been the cause of a greater number of accidents than any other, and causing the destruction of numberless bridles, halters, etc.

To break a horse of this habit properly and for all time, the first thing would be to investigate the cause, or why the horse pulls back on the halter. His natural instinct is to refuse to be held by the head. When the animal's head is fastened he will make an effort to get loose, and as long as he finds he is successful in getting loose he will continue to do so. Therefore, should he set back on the halter and attempt to get loose—his head being in a trap prepared for him, by the art of man—he will naturally pull to get his head out, and if any part of the halter should give way or break, his head will become free, and every time he gets free by pulling, he will be encouraged to pull harder the next time, until it will take a very strong halter to hold him, especially if he is a large, heavy horse.

There are various plans devised for the breaking of this habit.

No. 8.

Cut No. 8 represents a horse pulling on the halter while fastened according to my method of breaking this habit. Take a half-inch rope fifteen feet long ; double about one-half of it, and put the doubled end under the tail for a crupper, wrapping a piece of cloth around the crupper part to prevent the rope cutting his tail.

Pass the longest end of the rope around his neck from the off to the near side; tie it to the short end in a flat knot on the near side, and have the knot come about where you buckle the girth of the harness. Then take the long end and place it under the belly and tie it to the rope on the off side. This will make a girth or belly-band to prevent it from slipping up. When the rope is placed on in this way, as shown in cut No. 8, put on a strong rope or leather halter; take the lead of the halter, running it through a ring in the manger, tree, or side of the building. After running the lead of the halter through the ring fastened to either of the places named, tie the end of the lead to the rope in front of his chest, as shown in the cut.

Now the horse is not only hitched by the head, but to the rope running under the tail also; and when he starts to pull, the lead of the halter will slip through the ring. The rope will then catch him under the tail, and he will soon jump forward to relieve the pressure under the tail. When he does this, go up to his side near his head, patting him gently on the neck, allowing him to stand a few minutes; then take a cane or stick, and running up quickly to frighten him back again, and should he run back, strike heavily on the lead of the halter in front of his head until he jumps forward.

When he comes forward again treat him kindly as before, repeating this operation several times until he refuses to pull back. If the horse is afraid of an umbrella, blanket or anything of that kind, run towards him with the object in your hands and try to frighten him back, and when he comes forward repeat the rubbing on the neck as before, or until the horse refuses to pull or tighten on the halter. After this lesson he can be hitched at night in the stable without any danger of hurting himself.

This treatment will break the most confirmed "halter-puller" in existence after giving him a lesson lasting half an hour as above for one or two days.

If he pulls on the bridle and not on the halter, make a strong rope bridle and hitch the same with the bridle as you do for "halter-pulling" by running the rope lines through the ring and tie to the rope in front of the chest.

DIFFERENT DISPOSITIONS AND TEMPERA-MENTS OF THE HORSE.

The lesson on the management and training of the colt and horse would be incomplete without calling the attention of the pupil to their different temperaments and dispositions.

While all horses are governed by the same fixed laws and instincts, their temperaments and dispositions are as varied and numerous as those in man.

No. 9.

Some are naturally very quiet and gentle in their disposi-tions, so much so that it would appear as though they would never do anything wrong, but, by improper management on the part of the trainer or owner, they may become so vicious and bad as to make them almost as worthless as the horse Cognac, well known all over California, that became so vicious and unmanageble, that when he got loose and out of his stall, on the Fair Grounds of Petaluma, Sonoma County, he killed a man who undertook to return him to his stall.

This horse at one time was as tractable and gentle as it was possible for a horse to be, but by the improper treatment he suffered at the hands of his groom, while in Illinois, he became very vicious and unmanageable.

The groom, in order to show the intelligence of the horse, would put his arm up to the horse's mouth, coaxing him to take hold of it, in the same way as is often done by foolish people, who are not thoroughly conversant with the habits of the horse. In doing this, the groom succeeded in getting the horse to bite, or pinch him, on the arm, with his teeth.

One day Cognac bit him harder than usual. This enraged the groom, and he took the horse out of the stable and began to whip him in an unmerciful manner about the body and legs, until the horse lay down, squealing from the pain inflicted by the groom. And when he got up, the once gentle and kindly-disposed horse was transformed into a demon, with a disposition to eat up and destroy his master, who had wantonly and cruelly beat him, or any one who attempted to manage him.

It was considered, by numerous judges, that this horse had no sense, as the term is generally used among horsemen, but the writer looks upon this horse as having more sense than if he had allowed the groom to punish him wantonly and cruelly for doing that which he—the groom—had taught him to do, without making an effort to retaliate.

I was in Chicago in 1880, and my attention was called to another very bad horse, called the Duke of Normandy, that had previously got his groom under his knees and chewed him up, and had crippled and injured several other men.

He was led about from one stand to another by a jockey-stick, fastened to the bit, in order to prevent his jumping on the groom and killing him.

If the groom, having him in charge, should get on his back to ride him, he would reach around and bite him on the leg, consequently they were obliged to walk and lead him.

The owner of this horse lived at Norwood Park, about eleven miles from Chicago. I went one day to see him concerning his horse, and, in the course of conversation, I found that the horse would make a good subject to handle before my class, and the gentleman had him brought to my tent in Chicago, and in less than forty minutes from the time I began to handle him, the owner was on his back, riding around the ring, and the horse was perfectly gentle and quiet. I hitched this horse to a buggy and drove all through the city of Chicago, with perfect safety, also turned him loose in my ring and had him follow me around, without halter or bridle, perfectly quiet and gentle.

This horse was about seventeen hands high and weighed eighteen hundred pounds, and was naturally of a mild, even temper.

On investigating the early history of this horse, I learned that he was imported from France at the age of two years, and was pefectly kind and gentle, until he was spoiled by the unskillful management of his groom.

We could mention many such cases of good-tempered horses, having been ruined and made ugly by mismanagement on the part of grooms and others.

Then again there are other horses that are naturally stupid, sullen, and of treacherous dispositions. [See cut No. 10.]

These horses will require very little aggravation at the

hands of the trainer in order to draw out their mean traits.

If they are of the balky or sullen order, great pains should be taken by the trainer to overcome this as much as possible by studying how to get the best of them, and not allowing them to gain any points.

No. 10.

They will often attempt, while the trainer is handling them, to do just the reverse of what is required of them. This we must never allow them to do, but must work on that point constantly and firmly until they do as we are trying to teach them. Always treat the horse with kindness when he does that which we demand of him. If he is of a treacherous disposition, be very careful and see that he gets no advantage of you. Always be sure that you have every advantage on your side.

Some people are of the opinion that a horse knows when you are afraid of him. He knows nothing about your thoughts. He only knows what you can do with him, and if you should undertake to handle him and he finds out by experience that he can handle you, he will continue to do so as long as he finds your inability to force his submission. As soon as he finds your ability to force submission he will yield at once to your commands. I have handled hundreds of horses and made them perfectly submissive when I have been very much afraid of them. I have heard men say they never saw a horse they were afraid of. A man that will stand behind a horse and let him kick his head off has not as much sense as the horse. Always use great care and judgment in handling horses like the ones I have alluded to.

There is another class of horses that are of a nervous and high-strung temperament [see cut No. 11], that will fight

No. 11.

and resist every effort to confine them. While in San Bernardino, California, I came across a horse of this kind. He had been caught up wild, and resisted every effort made to domesticate him.

When I commenced to handle him in the way and manner I have laid down in the lesson for training the colt, he acted more like a hyena than a horse. Some of my class said he was crazy, or "loco" as it is expressed in that locality—this is a Spanish word for crazy. One of the class said he knew the band from which this colt was taken and that every one of them was "loco."

After I had handled him about thirty minutes he gave up the fight from the fact that he found out I was not going to hurt him. The next day I drove him on the streets and he acted like a good, sensible horse, and showed no signs of being "loco."

When I first came to California advocating my new system, there were quite a number of good horsemen who said:

Perhaps this man can handle the Eastern horses that are domesticated, but we don't think he will meet with much success in handling our "broncos."

But after staying in Los Angeles six weeks, handling their "broncos," and driving them through town with tin cans tied to their tails, they became satisfied that my system would break wild horses as well as those domesticated, as this article of January 2d, 1882, from the *Los Angeles Times*, will prove:

The citizens of Los Angeles witnessed one of the most interesting processions that has paraded the streets of this city for many a day, yesterday. For some time past Professor Sample has been in this city teaching the lovers of that noble animal, the horse, how to train him. From the exhibition yesterday it was fully proven to the satisfaction of the most skeptical that Sample is the most thorough horse-trainer in the United States, if not in the world. The owners of the horses in the procession will testify that less than thirty days ago every animal was ungovernable to a considerable extent. But the reader, if he saw the parade, noticed that every horse was led by boys not over twelve years of age. This is proof positive that every man should understand the *modus operandi* of taming horses. The procession started from Temple-street stable about 12 o'clock noon, and marched through the principal streets. The Professor led the caravan, seated in a fine buggy drawn by two magnificent black horses. The City Band followed : then came the riproaring mustangs that had been trained. The first one had a motto on his sides which read : " I was the boss of Denker's ranch, but Sample got the best of me." Then followed nine horses with mottoes which read like this : " I was the bucking bronco, that had my tail full of cuckle burrs and I have been Sampled ;" " I was a nullifier, but have been conquered ;" " I was Wild Bill of Temple-street stable :" " I was the worst pill in the box, but Sample got the best of me ;" " I was a balker, but Sample made me go ;" " I would'nt back, but I do now ;" " I am the one that crippled my master and killed my mate, but will never do it again." The last one had : " I was a high kicker, but Sample took it all out of me."

TO BREAK A HORSE THAT IS AFRAID OF A LOCOMOTIVE.

A horse that is afraid of a locomotive is a very unpleasant kind of horse to drive, and can be broken of the habit in a short time. One of the instincts of the horse is to be afraid of anything he does not understand ; in fact, fear, either directly or indirectly, is the cause of all bad habits. The natural instinct of the horse is to follow after any object he may not understand, providing the object is moving from him ; therefore, instead of forcing the horse up to the object when it is moving toward him, be it locomotive or what not, get the horse in a position that you can ride or drive him after the object.

If he is afraid of a band of music that is coming toward him, it will be best to take him around in some way and get in the rear of the band. In this way he will become familiar with the noise while following it. This is what we call educating the sense of hearing. If it is something that frightens him when he sees it, get him accustomed to the sight of it in the same manner that you accustom him to the sound—by letting him follow after it.

By way of illustration: a horse will follow a top-buggy on the road or street without becoming frightened, but should the same buggy approach him or come up behind him, he will become frightened, and thereby, obeying his natural instinct in attempting to get away from an object he does not understand. A couple of gentlemen, who took lessons from me some years ago, while I was illustrating this point, one said:

"That's so."

He went on to state to the class: "When myself and companion were traveling out West, we came up with a band of wild horses, and they followed us at a distance for two days; sometimes we would turn our horses around and start toward the band to get a good look at them, and they would invariably turn and move from us, but when we resumed our journey the wild horses would again follow us, always keeping off at a safe distance."

So, in accustoming a colt or horse to any object that would be inconvenient to use in the training-lot, proceed as directed above. In fact, to break a horse of any bad habit, such as shying on the road, refusing to stand quietly while being hitched or unhitched; being restless while you are getting in or out of the buggy, rearing up, running backwards, jumping over things in the road, or, in fact, any bad habit that the horse is subject to, can be thoroughly eradicated by putting him through a thorough course of training, as directed in the handling of the colt, thus getting him under your control.

Never go into partnership with your horse, or compromise with him when he disobeys, but let him know that you are what you were intended to be—his master, and he your *servant*.

After giving your horse a thorough course of training, if you ever have got into the miserable and uncalled-for habit of trying to make the horse go by jerking on the lines, as most ladies and quite a number of gentlemen do, by all means desist at once and never repeat it. The main object is to be uniform in your language and actions toward him. Never say whoa! to him unless you want him to stop, and if you should happen to say whoa when you did not want him to stop, stop him.

If you tell him to go and he refuses to obey, touch him with the whip, but do not jerk on the lines. By giving him the above lesson he will soon understand your commands, and will act promptly. You should be careful and not pull much on the lines, for his mouth will be a little tender after the lesson. Never use a severe bit, as it is unnecessary. The plain-jointed bit will be sufficient to hold any horse if he is properly drilled. Some people make their horses foolish by holding the lines tight when the horse starts.

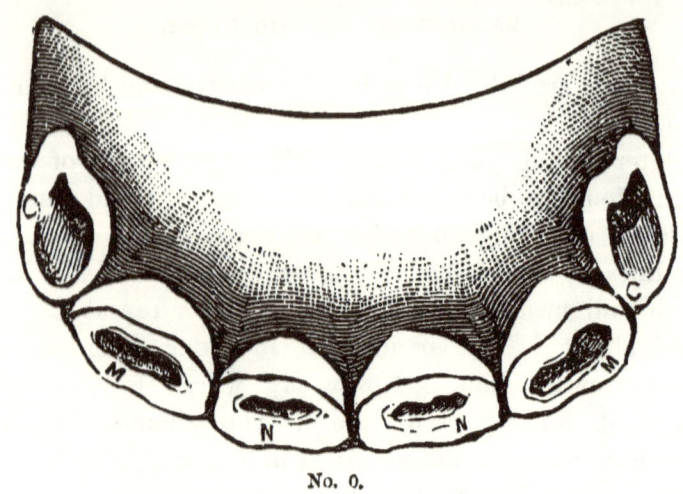

No. 0.

HOW TO TELL A HORSE'S AGE TO HIS TWENTY-FIRST YEAR.

There are few persons, even among veterinary surgeons, who are able to tell the exact age of a horse after he has attained his tenth year, and this being the case, how can we expect those who have neither anatomical nor physiological knowledge of the mouth to tell his age

Horse-dealers are frequently accused of deceiving their customers in the age of horses. The purpose of this lesson is entirely to set aside this deception, and to enable all, sellers, buyers, and those who never before knew anything about the age of horses, to thoroughly understand the age of all horses, from the time of foaling until he has reached his twenty-first **year.**

The writer, who has theoretically and practically studied the horse's mouth for eighteen years, has had opportunities of examining the mouths of thousands of horses of all ages, thus thoroughly convincing himself of the reliability of the rules he has laid down for telling the age of the horse.

He has been teaching this new system for nearly ten years, and has taught thousands of persons, and caused numerous discussions upon the subject.

While in Terra Haute, Indiana, there was no little excitement created by the teaching of this system. In fact, some of the horsemen who were skeptical on the subject, wrote to *Wilkes' Spirit of the Times* to ascertain if it were possible to tell the horse's age up to twenty-one years. The answer came, " No," with a long explanation, giving many reasons why it could not.

The principal point presented in *Wilkes'* argument was, that the cups or marks entirely disappeared in the teeth at nine years of age; and that, after the cups or marks were gone, it was impossible to ascertain with any degree of certainty how old the horse was.

(Every new invention, idea, and system of teaching any science or art, must have a discoverer or inventor; and as these new ideas, systems, and inventions are made public, there is, of course, much discussion, criticism, and opposition created by those familiar as well as by those unfamiliar with the subject.)

The writer contends that the horse's mouth undergoes a continual change from the time he is foaled to the day he dies; and that it is much easier to determine his age from ten years up to twenty-one, than it is from one to ten, and we feel confident that we will be able to substantiate these statements as we proceed with the lesson.

The horse has forty teeth, and, as we use only twelve of them to determine his age, we will have very little to say about the other twenty-eight, as it will have a tendency to confuse the reader. The twelve teeth we use to tell the age by are located in the front of the mouth, six on the upper and six on the lower jaw. [See cut No. 1, of lower jaw of foal six months old.]

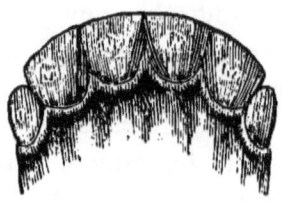

No. 1.

Outside view of a six months old colt's lower jaw.

We will name these teeth "nipper," "middle" and "corner" teeth—NN, the nippers; MM, the middle; CC, corner—as marked on the teeth in the cut.

The upper jaw has six teeth—the same as the lower. The cut simply represents the lower jaw, front view. There are six on the upper jaw that will be understood by the same names—nipper, middle and corner. The nipper, middle and corner teeth of the upper jaw will come directly over the nipper, middle and corner teeth of the lower jaw.

These twelve teeth are all that we use to determine the age of any horse, mare, mule, jack or jenny, and the first thing for the reader to do will be to familiarize himself with the names and location of these teeth—nipper, middle and corner, or N, M and C; so that, when we speak about nipper, middle and corner teeth, the reader will know just where to look in the horse's mouth for the teeth we are speaking about.

The rule we lay down for telling the horse's age applies to the mare as well as the horse. Mares do not generally have canine or hook-teeth, commonly called tusks or bridle-teeth.

This is one of the reasons for discarding those teeth in determining the age, as it would have a tendency to deceive or mislead the pupil. (See cut No. 2.)

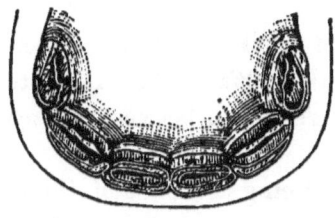

No. 2.

INSIDE VIEW OF THE LOWER JAW OF A FOAL'S MOUTH AT SIX MONTHS.—By looking closely at this cut it will be perceived that both the outer and inner edge of the nipper are worn, while only the outer edge of the middle is worn off, and the corner teeth have not yet come in contact with the upper jaw.

The average time for the foal to get his first four teeth, called nippers, is fourteen days. He gets the next four, called middle, between fourteen days and three months. Between three months and six months he gets the last four, called corner. So you will understand by this that the colt, at the age of six months, has twelve teeth. These are all the teeth we use to tell the age.

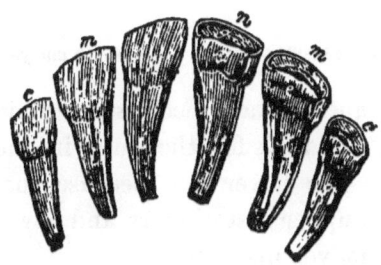

No. 3.

The colt's teeth as they appear when drawn out of the jaw.

This will represent six colt teeth as they would appear if pulled out of the jaw. The three on the left, marked II, represent the outside view of the crown. The three on the right, marked E, represent the inside view of the crown of the teeth. G represents the roots of the middle and corner teeth, from an inside view, and I represents the outside view of the roots.

By this cut the pupil will readily understand the anatomical structure of the colt's teeth. These teeth will all disappear from the colt's mouth between the age of two and five years.

By carefully noticing the ends of the teeth in cut No. 2, you will see that the crowns or part that the colt eats with has a hole or mark inside, and by the upper and lower jaw coming in contact with each other causing the teeth to wear off at the crown. These cups or marks will disappear, at the age of one year from the nippers of the foal. (See cut No. 4.)

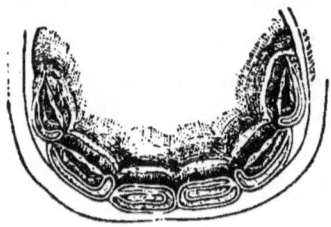

No. 4.

This is the inside view of a colt's mouth one year old.

The middle and corner teeth still retain the cups or marks. When we look for the cups in the colt or horse, always look on the lower jaw, because the lower jaw is movable and the upper is stationery and never moves except when the horse moves his head.

For this reason there will be more friction on the lower jaw than on the upper, hence the lower teeth will wear away sooner than the upper, and in looking for the marks or cups in the crown of the tooth always and invariably look on the lower jaw.

Cut No. 5 represents the lower jaw of a two-year-old, in which the edges of the nipper and middle teeth and their marks or cups are worn down, and the inner edge of the corner tooth is just commencing to wear.

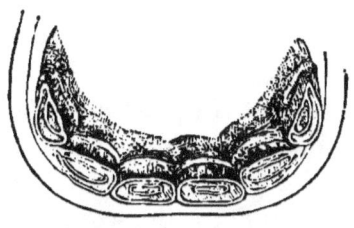

No. 5.

Inside view of a two-year-old, when the cups are worn off of the nipper and middle, a small cup remaining in the corner teeth.

At the age of two years and a half the colt teeth commence to drop out and horse teeth take their place ; this we call shedding the teeth.

There is a difference between the teeth naturally shedding and being knocked or pulled out.

Sometimes they are pulled or knocked out for the purpose of representing the animal to be older than he really is.

During the late war between the North and South there were a great many mules sold to the government that had their nippers pulled out, sometimes at the age of eighteen months, to make them appear as being two years and a half old, this age being the youngest at which the government would receive them. And thousands passed into the government employ for mules that were " coming three years," when really they were only from a year to eighteen months old.

While in Chicago I frequently visited the sale-stables. On one occasion I was an eye-witness to this circumstance :

A gentleman, wishing to purchase a horse, inquired the age of a fine large colt some sixteen hands high. The dealer informed him that the colt was five years and two months old. Out of curiosity I ventured to examine the colt's mouth, and found it was only three years old.

The dealer's object in representing the colt to be five years old when he was but three was, that the purchaser desired a horse of suitable age for work, whereas a three-year-old would not answer.

Had the Government Inspectors of horses and mules known that the animals brought to them were but eighteen months old instead of two and one-half years, they would have refused them as unfit for the work required. Had the Government Inspectors and the Chicago man we have alluded to been familiar with this method of telling the horse's age and the anatomical structure of the mouth, it would have been impossible for them to have been deceived as to the age of a horse.

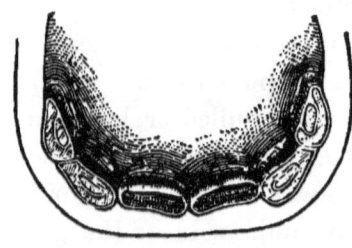

No. 6.

Inside view of lower jaw, when two and a half years old, with the horse-nippers just coming through the gum.

Cut No. 6 represents the lower jaw two years and a half old, with the colt teeth called "nippers" shed out, and the horse teeth of the same name have taken their place.

It will be seen, by carefully examining the above cut, that the horse teeth now coming in have not filled up all the vacancy in the horse's mouth caused by the shedding of the colt teeth.

When the horse teeth on the lower and upper jaws come

in contact with each other, and are worn perfectly straight across the crown, so as to fill up all the vacancy caused by the colt teeth "shedding out," the colt will then be three years old. At this time the colt will have four horse teeth and eight colt teeth. In other words, the nippers above and below will be horse teeth, while the middle and corner teeth above and below will be colt teeth.

No. 7.

Inside view of the lower jaw, three years and a half old.

The way we distinguish the horse teeth from the colt teeth, is by the horse teeth having a groove running down the center of the tooth from the crown to the gum on the outside surface, while the colt teeth are smooth on the outside surface, resembling your finger-nail, as shown in Cut No. 1.

Cut No. 7 represents the lower jaw of a colt three years and a half old.

The colt teeth, called "middle," are gone, and the horse teeth have cut through the gums. At four years old, these horse teeth, called "middle," shall have filled up all the vacancy, and be perfectly straight across the crown. Then the colt will show four horse teeth on the lower and four on the upper jaw, with only four colt teeth remaining, namely, the four "corner" teeth. When the colt is four years old, it will be seen, by a close examination of the colt's mouth, that he will have eight horse teeth and four colt teeth; the four nippers and four middle will be horse teeth, showing a groove on the outside surface; while the four corner teeth

that remain in the jaw will be colt teeth, with no groove on
the outside surface, and the crown of the tooth will be worn
perfectly smooth, as represented in cut No. 7.

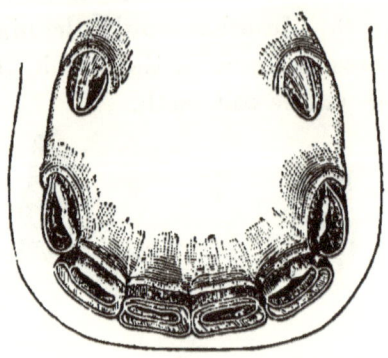

. No. 8.

Inside of the lower jaw of a colt four years and a half old, with the tushes
and corner tooth through the gum.

Cut No. 8 is a representation of the lower jaw of a
four-and-half-year-old colt. It will be seen by the above
cut, that all the colt teeth are gone, but the corner teeth
are not yet fully developed. These corner teeth will be full
size at five years. Then, all the teeth, nipper, middle, and·
corner, will be horse teeth, and will all show the groove on
the front except the corner teeth.

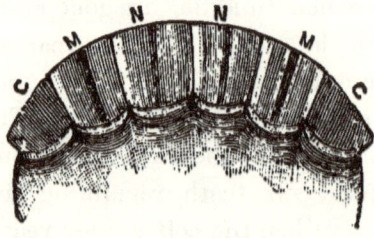

No. 9.

Outside view of lower jaw at five years of age.

The above cut is a correct likeness of the outside view of
the lower jaw of a five-year-old horse, showing the grooves

in the nippers and middle teeth, while showing the corner teeth as smooth. The corner teeth of the upper and lower jaw at five years are just commencing to wear, and it will be seen by Cut No. 9 that the corner teeth are wider than they are long.

The length of the tooth is from the gum to the crown, and the width is across the crown. The tooth marked c is wider than it is long.

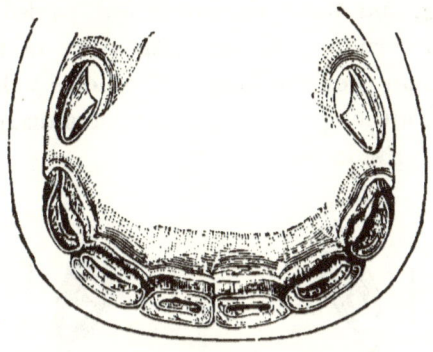

No. 10.

Inside view of the lower jaw at five years.

This cut shows the inside view of the lower jaw at five years of age. There is but slight difference between this and the six-year-old.

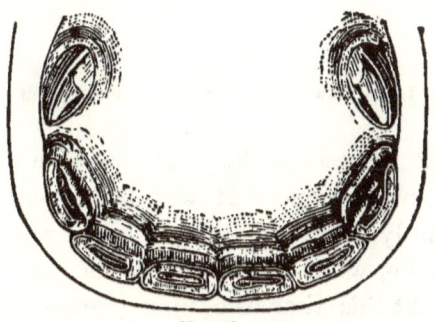

No. 11.

Inside view of a horse's mouth at six years.

Cut No. 11 shows the lower jaw of a six-year-old horse.

By examining this cut it will be noticed that there is a large cup in the corner teeth, and a small one in the middle teeth. The cups have almost disappeared from the nippers, and sometimes at six years the cups are gone entirely from them, which would represent a seven-year-old horse. But if the pupil has a doubt as to the horse's age he can determine by the examination of some of the other teeth. We have shown that the corner teeth at five years old are wider than they are long, and until the horse has passed six years of age the upper corner teeth, on both sides of the jaw, will show wider than they are long. The horse will not be over six years old, although the cups may have disappeared from the nippers of the lower jaw.

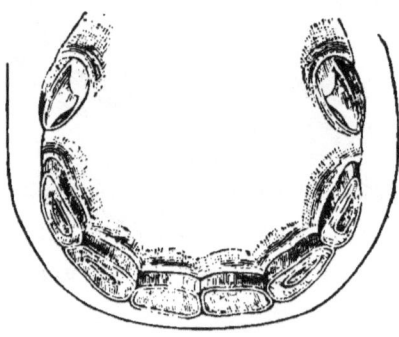

No. 12.

Inside view of horse's mouth at seven years.

Cut No. 12 represents the inside view of the lower jaw of a seven-year-old horse. It will be noticeable that the cups are entirely gone from the nippers, and almost gone from the middle, while the corner-teeth are worn dull on the inside. At this time the upper corner-tooth will show longer than it is wide. This is the only difference perceptible between the six and seven-year-old horse.

Cut No. 13 shows the lower jaw of the horse, aged eight years, in which the teeth have all become equally worn, and in the corner-teeth alone is to be found any trace of the

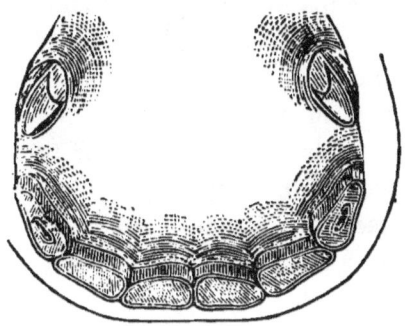

No. 13.

Inside view of a horse at eight years.

cup. The lower-jaw will be smooth at this time except the corner-teeth, which will show a small cup.

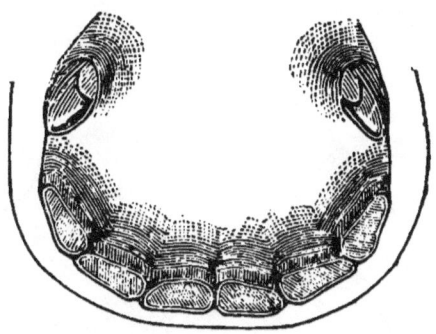

No. 14.

The above cut shows the lower jaw of a nine-year-old horse, where all the teeth have become smooth.

This is the general rule—but there are exceptions; at least, there are shell-teeth, or holes in the teeth, that would tend to deceive the beginner, and if we had no other marks to go by, except the cups, we would find it a difficult task to determine the horse's age with any degree of certainty. But we understand other marks that are more reliable than the cups we have just spoken of.

Some unprincipled men might make false cups in the teeth to make the horse appear younger to those persons not fully conversant with all the marks in the mouth. It will be noticed, by examining the outside of the teeth of horses between the ages of five and ten years, that they have smooth corner teeth, as shown in cut No. 9.

At ten years of age there will appear a small groove on the upper corner tooth close to the gum, about half the size of a grain of wheat, and this groove will appear longer as the horse advances in age; and when he arrives at the age of twenty-one years, this groove will show all the way down the tooth, as it appears in the nipper and middle teeth of the following cut.

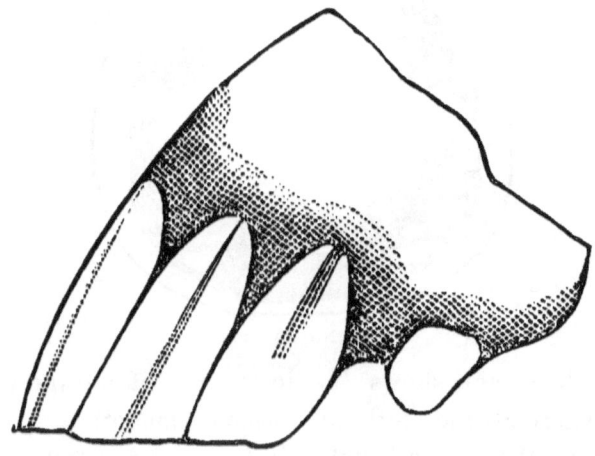

No. 15.

Side view of the horse's jaw, at the age of fifteen years.

The above cut represents the side view of the upper jaw of a horse fifteen years old, with the groove half-way down the upper corner tooth; or, in other words, to make it plain, the groove shows down the tooth one-half the distance from the gum to the crown. In measuring the length of the tooth in this case, we always measure from the gum to the longest point of the tooth; but, to be better understood, we will say, measure the longest side of the tooth to get the proper length. If this groove should show half-way down the longest side of the tooth, as represented in cut 15, the horse will be fifteen years old without a doubt.

If it shows three-fourths of the way down the longest side, he is eighteen years; and if it shows all the way down he is twenty-one years old. According to this, it will be seen that the groove starts close to the gum at ten, and will reach down to the crown at twenty-one. It takes eleven years for the groove to reach the crown, hence, one-eleventh the length of the tooth represents one year; two elevenths, two years, and so on, and when the groove is half way down the tooth, as represented in cut 15, the horse is then fifteen and a half years old—providing we count the fraction—from the fact that one-half of eleven is five and a half, and the groove not making its appearance on the tooth until the horse arrives at the age of ten; adding the ten to the five and a half, counting the fractions, makes him fifteen and a half years old.

But as we are perfectly satisfied to be able to come within a year of the horse's age, we will throw this fraction out and simply say fifteen years old. We will lay down a simple rule to examine this tooth and groove by:

If the groove is just starting on the tooth, the horse is ten years old · one-eleventh down the tooth, he would be eleven years old; two-elevenths, he would be twelve years old; three-elevenths, thirteen years old; nearly half-way, fourteen years old; half-way, fifteen; a little below half-way, sixteen years; still a little farther down, seventeen years; three-fourths of the way down, eighteen years; a little more than three-fourths of the way, nineteen years, and almost to the crown, twenty. When the groove reaches from the gum to the crown, he is twenty-one, measuring with the eye. This being as far as we propose to teach, scientifically, the horse's age, the reader, by a close examination of horses' mouths that he knows the age of positively, and comparing them with the above rules, will soon be able to tell correctly the age of any horse from the time he is foaled to twenty-one years.

We have endeavored, in the above instructions, to give in plain language the simplest, yet the most scientific method of telling the horse's age known.

In order to still further explain the anatomical and physiological structure of the teeth, we will refer the reader to the following illustrations :

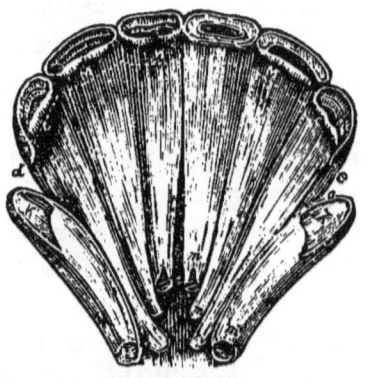

No. 16.

Teeth as they are located in the jaw.

Cut 16 represents the way and manner in which the teeth are located in the jaw of the horse. The roots, as they are commonly called, are narrow at the ends, while the crown of the tooth is much wider. The dotted line, from D to E, represents that portion of the tooth which extends above the gums, and the lower parts are buried beneath the gums in the jawbone. K K represent the tusks or hook teeth, commonly called bridle teeth, just about to cut through the gums, and as there is no certain time to be relied upon for these teeth to cut through, we will say nothing more about them, as this would mislead the reader.

The six teeth are marked NN, MM and CC. The three on the left show the shape of the teeth, on the crown, as they come through the gum, while the three on the right show some little wear by coming in contact with the upper jaw.

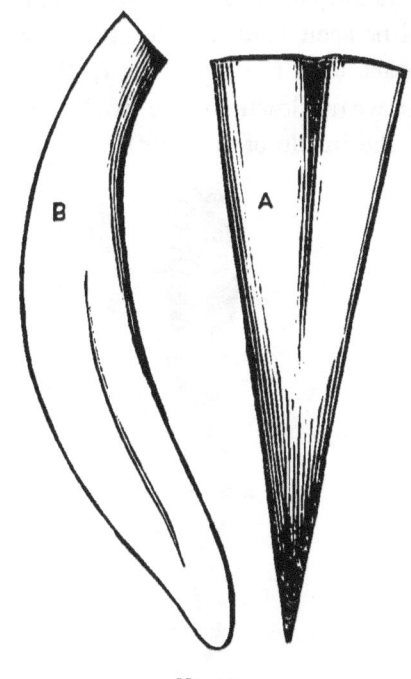

No. 17.

Full-size front and side view of nippers as they appear when pulled out of jaw.

Cut 17 is the full-size, front and side view, of the tooth called nipper. A represents the front view, and B shows the side view of the same tooth.

By noticing the front view, marked A, of the nipper-tooth, in Cut No. 17, you will see that at the crown or top it is quite wide, and gradually tapers to the root, where it is quite pointed, and the black mark, beginning at the crown and running down near the whole length of the tooth, represents the groove we dwelt upon before.

The representation in Cut 17, marked B, gives you a side view of the same tooth, and shows the top or crown to be much narrower on the side than on the front, and instead of gradually tapering down to a sharp point, it bulges out, or becomes thicker, near the middle than at either end. By this it will be seen that as the tooth wears away, by coming in contact with the upper jaw, the crown becomes narrower, as it wears down to the root, and thicker from the outside to the inside of the tooth.

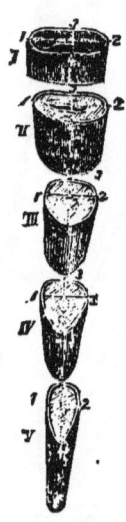

No. 18.

Shows nipper as it appears at three, six, twelve, eighteen and twenty-four years.

Cut 18 shows the shape of the crown of the nipper tooth at different ages. The upper section of this tooth shows a three-year-old tooth.

The width is from figure one to figure two, while the thickness is shown from figure three to figure four. The second section of this tooth shows a six-year-old, and the third section shows a twelve-year-old tooth. The fourth shows eighteen years old, while the fifth, and lower section, shows twenty-four years.

If the reader will carefully examine this illustration he will notice that the upper section from one to two is twice as wide as it is thick, while the lower section, showing the same tooth at twenty-four years, will discover that it is twice as thick as it is wide.

The width is from one to two, and the thickness from three to four.

We will next call your attention to cut 19.

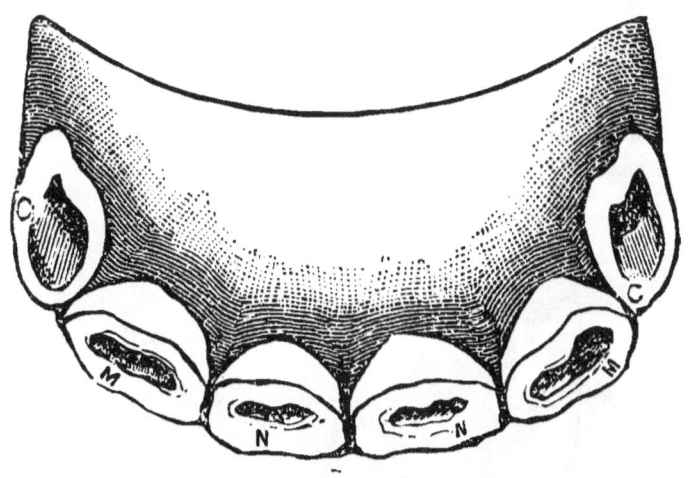

No. 19.

Life-size inside view of five-year-old.

This cut will represent a life-size, inside view, of the lower jaw of a five-year-old, showing all the cups or marks in the teeth as they would appear in the five-year-old mouth. N N the nippers, M M the middle, C C the corner teeth.

Cut No. 20 shows a life-size outside view of the lower jaw of a colt five years old.

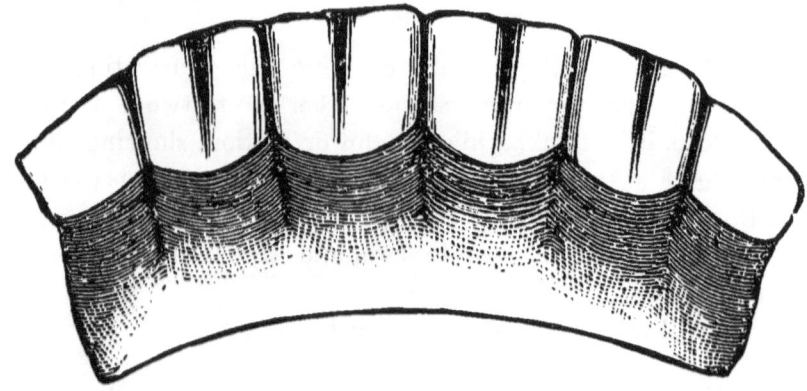

No. 20.

Life-size outside view of a five-year-old.

Cut 21 shows a life-size inside view of the lower jaw of a horse twenty-four years old.

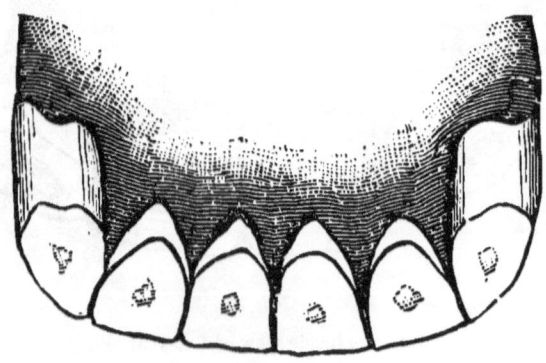

No. 21.

Life-size inside view of a twenty-four-year-old.

Cut 22 represents the outside view of the lower jaw of a horse twenty-four years old.

These last six cuts, 17, 18, 19, 20, 21 and 22, are not in-

serted to show any particular age, but to post the pupil
more fully in regard to the shape and form of the teeth at
different ages, showing the two extremes, the very young
and the very old.

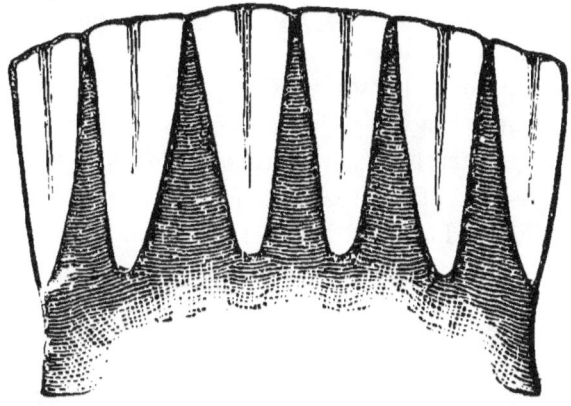

No. 22.
Life-size outside view of a twenty-four-year-old.

By closely observing the cuts above mentioned, more particularly the last four, it will be seen that the five-year-old
shows very wide across the crown, while the twenty-four-
year-old shows very narrow across the crown, both the inside
and outside views. This is caused by what is called the
alveolar process.

It will be more fully understood by the pupil to say, the
teeth in the young horse are long, while those in the old
horse are short, as shown in Cut No. 18.

Most people are under the impression that young horses
have short teeth, and that old horses have long ones. It is
just the reverse. The old horses have the short teeth and
the young ones the long, as will be seen in Cut No. 17. A
shows the front and B the side view of a full-size tooth of a
young horse, which averages in length from 2½ to 3 inches.

While Cut No. 18, lower section, represents the horse
when he is very old —three-fourths to one inch long.

The reason people call the old horse's teeth long is because they show further out from the gums, while the young horse's teeth are buried in the jaw-bone and covered by the gums. For this reason the young horse's teeth appear short, while the old horse's teeth look longer because they project farther out from the gums.

There are some horses that have what are called parrot-mouths, where the upper jaw teeth extend over and beyond the lower jaw teeth. Should this be the case, they will not wear off short, but the teeth of a horse eight or nine years old will show as long as a horse of twelve or fifteen will, where the teeth come together and wear off properly on the crowns.

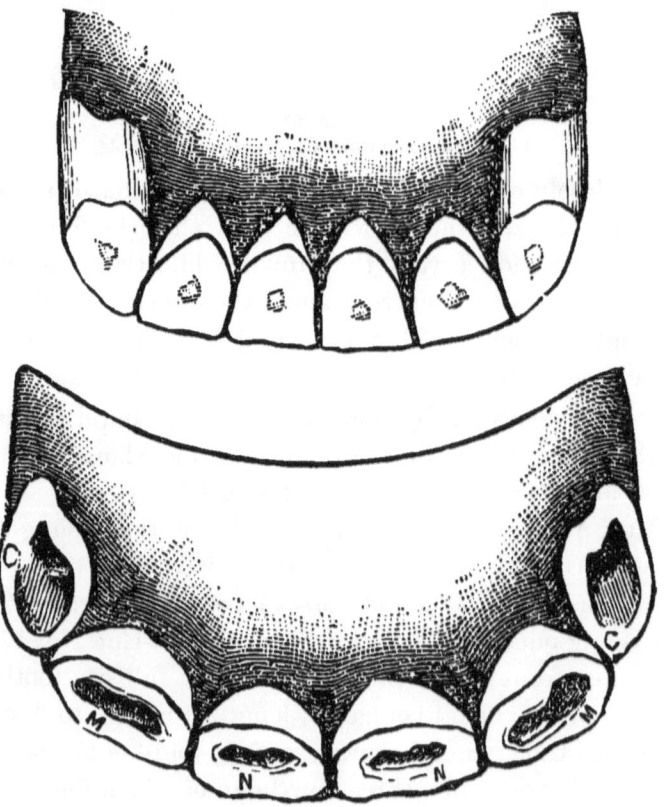

Page 74 shows the two inside views of the lower jaw together, so that the pupil can see the contrast between the old and young mouth.

We will also put the two outside views together on this page, so the pupil can see the width and shape of the teeth and gums. By noticing closely, it will be seen that the gums in the young mouth are nearly straight across, while the old mouth shows the gums extending up between the teeth.

The upper view on page 74 shows twenty-four years old; the lower view, only five. On page 75 the upper view shows five, and the lower one twenty-four years.

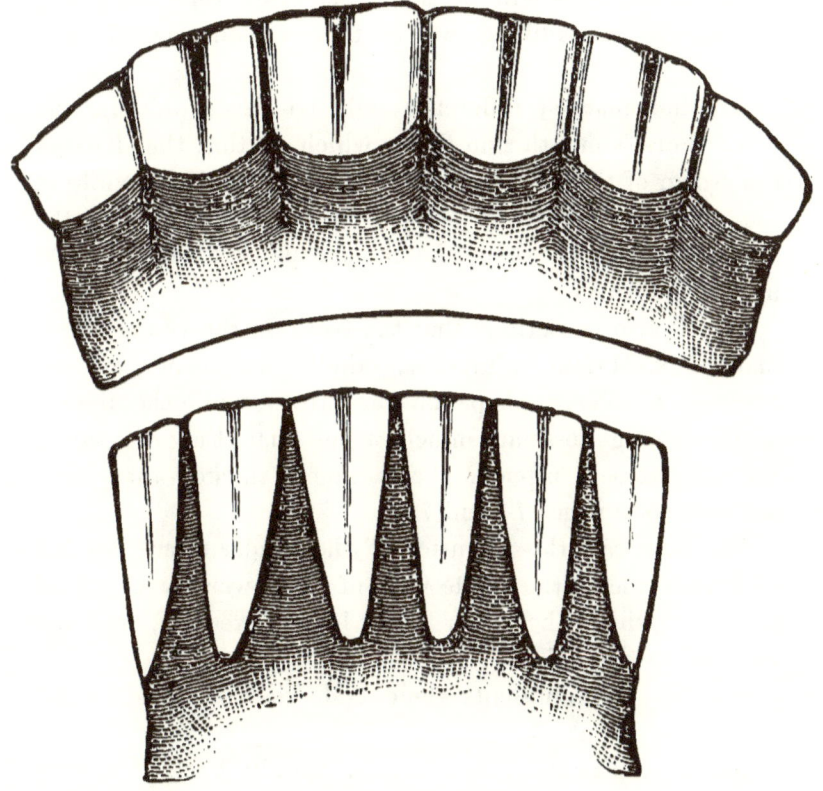

We will next proceed to explain as well as possible to the pupil what is meant by the alveolar process.

In the human as well as in the horse, the teeth are constantly and slowly, as nature directs, moving up out of the sockets, and as the teeth in the horse are smaller at the roots than at the crown (as shown in cut No. 17), it will be understood, as they move out of the sockets, that the further out they get the narrower the mouth will show.

The jaw-bone naturally contracts to fill up the space left by the teeth coming out of their sockets, and as this is a gradual process from the time the horse is fully developed, the older he gets the narrower the jaw will show. Hence the old horse's jaw will be much narrower than the young one, as will be readily shown by the cuts on pages 74 and 75.

Another marked difference will be perceptible in the young horse's mouth and teeth, which is, that the shape of the crown of the teeth will be that of a half-circle, while in the old horse they will show almost straight across the crown, showing the shape the alveolar process leaves the old horse's mouth in.

It will also be noticed that the teeth in the young horse, marked N, M and C, nippers, middle and corner, are entirely of a different shape on the crown, while the nippers of the young horse are much wider than they are thick, the old horse's nippers shows much thicker than they are wide (see pages 74 and 75).

We next call the attention of the reader to cut No. 23, which represents the inside view of the lower jaw of an old horse, in which the teeth have been sawed off, and not naturally worn off.

Cut No. 24 represents the outside view of the same jaw illustrated in cut 23.

Many unprincipled men have a rascally trick of sawing

off the horse's teeth and cutting holes in the crown, and then putting a red-hot iron in the holes to make black marks or false cups.

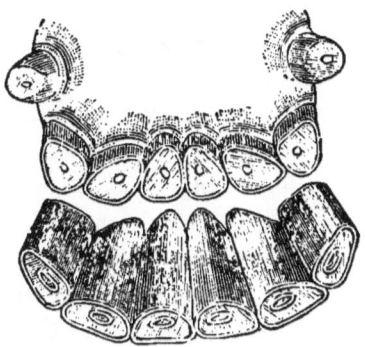

No. 23.

This is called "Bishopping," because the man who first practised this fraud was named Bishop. When this operation is performed on a horse that is getting along in years, it might deceive those that are not familiar with the formation and structure of the teeth ; but, after a close investigation of the young and old mouth, as shown by cuts 19 and 20, it will be impossible to deceive the pupil.

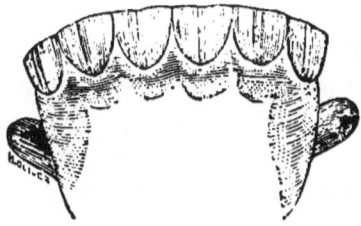

No. 24.

These simple but practical rules can become understood thoroughly by examining the mouths of different-aged horses.

I would advise the pupil to first examine the mouths of horses whose ages are well known to him, and compare with these instructions; then he might examine the mouths of different horses that he knows nothing about; and if these rules will hold good in describing the marks in the mouth that is well understood by the pupil, they will hold good in determining the ages of horses he knows nothing about.

The way that the author found out how to tell an old horse's age was by examining every horse he could find, if the horse's age was positively known by the owner. He then observed the different marks as described in this lesson, and now feels satisfied that by these rules the old horse's age—say up to twenty-one—will be known as well as the horse from one to ten. We are so positive that we will invite any scientific horsemen or others to make the test.

In regard to the different ages of horses we will give a few words of advice. Most people, in buying horses, prefer to get a young horse—from four to five years old. If a gentleman intends purchasing a horse for light work, intending to have him under his own care, it would perhaps be well to buy such a horse, because the young horse would be likely to improve in value, if properly cared for, and the work light and easy; but if he were going to purchase a horse to do hard, steady work, it would be better to get one seven or eight years old.

Many persons, inexperienced in handling and working horses, imagine that when the horse is nine or ten years old, he is rather an old animal, but experience has taught me, if he has not been crippled and injured, by working him when too young, that he is just in his prime.

If the horse is to be used for staging, street-cars, omnibusses, hacks, or any kind of constant or hard work, a sound ten-year-old horse is the right horse in the right place.

In traveling through Wisconsin, last year, at a small town called Sharon, where I formed a class, a gentleman, named Lowell, had a very fine stallion, that was twenty-one years old, sired by old Lexington, the celebrated running horse. He hitched him up to a "buckboard," and the horse got to kicking. Some of my scholars, knowing of this, got Mr. Lowell to bring him to Sharon, to have him handled before the class, and when he led the horse into town he looked like a young colt, and was one of those high-strung, well-bred, fully-developed, symmetrical horses that would furnish a fine subject for a picture to adorn any art gallery.

After handling this horse a few minutes, I hitched him to a buggy and drove him up and down the streets. I liked the horse so well that I persuaded Mr. Lowell to let me take him and drive him through the country. I drove him two or three months, and gave him some very long drives, which appeared beneficial to him rather than otherwise, and would have severely tested the endurance of many much younger horses.

Flora Temple, when nineteen years old, made her fastest time—2:19¾—which was the fastest mile ever trotted by any horse, mare or gelding, young or old, up to the year 1856.

Goldsmith Maid, at the age of nineteen, also made her best time—2:14—which was considered wonderful, as she beat all former records. In fact, the writer has seen horses working every day on the streets, and performing the work of ordinary horses, at the advanced age of thirty-three years. So, in buying a horse, be careful in discarding him solely on account of his age.

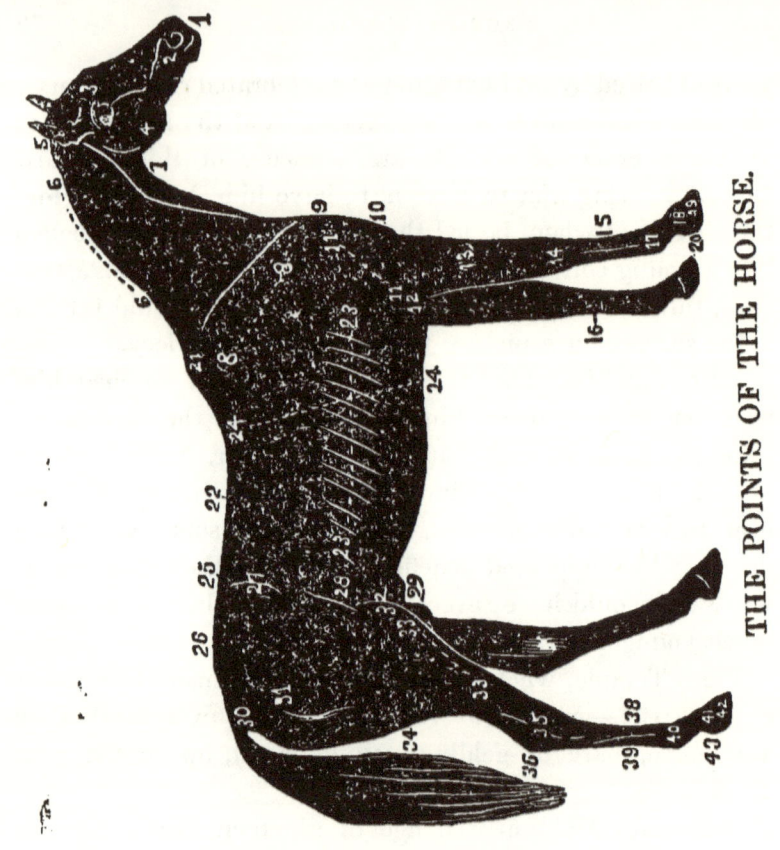

THE POINTS OF THE HORSE.

REFERENCES TO OPPOSITE CUT.

HEAD.

1. Muzzle.
2. Nostril.
3. Forehead.
4. Jaw.
5. Poll.

NECK.

6. 6. Crest.
7. Thropple or windpipe.

FORE-QUARTER.

8. 8. Shoulder-blade.
9. Point of the shoulder.
10. Bosom or breast.
11. 11. True-arm.
12. Elbow.
13. Fore-arm (arm).
14. Knee.
15. Cannon-bone.
16. Back sinew.
17. Fetlock or pastern-joint.
18. Coronet.
19. Hoof or foot.
20. Heel.

BODY OR MIDDLEPIECE.

21. Withers.
22. Back.
23. 23. Ribs (forming together the barrel or chest).
24. 24. The circumference of the chest at this point, called the girth.
25. The loins.
26. The croup.
27. The hip.
28. The flank.
29. The sheath.
30. The root of the dock or tail.

THE HIND-QUARTER.

31. The hip-joint, round, or whirl-bone.
32. The stifle-joint.
33. 33. Lower thigh or gaskin.
34. The quarters.
35. The hock.
36. The point of the hock.
37. The ball.
38. The cannon-bone.
39. The back sinew.
40. Pastern or fetlock-joint.
41. Coronet.
42. Foot or hoof.
43. Heel.

DISEASES OF THE HORSE AND THEIR TREATMENT.

The treatment and remedies given in this book, I have secured at great loss of time and money. I have been treating my own horses for nearly twenty years, and have used the remedies in this book with great success.

Many of the remedies included are worth much more than the cost of five of these books.

My principal desire in the production of this book is to benefit my patrons. Hence the reader may feel assured that no remedy will be placed in it, not known by me to be valuable and reliable.

It is an old maxim that reads: "An ounce of prevention is worth a pound of cure," and I would urge the necessity of at least ordinary care in preventing colds and sickness by guarding against exposure or mercilessly driving until the horse is in a high state of perspiration; then leaving him where some cold, bleak wind will strike him, perhaps without even putting a blanket or covering over him.

If covered at all, the blanket may be thrown on carelessly, and the driver or groom goes off to enjoy himself with his friends, taking his toddy, or toasting his shins, while the poor animal stands shivering in the street.

The effect of such treatment will not then have time to fully develop itself, but will be seen afterwards, when perhaps it is too late.

This is the cause of *Acute Laminitis* (founder) and of

Pleuro-Pneumonia (Pleurisy.) The principal points in securing the health of a horse, are exercise, pure air, and good feeding.

In the first place irregularity in exercising the horse will certainly produce diseases, and in the second place, the stable should be ventilated so that it will be neither too hot nor too cold. If this is not looked to, the animal will show the effects in a short time, by coughing or having a slight irritation of the mucous membrane of the throat.

A horse will take cold very easily by going out of a hot stable into the cold air, or from the cold air into a hot stable.

It is the sudden atmospheric change that produces the change on the mucous coat of the larynx and throat.

The clothing or covering of the horse in a stable should be neither too warm nor too cold.

A great deal depends on the care and attention that is paid to the horse in this respect. Whenever the laws of nature are violated, and the horse is caged or housed up by man, the same care and attention should be given him that we would give ourselves, when apprehending a return of previously endured hardships occasioned by exposure and neglect.

Another point that should always be observed in keeping a horse in condition and good health, is regular feeding and paying strict attention to him immediately after a long or hard drive, especially if he has been exposed to wet and cold weather.

Anticipate and look for a chill. Blanket him warmly and also give him a little fever medicine and a bran mash. By these timely precautions a severe attack of pneumonia may be averted.

Lung Fever.

Lung fever is an epidemic prevalent throughout the United States and Canada, and is considered contagious and generally proves fatal. It, however, has its causes of production in all countries, some of which I will describe first. Sudden changes from heat to cold; after severe cold weather it turns suddenly warm, the atmosphere is damp, the walls of stables are damp, the miasm and stench which arise from close stables produce a poisonous effluvia, which is inhaled by the horse, and produces disease. Again, changing horses from warm, comfortable stables, to cold, damp ones, often produces it. Driving your horse hard,

First stages of Lung Fever.

getting him warm, and then leaving him in a current of cold air, or giving him a heavy draught of cold water when warm, and allowing him to stand afterwards to chill taking him out when he feels well, in the rain, or turning him out in a paddock when he feels fresh, allowing him to take severe and quick exercise under exciting circumstances; causing undue excitement, affecting the lungs by rapid respiration. It is frequently caused by sudden fright, holding and compelling horses to remain in close proximity with whatever they think will harm them, producing heat and excitement; overdriving and exhaustion without sufficient care after the drive; too hard driving on a full stomach; injuries received on the head, back or limbs; crowding too many horses in small stables without sufficient ventilation; keeping one diseased horse in a herd or stable with other horses. It is found to prevail mostly in crowded cities; seldom attacks horses on the farm, where they have plenty of clean water and pure air; the damper the stable, the more liable is the horse to disease. It frequently attacks other parts of the horse, as well as the lungs.

Symptoms.

The horse breaks out in a cold, clammy sweat, accompanied with a severe chill. The ears, legs and head become deathly cold; he hangs his head down, or rests it on the manger; nibbles a little at his hay, refusing to eat any quantity; stands perfectly still, never moving unless compelled to; he is exceedingly stiff and weak; has a quick, weak pulse, hot mouth, shivering, dullness, watery eyes, accompanied by watery discharge from the nostrils, which soon becomes purulent; sore throat, difficulty of swallowing; loss of appetite, bowels costive; invariably dying upon his feet. In some cases the chest fills with water; the heart and its coverings are severely involved; the eyelids

Second stage of Lung Fever.

and the head are distended with fluids. It occurs generally in spring and fall, but may occur at any season of the year. It has been often mistaken for ordinary founder. Horses generally live from eight to fifteen days; but if they are not relieved during the first three or four days, their case is hopeless. Running, trotting, livery, and fancy horses are the most liable to take lung fever. The celebrated Canadian trotting-horse, St. Lawrence, died at Kalamazoo, Michigan, in 1860, from lung fever, produced from cooling off too suddenly after his race. The American trotting-horse, George M. Patchin, died from the same cause; Royal George died at Buffalo, in 1867, from the same cause; the Maid of Orleans died from the same cause, after running her four-mile race. Livery horses are subject to it, because they are so often over-heated, and left standing in the cold by careless drivers.

Fancy horses that are kept in warm stables with two or three heavy blankets on, when brought in contact with the air, chill very soon, unless kept in rapid motion. No horse should be blanketed in the stable generally. If kept in a good stable without clothing, and clothed whenever he is obliged to stand in the air, it would be better. Never expose your horse to sudden changes; they affect his general health and spirits. Horses that are regularly fed and worked, seldom if ever need any medicine.

All horses should have plenty of exercise in the open air. Colts should never be housed up or confined; nature intended they should have a certain amount of exercise to develop their muscles and lungs, to keep them in condition. This is why wild horses excel tame ones; they commence to run from the time they are foaled, so that by the time they are four years old, they are well developed.

Treatment in Lung Fever:

Tincture of aconite........................1 oz.
Tincture of veratrium.....................¼ oz.
Aqua......................................4 oz.

Dose from fifteen to twenty-five drops on the tongue every thirty or forty minutes.

This dose can be increased or decreased according to the severity of the case. Blister his sides just behind his forelegs ; bathe his throat with some strong liniment, and give him plenty of good pure air; do not stand him in the draught ; rub his legs well with some stimulating liniment, remembering that good care is one-half the battle.

Spasmodic Colic.

One of the most dangerous and common diseases to which the horse is subject, is the Colic, both spasmodic and flatulent. Spasmodic Colic, if not relieved, will, in severe cases, cause inflammation of the bowels and speedy death.

Flatulent Colic, while exhibiting the general symptoms, shows marked enlargement of the belly, from generation of gas, which, when not checked and neutralized, results fatally by rupturing the diaphragm, causing death.

The causes of colic are drinking cold water when in a heated condition, costiveness, unwholesome food, and the application of cold water to the body, etc.

Premonitory symptoms are sudden. The animal paws violently, showing evidences of great distress, shifting his position constantly, and manifesting a desire to lie down.

In a few minutes these symptoms disappear and the horse is easy.

He may also act as if he desired to make water, which he is unable to do, there being a spasmodic contraction of the urethra. Hence the desire to give diuretic medicine. Straining in this way is usually prompted by a desire to relieve the muscles of the belly. No diuretic remedy should be given the horse, as he cannot pass the urine until the attack of colic ceases, or it is taken from him with a catheter.

But the same uneasiness soon returns, increasing in severity until the animal cannot remain on his feet; the pulse is full, scarcely altered from its normal condition.

A cold sweat breaks out over the body; the temperature of the legs and ears natural.

First stage of Spasmodic Colic.

As the disease advances the symptoms become more severe, the animal throwing himself down with force and looks anxiously at the sides, snapping with his teeth at his sides, looking anxiously at his belly, and striking upward with the hind feet, showing almost the same symptoms as in inflammation of the bowels.

To better point out the peculiarities or characteristics of each trouble, I will say :

Colic is sudden in its attacks. Legs and ears of natural temperature. Rubbing the belly gives relief. Relief obtained from motion. Pulse, in the early stage of the disease, not much quickened or altered in its character. Intervals of rest. Strength hardly affected.

Inflammation of the Bowels : Gradual in its approach, with previous indications of fever. Pulse, much quickened, small, often scarcely to be felt. Legs and ears cold. Motion increases pain.

Rapid and Great Weakness. Constant Pain.—This disease being wholly of a spasmodic nature, it must be counteracted by anti-spasmodic treatment; and laudanum being the most powerful and reliable anti-spasmodic, it is here indicated.

Treatment.—Give in a pint of raw linseed oil, from two to three ounces of laudanum.

If not better in an hour give two ounces each of oil and laudanum.

The following remedy is considered one of the best in use for the cure of either form of colic:

Colic Remedy.

Opium . . . . $\frac{1}{4}$ lb.
Sulph. ether . . . . 1 pint.
Aromatic Spirits Ammonia . . . . 1 pint.
Sweet Spirits Nitre . . . . 2 pints.
Asafœtida (pure) . . . . $\frac{1}{4}$ lb.
Camphor . . . . $\frac{1}{4}$ lb.

Bottle and let it stand fourteen days, with frequent shaking, and it will be fit for use.

Dose—One ounce, more or less, according to severity of the case, once in from thirty minutes to an hour. Give in a little water.

To enable its immediate use, substitute same proportion of tincture for the gum.

Flatulent Colic.

Same symptoms as spasmodic colic, except that the accumulation of gas in the stomach and intestines is such as to cause the belly to swell.

This disease often proves fatal in two or three hours.

Generally it attacks the horse very suddenly, often occurring while the animal is at work, particularly during warm, or changeable weather, from cold to heat. Indigestion is a general cause, producing gas in the stomach and bowels.

The two locations and causes for this disease are—the stomach, colon and cœcum.

When in the stomach it will be known by eructations or belching of gas through the esophagus or gullet.

If from the coecum or colon, the horse is violently swollen along the belly and sides.

The pulse rarely is disturbed until the disease advances, when it will become quickened, running to its height quickly and receding as rapidly if fatal.

First stage of Flatulent Colic.

If to terminate fatally it will become weaker and slower until it is almost imperceptible.

Should the animal suddenly fall down during great pressure of gas against the walls of the stomach, there is danger of rupturing the diaphragm, causing almost instant death from suffocation.

Treatment—Keep up evaporation of the body as much as possible by sweating with blankets. A hot bath would be still better. If you have on hand the remedy recommended for spasmodic colic, give at once as directed. Should it not be available, give a drench of the following:

Sulph. ether.............................2 oz.
Peppermint..............................2 oz.
Laudanum................................1 oz.
Soft water..............................1 pint.

If the horse is not too sick to get up during the intervals of administering the mixture, keep him in motion. Repeat the dose in half or three-quarters of an hour if not improved.

There is great danger of the diaphragm being ruptured, through the distention of the intestines, in this disease.

To keep the animal on his feet in the stall, and prevent those violent falls and rolling about, and to avoid irritation or action on the bowels, it would be advisable to walk the

Last stages of Colic.

horse as slowly as possible, led by the head to prevent falling or rolling, until such time as the treatment has had the desired effect.

Catarrh or Cold.

Colds, if neglected, may lead to serious consequences, and are of common occurrence. By a little rest and nursing, in time the system will soon resume its normal condition.

Usually, the symptoms are a slight increase of the pulse, followed by a slight discharge from the nose ; loss of appetite ; hair roughed ; and a cough, which sometimes is quite severe. Give aconite as for a fever, and blanket warmly. Give bran mashes, etc. In serious cases, it may run into inflammation of the air passages, as bronchitis or laryngitis. Give fever medicine, and alternate with belladonna. Aim to keep up the strength. Put on a bag made of coarse, loose cloth, into which put some hot bran, on which throw an ounce or two of turpentine. Hang the sack on the horse's head, being careful to leave an opening to allow some of the steam to escape, so it will not scald his nose. A repetition of this treatment a few times will start the nose running freely. Complete this treatment with judicious rest and care.

To relieve obstinate inflammation of the throat and air-passages, apply a good liniment to the throat and chest. This will stimulate the surface.

Strangles, or Distemper.

This form of sore throat has for its design the throwing off of some poisonous matter from the system. You should keep up the strength of the animal, and hasten suppuration. The horse's neck becomes sore and stiff, and there is an enlargement which is hard at first; the nose discharges

Strangles, or Distemper.

matter. The horse generally becomes worse, and, when very bad, causes suffocation; he is able to eat very little, and he loses strength rapidly. A poultice of warm vinegar and bran, freely used and changed as often as it becomes dry, will do much good if applied until the enlargement becomes soft, and can be opened.

Another treatment is to take spirits of camphor, one part; spirits of turpentine, two parts; laudanum, one part. Apply to the neck with a brush three or four times a day until soreness is produced. After each application, put three or four thick pieces of flannel over the parts, binding them on with a bandage. When the tumor comes to a head or point, open it to allow the matter to escape thoroughly. In case the swelling is very deep, and causes serious soreness and swelling of the throat, nurse the horse carefully by feeding with warm gruel, give warm drink, tempt his appetite with grass, etc. Rubbing the enlargement with fly-blister, to bring it to a head, is often resorted to. No physic should be given.

Poll-Evil and Fistula of the Withers.

The treatment of these difficulties is the same for one as for the other—their characters being the same.

Poll-Evil is oftentimes caused by the poll striking a beam or against the floor. Sometimes it may be the result of constitutional predisposition.

When the enlargement and inflammation are first noticed, you may be able to dispose of it by giving a dose of physic and applying cooling applications to the part.

If the inflammation has not become reduced, clip the hair from the part and rub on some blistering ointment.

Should the swelling enlarge, open and allow the pus to escape.

In the treatment of all ulcers keep one point in mind, which is, to make an opening at the bottom if you can, to allow the matter to run out, as matter will always burrow toward the bottom.

This is done by running a seaton through, bringing it out just below the bottom of the wound.

Wash out the sore clean. It should be afterwards bathed with any of the healing preparations for ulcers given in another page.

If pipes are formed requiring caustic medicine, use either chloride of zinc, corrosive sublimate, or any strong escorotic to destroy this growth, after which treat as before.

These difficulties require proper dressing daily.

Fistula of the Withers should be treated in the same manner.

The principle of treating these difficulties is the same as that for deep-seated ulcers.

Special directions for the treatment of them will be found under the head of Ulcers, etc.

Sweeny.

All reliable practitioners have discarded Sweeny as a fictitious disease. It is claimed that Sweeny is the effect of diseases of the feet, such as ossification of the lateral cartilage, contraction, corns, navicular diseases, etc., producing atrophy of the muscles of the shoulder, and their treatment would be to remove the cause, and the effect would disappear.

To follow a local treatment of Sweeny, or filling-up of the shoulder, you do so by the application of most any stimulating treatment.

The simplest and best, never-failing remedy is the application of soft-soap.

Horsemen consider it invaluable. Add a little salt to soft-soap, and rub on the parts thoroughly four or five times during the week.

Four or five applications will fill up the depression of a bad case.

The regular treatment consists of seatoning and blistering, but the above will answer for local treatment.

Spavins—two kinds.

There are two kinds of Spavin, jack and occult or consolidated joint.

The first is situated at the upper portion of the metatarsal bone at its juncture with cuboid bones.

Spavins of both kinds have their origin from the same

causes—inflammation of the cartilage of the joint in the first instance, and extending to ulceration of the bone, consequently bony matter is thrown out, uniting more or less of the hock and excess of matter and ulceration of the bones from the enlargement.

The causes of Spavin, though numerous, are traceable principally to sprains, blows and hard work, or any cause exciting inflammation of this part.

Bone Spavin.

At the beginning, the symptoms are treacherous.

Horses are often treated for hip lameness before any enlargement makes its appearance.

The horse, while laboring under acute inflammation of the hock joint, is at first very lame.

Generally, the tumor makes its appearance from the fifth to the eighth week. At times, the lameness is gradual—hardly perceptible at first—becoming worse until there is a decided lameness at starting, which will in a short time wear off as the horse becomes warmed up.

There are various remedies and applications. Some men pretend to remove spavins. The skillful practitioner knows better. It will be seen that if such people *can* remove the external tumor, they *cannot* separate the bones that are united, and horses may be spavined without any visible enlargement.

Blood Spavin.

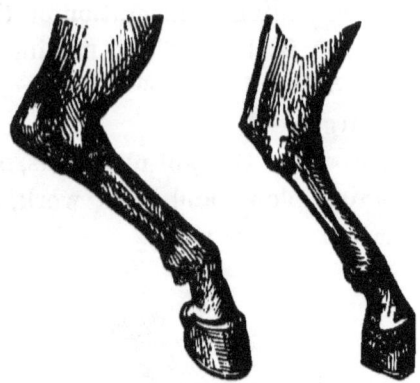

Natural action.   Spavined leg.

Take cantharides 2 oz., mercurial ointment 4 oz., tincture of iodine 3 oz., turpentine 4 oz., corrosive sublimate 3 drams; mix well with 1 ℔ lard. After well blistered, dress with calomel salve.

Blood Spavin.

This disease, when once well seated, is incurable; but if taken in its acute state, bandaging tight and kept wet with cold water is the best treatment.

Heaves

Are produced by driving the horse against a heavy current of air, and inhaling an excess of air; thus overcharging the lungs, they become ruptured, and when once ruptured, can never be cured. The food should be well wet, so that he will inhale no dust while eating, as it is very injurious.

The dust of a threshing-machine for one day is worse than to feed with clover-hay for a month.

Glanders.

Glanders is an affection of the glands of the head, and may be known by a flow of white matter from one or both nostrils, accompanied by an offensive smell. It may be told from common distemper, as the secretions from distemper will float on water, while that from glanders will sink immediately. It cannot be cured, but may be relieved.

Lockjaw, or Tetanus,

Is produced from some injury received by the nervous system, injury to the spinal column, a rap on the top of the head, a nail driven into the quick by the smith, or one picked up on the road.

Symptoms.

He stretches himself at full length, hangs his head down, is stiff all over, his jaws immovably fixed.

Treatment.—Open his bowels with a drench of ten drams of aloes, three drams calomel, in one pint of linseed oil. Keep him in a comfortable box, feed him on whatever he can eat—bran mashes, boiled oats, or, if he is very bad, give him a sloppy drink of oat-meal, rye-meal, or linseed-meal, whichever he can take.

Bots.

Bots are one of the natural appendages of the stomach of a horse—as much so as his lungs, arteries, nerves, or any other essential part of his vital organism. They never injure the horse.

They have been placed in the stomach of all horses by nature, for a specific purpose, and no horse can live without them in the stomach.

They are in the stomach of all horses at the time of

foaling, and number about the same—or no more or less—
at any age of the horse. They never lose their hold of the
lining of the stomach under any circumstances. The heart
was given to propel the blood ; the lungs, to breathe ; the
eye, to see ; the ear, to hear ; and the bots, to aid digestion.
The life and health of the horse is dependent upon the bots.
When the horse is sick the bots are sick ; any description of
food good for the horse is good for the bots. They never
injure a horse except when they become diseased—the same
as any other vital part. If your horse is over-heated or
exhausted from work, and is attacked with colic or any
description of inflammation, the bots suffer equally with the
horse; anything given the horse that will kill the bots, is
liable to kill the horse also. When you keep your horse in
good condition, well and regularly fed, there is no danger.
Bots have been used heretofore to cover up the ignorance of
the farrier. If your horse dies of inflammation of the brain
they would say he died of bots ; if he dies of lung fever the
same thing is said ; if he dies of colic or anything else, it is
always attributed to the bots—when, in fact, no horse ever
died directly from their effects.

The quid has been given to the sheep and cow, so that
they may belch up their food and ruminate or re-chew it,
thereby preparing it for the digestive organs, while the bots
have been given to the horse to perform the same work for
him, without taxing him with the labor of re-chewing ; besides, his owner might require some hard or fast work of
him, just at the time when he should be re-chewing his food.
The gad-fly or nit-bee has nothing to do with the production
of the bot, no more than the horse-fly, buffalo-gnat, or any
other fly ; all the harm they do is the tickling and buzzing
sensation that they produce in the particularly ticklish portion of the horse that they visit; the wasp, hornet, and
other insects, torment horses, yet there are no bots ever at-

tributed to any of them ; you can punish a horse as much
with a fine straw or a piece of paper twisted to a point, by
tickling him under the throat, in the flank, or upon the legs,
as much as the gad-fly does, or by catching a fly and holding
close to his ear while it makes a buzzing noise, all of which
he attempts to escape from, as much as from the presence of
the gad-fly. It is impossible for him to lick or bite the nits
from off his legs, belly or throat, without pulling the hair
off, and as no horse ever swallows any hair, it is impossible
for them to be carried into the stomach ; besides, there are
thousands of horses in warm climates, and in stables, that
never see any gad-flies, yet all horses have bots.

All that has been written in connection with the gad-flies
producing bots, and all of the technical terms used to illustrate
them and their effects, have been to till works upon the
horse.

Bots, as a disease in horses, like that of the lampass and
many other old notions, will soon be obsolete.

Lampass.

Lampass is a fullness and inflammation of the front portion of the roof of the mouth, near the teeth.

I here have to combat with an old-established opinion,
that lampass is a disease in horses; but eighteen years' experience has taught me that there is no such disease.

The gums of all young horses are swollen below the
teeth, as nature intended they should be, and all of the dis-
comforts of the horse attributed to lampass, is the effect of
improper feed and bad care. You never find a horse of five
years old with lampers ; at this age the gums recede above
the teeth, and continue to do so as they grow older.

The practice of burning colts for the lampass is a severe and
savage practice, destroying the roof of the mouth, and the
power of rataining the food until it can be well masticated.

The hard gristly bars in the roof of all colts' mouths, have been placed there by nature for specific purposes. 1st, it is quite insensible to the touch, and with this hard bar he picks grass and grinds his feed while his teeth are tender and being shed ; 2nd, a large artery terminates in the roof of the mouth, and those bars have been placed there to protect it from rupture. To relieve him, give him plenty of oats and bran well wet up ; give him plenty of carrots, turnips or potatoes, plenty of nice clover hay, clean water, fresh air, a dry bed, and you will never be troubled with lampass. You might as well burn off one ear, or burn out one eye (then he would have one ear to hear with, and one eye to see with); but when you burn out his mouth, he has nothing to supply it with, and you disable and perpetually torture him.

To Strengthen the Tendons After Hard Driving, and Reduce Swelling of the Legs.

Camphor Gum......................½ oz.
Gum Myrrh........................1 oz.
Oil of Spike......................1 oz.
Alcohol...........................1 pt.
Organum..........................1 oz.
Beef's Gall.................... 1 ordinary size.

Wash and rub dry, then apply the liniment ; after which rub dry ; again apply the liniment to the limb and bandage moderately tight.

This remedy I consider the best ever used for the purpose recommended.

Grease Heels.

This is a greasy, white, offensive discharge from the heels of the horse. The skin becomes tender, hot and swollen. The acrid character of the discharge causes portions of the skin to slough away, leaving an ugly sore.

Treatment—with the following ball open the bowels :

Pulverized Gentian Root..............2 drams.
Barbadoes Aloes........................1 oz.
Pulverized Ginger....................1 dram.
Water.............sufficient to make the ball.

Poultice and wash the parts well for two or three days with the following : Flaxseed meal, mixed with a solution of 2 drams sulphate of zinc, to a pint of water, which—keep clean—bathe often with a solution of chloride of lime or of zinc. Glycerine can also be used.

Scratches—Cure.

Glycerine...............................4 oz.
Tincture Arnica.......................4 oz.

In severe cases, where heels are cracked, add :

Tincture of Myrrh.....................2 oz.
Iodine..................................1 oz.
Gunpowder (powdered fine).............½ oz.

Put in bottle and shake well.

Apply two or three times a day. First, give the horse a few bran mashes.

Quitter.

This is a formation of pus between the hoof and the soft structure within. A sore at the coronet, or upper part of the foot, which at first is a hard, smooth tumor, soon becomes soft and breaks, discharging quantities of pus.

Treatment.—Poultice the foot for several days with flaxseed meal. As soon as the hoof becomes soft, cut away the loose portions, but no more, and inject with a syringe the following once a day:

Nitrate of silver, 2 drams in a pint of water; or
Chloride of zinc, 2 drams dissolved in a pint of water; or
Sulphate of zinc, 1½ drams in a pint of water.
Glycerine is sometimes used advantageously.

Clean the foot well with castile soap and water before using the wash.

Mange.

Place your horse in the sun and scrub him thoroughly with castile soap and water; then wash him well with gas water, putting in the water 2 drams of white hellebore to the gallon. Then change him from his old stable to another one. One washing generally cures permanently.

Thoroughly scrub the harness and put it away for six or eight weeks, as a necessary precaution against the disease.

Mange Treatment No. 2.

Linseed Oil............................6 oz.
Oil Turpentine ....4 oz.
Oil Tar ....4 oz.

Mix.

Fatal Disease of the Foot.

The report of the Statistician of the Department of Agriculture, in the Commissioner's report of 1869, states that a number of horses have died of a peculiar disease of the foot, and says that diagnosis shows a separation of the ligaments of the coffin-joint and the foot.

It reads: "The foot turns up, causing the animal to walk on the ankle. The flexor-tendons are literally severed from the laminæ, and the foot will drop off by simply cutting through the skin with a knife. None have ever been cured and no one appears to know the cause of the difficulty.

No cases so extreme as those described by the Statistician have come to our personal knowledge, but we have little doubt that it will prove on investigation, which we are making, that the cause of the terrible malady is in the use of shoes of improper construction, neglect of the form of the foot, a proper form of which is so essential to health, and the too liberal use of cold water on the feet and legs, when the animal was in a heated condition, or too much dampness of the stable or pastures in which the animals were kept, or, perhaps, all combined.

Nasal Gleet.

The result of neglected catarrh is a chronic discharge, from one or both nostrils, of a whitish, muco-purulent matter.

The animal looks, feeds and works well, though he has this discharge, which is caused by weakness in the secretory vessels of the lining membrane of the nose.

A treatment on the tonic principle has been successfully used in this disorder. Purging and bleeding are decidedly hurtful.

Give one of the following powders night and morning :

Carbonate of Iron.......................1 oz.

Gentian, pulverized ....1 oz.

Quassia,   "   ....1 oz.

Divide into four powders.

Or—

Sequin-chloride of iron..................2 oz.

Cinnamon.............................1 oz.

Divide into four powders.

Or—

Nux Vomica, pulverized..................½ oz.

Linseed Meal..........................2 oz.

Divide into eight powders.

Or—

Muriate of Barytes.....................½ oz.

Linseed Meal..........................1 oz.

Divide into eight powders. The best known. One should be given night and morning.

Cure of Farcy.

Black Antimony.......................1 oz.

Saltpetre.............................⅛ lb.

Sulphur..............................¼ lb.

If acute : Dose—One tablespoonful twice a day. If sub-acute, once or twice a week.

I give for this formidable disease :

Three drams powdered sulphate of copper, given every night in the food until the horse refuses to eat.

Repeat in a few days, but if the case is bad, give the medicine in water as a drench, for ten days, if he will not take it in his food.

Ringbone.

Many have supposed and asserted that this unsoundness in the horse was inheritable. This is erroneous, as Ring-bones are the result of injuries, and often occur when the colt is but a few days old, especially if it is compelled to follow the dam too far on a hard road, before the feet have acquired sufficient strength and solidity. Requiring the young foal to stand on a hard floor will also produce them. They are produced in the horse, after he has arrived at the age to be shod, by allowing the toes of the feet to get too long; from slipping on the ice; shoeing without support to the soles; tramping on the feet by other horses, and various other causes.

The Ringbone is a knot, or excrescence of ossified bone, usually forming in the region of the articulation of the coffin and lower pastern bones; hence, they destroy, in a greater or less degree, the action of that very important joint, and generally produce permanent lameness.

Prevention by care and good management is more simple than cure.

In purchasing a horse it will be prudent to examine all the feet by the pressure of the finger on the skin all around the pastern, from the lower margin of the hair to the height of three inches, as Ringbone may sometimes be detected in this manner when it is not visible, especially in the incipient state. We have seen excrescences form on the bone near the foot from bruises, which never produced lameness, though they are suspicious blemishes.

Use a strong blister in its acute state : if of old standing its cure is difficult and doubtful.

Sprains in the Stifle.

Symptoms.—The horse holds up his foot, moans when moved, swells in stifle ; this is what is called stifling. There is no such thing as this joint getting out of place. It gets sprained the same as any other joint, and the patellar may slip from its place, which acts as a stay to the joint.

The tendons and ligaments become contracted, and lameness follows. To relieve it, foment the joint well, stimulate it with some strong liniment or a slight blister.

The Nerve Operation.

A most barbarous operation called "nerving," or "neurotomy," was discovered in England, and was subsequently introduced into this country ; nothing more disgraceful was ever imported into any country claiming civilization.

It consisted in laying bare, taking up and cutting out from an inch to one and a half inches of the metacarpal nerve, producing the most excruciating pain. We illustrate the operation for the purpose of exposing the cruelty of it, that no one will ever be guilty of such wanton torture again.

By reference to the annexed plate (page 106), it will be sufficiently explained.

We would suggest as a humane substitute for this operation, to shoot the horse in the brain, and thus put an end to the suffering of the pitiable animal as speedily as possible.

If a proper shoe is applied when the horse is first shod, and its use continued, all the organs of the foot will be maintained in their natural, respective and relative positions, and health, vigor and protracted usefulness will be secured, and there will be no necessity for the brutal operation of neurotomy.

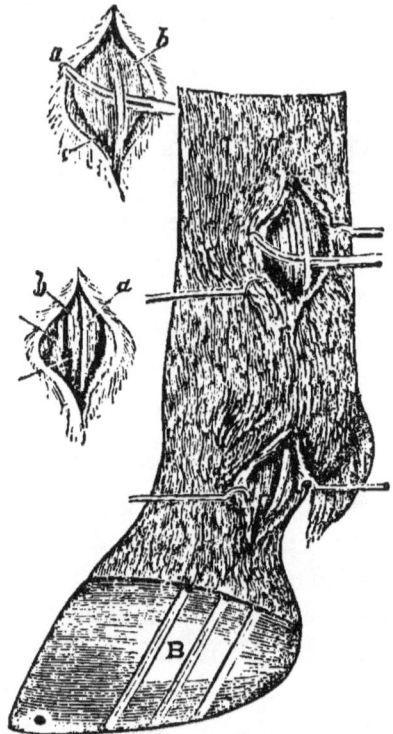

REFERENCES—*Upper Section.*—*a*, A prober passed under the nerve; *b*, the nerve; *c*, the artery; *d*, the back sinews, or flexor tendons.

Lower Section.—*a*, The nerve; *b*, the artery; *c*, the vein; *d*, a branch of the nerve between the vein and artery, not divided in the low operation.

How to Treat Contracted Feet.

By reference to the foot in the plate illustrating the process of nerving, three grooves will be seen in the wall.

These *grooves* we make in the hard crust of the foot of patients suffering from long standing, and severe contraction of the heels. The forward groove is placed directly over the points or wings of the coffin-bone, where the pressure of the contracted wall is most severe on the metacarpal nerve; back of this we cut two others parallel. These grooves should be cut from one-eighth to one-fourth of an inch in depth and the same width, according to the strength of the wall and the extent of the contractions. We use a narrow gouge with which to cut the grooves, and cut them before the shoe is set, by placing the bottom of the foot on a block some twenty inches in height, and use a light mallet to drive the gouge.

The operation of grooving, three on the outer and two on the inner sides of the foot, does not require more than five to ten minutes, and may be done by any person of ordinary judgment, as it only requires a little care not to cut the groove so deep as to disturb the sensitive portion of the foot, which will be indicated by blood showing in the bottom of the groove, a slight show of which need not alarm the operator, though it is preferable to take sufficient time and care in performing the operation, to do it in the best

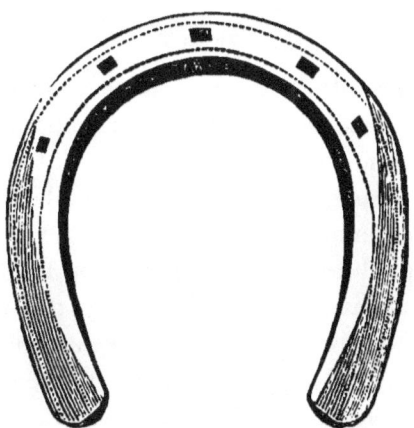

Shoe for Spreading the Heel.

possible manner, as it doubles the value of the horse the instant the operation is completed and our shoe for spreading the heel is properly set. The above cut is a drawing of this shoe, with five nail-holes in front and none in the heels.

This shoe is generally understood by the skilled blacksmith, and requires great care in the fitting to make it perform its desired work, which is to spread the heel slowly.

It will be seen by the cut that the portion of the shoe resting on the heel is about one-eighth of an inch higher on the inside than on the outside at the heel. In fact, the shoe is convexed from the last nail to the heel. The cut represents the surface of the shoe next to the hoof. The shoe should be a trifle wider at the heel than the hoof. Care must be taken that the shoe does not rest on the sole of the foot, but bear on the wall.

The best way to fit this shoe is to fit it cold as well as you can. Then heat it and apply it to the hoof, and make an impression on the foot with the hot shoe. This will enable the smith to get a better fit than he could by fitting it cold. After these grooves are made in the hoof, and the above shoe properly fitted, it will at once double the value of the horse.

Founder.

Founder is produced by the sudden transition from heat to cold. For instance, by driving a horse until he is hot, then allowing him to stand in a cold current of air, or giving him a heavy draught of cold water while warm, thereby checking the circulation of the blood to the extremities. It is frequently produced by driving fast on hard roads, which produces inflammation of the delicate plates called laminæ, by which the hoof is attached to the sensitive foot. It also occurs from overloading the stomach by too much wheat, oats, barley or peas, as is often seen when a horse gets loose during the night, getting to the grain-bin; the food, taken into the stomach in such large quantities, and a portion of it dry, when wet by the stomach, swells to such an extent that it prevents the blood from circulating, and produces founder.

No horse will be foundered from giving him his ordinary amount of feed at any time. Symptoms : Shivering and uneasiness ; he refuses his food, moves about with the fore-feet, and seems restless; the mouth is hot, the pulse full and quickened ; soon the pain in the feet becomes evident, he sometimes inclines to lie, points with the muzzle to the feet, which are found hot and tender ; he advances

them in front, resting principally on the heels; while the hind-feet are well drawn under him ; on backing him, he backs with reluctance : when forced back, he drags one foot after the other, evincing considerable pain in so doing.

When moved forward he walks on the heels, his movements being slow and difficult. The bowels are costive and fever runs high.

Treatment.—Give the horse a good bedding of straw, in a large, well-ventilated stall, so as to encourage him to lie down, which, by removing the weight from the inflamed parts, will relieve his sufferings very much, and assist in hastening the cure. As soon as his bed is fixed, give him twenty drops of the tincture of aconite-root in a half-pint of cold water, poured into his mouth with a bottle having a strong neck, and repeat this dose every four hours until six

or eight doses have been given.   Also apply a cloth wet in
ice-water to the feet, and keep wet with the same for several
hours until the severe pain has been relieved.   Wet the
cloths often, and continue for two or three days, or longer if
necessary.   Give plenty of cold water to drink.   The above
treatment should be adopted as soon as possible after the
horse has been attacked with founder.   Let the horse have
rest until he has fully recovered.   Give grass or mashes for
two or three days, and then give a good and fair amount of
feed.

Ringbone.

This cut represents the seat of the ringbone.   Fig. 1, the
joint between the pastern-bones; Fig. 2, the joint between
the lower pastern (or small pastern) and the coffin-bone.

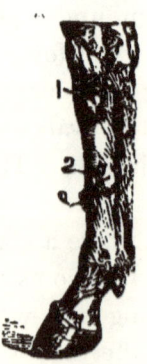

Splints.

This cut shows the location of the different splints on the
fore leg.   Fig. 1—A splint near the knee; Fig. 2, a low

splint; Fig. 3, a small bony growth on the front of the leg, also called splint.

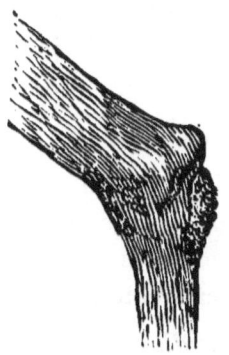

Curb.

This is one of the many diseases of the hock-joint, and consists of an enlargement or gradual bulging out at the posterior part of the hock.   [See above cut.]

Shoulder-joint Lameness.

This difficulty, being located in the joint, is much more serious than the shoulder lameness just described, and it is more difficult to effect a perfect cure of it.

Symptoms.—The animal drags the leg, with the toe on the ground, and throws the leg out in attempting to move it. It is with great difficulty that he can raise his foot.

Treatment.—If the treatment is not put off too long, a cure may reasonably be expected, if the following directions are followed. This disease, being similar to a spavin in the hock-joint, should have similar treatment. If the part is very hot, reduce the temperature by cold cloths; or perhaps hot fomentations may work well instead of the cold; then apply a mild blister.

To Kill Lice on Horses.

Place your horse in a warm place and wash him thoroughly with 1 ounce of arsenic dissolved in a pail of water.

Hen and human lice thrive well on horses, and the above recipe will always exterminate them.

Condition Powders.

Gentian Root, pulverized..................2 oz.
Anise Seed, pulverized...................1 oz.
Ginger....................................1 lb.
Fenugreek Seed...........................1 oz.
Seed of Sumach Berries, pulverized........1 oz.
Antimony.................................1 oz.

Mix with one pound of brown sugar. Nothing better for colds and coughs, and to improve a horse's appetite.

Liniment of Extraordinary Merit for all Purposes.

Turpentine..............................1 pint.
Apple Vinegar...........................1 pint.
Eggs....................................1 pint.
Chloroform..............................1 dram.
Carbolic Acid...........................1 dram.

Bottle tight and shake well before using.

Condition Powder.

Ashes...................................1 quart.
Flax-seed Meal..........................1 quart.
Salt................................2 tablepoonsful.
Mustard.............................1 tablespoonful.

Saltpetre....................1 tablespoonful.
Cayenne Pepper................1 teaspoonful.

Dose—Two tablespoonsful once a day.

Diuretic Drops.

These drops will be found good for the stoppage of water, foul water, or inflammation of the kidneys.

Gum Camphor, pulverized................1 oz.
Sweet Spirits of Nitre.................4 oz.

Treatment for Cuts or Wounds.

If the wound or cut is very bad, trim the hair off closely around the edges, and wash carefully with castile soap and warm water.

The object next is to produce a granulating process.

In all cases of wounds, cuts or ulcers, of any kind, you should bear in mind that the importance of washing the matter, or syringing it, from the affected part, with castile soap and warm water, daily, and a dependent opening must be made to allow the matter to escape from the wound.

Matter, in every case, burrows or pockets, and the principle is the same in every case.

Use caustics to cut out all fungus or diseased growths, and using, proportionately, more stimulating medicine for indolent ulcers than for those in a fresh state.

The following ointment is unsurpassed for curing cuts and fresh wounds on horses :

Beeswax ....¼ lb.
Palm Oil............................2½ lbs.
Lard...............................2 lbs.
Gum Turpentine......................½ lb.
Calamine...........................1 lb.

Simmer over a slow fire and stir well together until thoroughly mixed.   Wash the wound well with warm water and castile soap, and apply the ointment once a day.

A Simple Healing Preparation.

Water ....½ pint.
Tincture Myrrh........................1 oz.
Tincture Aloes........................2 oz.

Mix, and apply once a day.

Ointment for Healing Cuts, Galls, Etc.

Carbolic Acid.......................6 grains.
Lard ....1 oz.
Oxide of Zinc, pulverized fine   .....4 drams.

Melt the lard and stir in the zinc.

Add the carbolic acid and mix thoroughly.

By applying this ointment once or twice a day to the injured part, it will cause a healthy discharge from a foul ulcer.

Liniment for Open Wounds.

White Vitriol.........................2 oz.
Sulphate of Copper....................1 oz.
Muriate of Soda (Salt)................2 oz.
Linseed Oil...........................2 oz.
Orleans Molasses......................8 oz.

Boil the above ingredients in a pint of urine, for fifteen minutes.   When nearly cold, add 1 oz. oil of vitriol and 4 oz. spirits of turpentine, and bottle for use.

To quickly set the wound to discharging, apply the liniment to the wound with a quill, which will perform a cure in a few days.

Valuable Wash for Fresh Wounds.

Copperas............................1 teaspoonful.
Fine gunpowder.................2 teaspoonfuls.
White Vitriol....................1 teaspoonful.

Add 1 quart of boiling water. Let it stand until cool.
For deep wounds apply with the syringe.

Liniment for Foul Ulcers.

Nitric Acid ....½ oz.
Sulphate of Copper ....1 oz.
Water ....8 to 12 oz.

Cooling Liniment for External Inflammation.

Vinegar...............................2 oz.
Spirits of Wine.......................3 oz.
Goulard extract.......................1 oz.
Water............................. 1½ pints.

Apply with a bandage.

For Inflamed Leg, Galled Back or Shoulders.

Spirits of Wine.......................2 oz.
Vinegar...............................4 oz.
Sal. Ammoniac.........................1 oz.
Tincture Arnica.....................2 drams.
Water...............................½ pint.

Mix and bathe often and thoroughly.

Sticking Plaster for Cuts and Wounds.

Tallow................................2 oz.
Burgundy Pitch........................4 oz.

Spread on linen while hot. Cut in strips of proper length
and width. First, draw the cut together, warm the strips and
apply them. Cut the hair short where you apply the strips.

Wash for Reducing Inflamed Wounds.

Crotus Martes.........................1 oz.
Sulphate of Zinc......................1 oz.
Sugar of Lead.........................½ oz.
Water.................................1 pint.

Prevents bad smell in sores.

To Prevent Swelling, Following a Bruise or Sprain.

Tincture Arnica.........................2 oz.
Cold Water.............................1 qt.

Anodyne Stimulating Liniment.

Sulphuric Ether.........................1½ oz.
Spirits of Turpentine....................½ oz.
Spirits of Hartshorn.....................1½ oz.
Sweet Oil. ....¾ oz.
Oil of Cloves...........................½ oz.
Chloroform ....1 oz.

This liniment relieves pain and is unsurpassed for strains, lameness and soreness. Put the liniment in a strong eight-ounce bottle, cork tight, and keep in the dark. When used rub in well. .

Magic Liniment.

Organum................................2 oz.
Hemlock ....2 oz.
Oil of Spike............................2 oz.
Sweet Oil...............................4 oz.
Wormwood ....2 oz.
Spirits Ammonia.........................2 oz.
Spirits Turpentine ....2 oz.
Gum Camphor...........................2 oz.
Proof Spirits (90 per cent)...............1 qt.
Bottle tight after mixing.

It is beneficial for bruises, sprains, etc., and a fine counter irritant for inflammation and pleurisy.

For New Strains.

Carbonate Ammonia......................2 oz.
Apple Vinegar ....½ gill.
Rub in well.

Healing Compound.

Calamine, pulverized................2 drams.
Gum Camphor.....................1 dram.
Prepared Chalk....................1 oz.
Burnt Alum.........................½ oz.
Mix.

Sprinkle on the affected part, and in a few hours it will heal. Good for collar or saddle galls, fresh wounds, and for any sore or lacerated mouths, or any trouble requiring great astringent healing properties.

This wonderful powder is well known by having been extensively advertised through this country.

Caustics.

Substances used to burn away tissues of the body by decomposition of their elements are termed caustics, and are valuable in destroying fungus growth and renew a healthy action.

Nitrate of silver is excellent to lower granulation.

Corrosive sublimate in powder acts energetically.

Sulphate of copper is not so strong as nitrate of silver, but good.

Chloride of zinc is a powerful caustic. It may be used in sinuses; in solution, 7 drams in a pint of water.

Mild Caustics.

A wound or ulcer will not heal while there remains any foreign substance in the shape of splinters, pieces of bone, hair, etc.

No matter what treatment you subject the wound to, it will not heal so long as foreign substances remain in the cut.

Wash with, or inject, warm water and castile soap, after which the regular digestive ointment can be used. But if fungus growths cannot be removed with the knife, use a caustic—a little of which is to be put on the part or in the sinews.   Carrying this treatment in the extreme implies using a hot iron (the actual cautery).

Balls for Farcy.

No. 1—Calomel...........................20 grains.
  Common Turpentine ....3 drams.
  Sulphate of Copper..................1 dram.
 Syrup and liquorice to form a ball.
No. 2—Iodide of Potassium..............10 grains.
  Sulphate of Iron....................2 drams.
  Gentian........................2 drams.
  Ginger...................... ....1 dram.
 Treacle to form a ball.

Another Diabetes Remedy.

 Alum.... ....$\frac{1}{2}$ dram.
 Catechu................................$\frac{1}{2}$ oz.
 Sugar of Lead......................10 grains.
 With conserve of roses to form a ball.

Cough Balls.

No. 1—Digitalis........................$\frac{1}{2}$ dram.
  Nitre........................$1\frac{1}{2}$ drams.
  Tartar Emetic......................$\frac{1}{2}$ dram.
 Tar enough to form a ball.   One every night.
No. 2—Gum Ammoniac ....3 drams.
  Opium....................... ....$\frac{1}{2}$ dram.
  Powdered Squills...................1 dram.
 Syrup to form ball.

For Bloody Urine.

 Sulphate of Zinc...................40 grains.
 Catechu............................4 drams.
 Acetate of Lead...................10 grains.
 Conserve of roses to form a ball.   Give one daily.

Condition Powder.

This is the best tonic Condition Powder ever used, and is sold in the Eastern cities at a high price, under various names, such as Condition Food, etc.

Salt.....................................1¾ ℔s.
Common Brown Sugar...................6 ℔s.
Carbonate Soda..........................6 oz.
Ginger (ground)..........................½ ℔.
Gentian (powdered)......................¾ ℔.
Cummin Seed (ground) ....6 oz.
Fenugreek (ground).......................6 oz.
Grains Paradise (ground)..................½ ℔.
Meal....................................100 ℔s.

Dose—One pint with the food.

Incurable Diseases.

There are some diseases or afflictions to which the horse is subject, which, when thoroughly established, are incurable ; among which are heaves, cribbing, thumps, windsucking, bog and bone spavins, curbs, ringbones and exosotosis on the joints. This latter class of unsoundness may, however, be palliated in incipiency, by blistering, but it should be administered by a skilled veterinarian. If not, the effect of the treatment may be worse than the disease.

Watering Horses.

The water from ponds, streams or rain-water cisterns, is much preferable to that from cold springs or wells, as the temperature of it is more natural and more conducive to health than cold water, and it is generally softer, a desirable quality of water for all animals. If the horse is to be driven rapidly, he should be watered frequently with tepid water, and there is great economy in removing the chill from the water used for idle animals in cold weather.

The food saved by observing this, will pay many times the cost of tempering the water drank. It is very injudicious to water horses when away from home, with cold water, when they have been accustomed to warm water at home, as it is liable to produce lung fever, chills and severe colic.

Bare Feet for Farm Horses.

Horses used only on the farm and earth roads are better off without shoes in summer, unless the land is very rough and stony. There is not only the saving of the cost of shoeing, but all the destructive effects arising from shoeing in the ordinary way will be avoided. By working the horse barefooted, the natural organs of support are used, and a healthful condition of the feet is maintained.

It is well, however, to examine the bare feet twice a year, and in case they wear or grow irregularly, they should be pared to the proper shape.

Horses used for the road in winter should be sharp shod, but these shoes should be removed at the commencement of the plowing season.

A VALUABLE ESSAY

ON

HORSE-SHOEING.

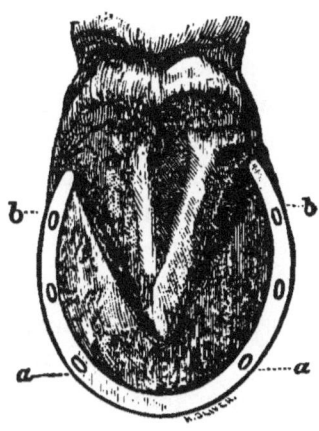

A few years ago the Scottish Society for the Prevention of Cruelty to Animals offered a series of prizes for the best and most practical essays on horse-shoeing, in connection with comfort and soundness of the horse. About fifty essays were sent in, and were submitted to Prof. Williams, Principal of the Edinburgh Veterinary College; Mr. W. Robertson, M. R. C. V. S., Kelso, and Mr. B. Cartledge. M. R. C. V. S., Sheffield, Examiners of the Royal College of Veterinary Surgeons, and Mr. J. C. Broad, M. R. C. V. S., London, by whom, after a very patient and careful examination, the first prize was awarded to Mr. George Fleming for the following essay :

It requires but little observation and reflection, one would think, in order to arrive at the conclusion that the art of horse-shoeing is not only an important one, so far as civilization and the ordinary every-day business of life is concerned, but that the successful utilization of the Horse, together with its welfare and comfort, in a great measure depend upon the correctness of the principles on which its practice is based, and the mode in which these principles are carried out by the artisan.

For proof of this we have but to glance at the immense traffic in our great towns and cities in which the horse figures so·prominently, at the same time remembering that, without a defence to its hoofs, this invaluable animal would be almost, if not quite, valueless, in consequence of the hardness of our artificial roads, and the great efforts demanded from him ; or, studying the anatomy and functions of the limbs and feet, to call to mind how these are wonderfully calculated to serve most essential purposes in locomotion and weight-sustaining, and how necessary it is, at the same time, that their natural adaptability be as little as possible thwarted or annulled by the interference of man in his endeavor to protect or aid them.

From the earliest ages, the horse's foot and its envelop, the hoof, have been looked upon by horsemen as the principal region of the animal's body to which care and attention should be directed ; as, when these become injured or diseased, no matter how perfect and sound the other parts may be, the quadruped's services are diminished or altogether lost.

Consequently, the preservation of these in an efficient and healthy state has ever been the aim of those who valued the Horse for the immense advantages his services were capable of conferring on mankind ; and in later years, those who have been moved by the sacred impulse of humanity toward the lower creatures have not forgotten how much the noble animal may suffer from unskillful management of its feet, through the neglect or ignorance of those who have the special care of these organs.

At a very early period in the domestication of the Horse, and particularly in western regions, it must have been soon discovered that, at certain seasons, on particular soils, and especially when called upon to perform any great amount of traveling and load-carrying, the horn composing the hoof underwent an amount of wear greater than nature could compensate for, and that the living sensitive structures within, becoming exposed and irritated by contact with the ground, gave rise to pain, lameness and inability to work.

To guard against this serious result, the ingenuity of man must have been severely tested in devising a suitable and durable protection for the ground-surface of the hoof, and among the many contrivances proposed, the most notable, and by far the most valuable, has been the device of nailing a plate of metal to the outer margin or *wall* of the hoof.

The antiquity of this invention is very great, and it is probable that for many centuries the shoe was considered as nothing more than a simple defender of the hoof from the damaging effects of attrition, and occasionally as an aid in securing the animal's foothold during progression on slippery ground.

As time advanced, however, and the services of the Horse became increased a hundredfold by the application of this ingenious and simple expedient, the sciences of anatomy and physiology began to embrace the Horse in their domain, and, crude as they were at first, it is to be feared that, when they were extended to the investigation of the structure and functions of the foot, the useful and comparatively harmless protection of early days was made subservient to the most varied and fantastic theories ; and it must be admitted that for many years horse-shoeing, so far from proving a boon to horse-owners and a preserver of horses' feet, has been far from yielding the benefits its scientific and reasonable application should afford. Indeed, it would be no exaggeration to assert that the predominating principles and practice of this art have been eminently destructive to horses and a source of great loss to their owners.

These principles were founded on a misconception of the functions of the foot and of the part assumed by the hoof in locomotion, and their speedy popularization was due to the fact that they were congenial to the whims of fashion and were deemed essential to the improvement of nature, commending themselves to unreasoning and unreasonable minds like the fashions of cropping horses' and dogs' ears, cutting, nicking and docking tails, and other cruel fancies of depraved tastes.

The amount of injury inflicted by an unscientific method of shoeing may be very much greater than a cursory inquiry would lead one to believe. To those experienced among horses, and who have directed their attention closely to the subject, the proportion of animals whose utility is directly or indirectly impaired by improper treatment of their feet must appear excessive, when compared with the other causes of inefficiency. Indeed, maladies of the feet and limbs, due, more or less, to faulty shoeing, form a very large percentage of the cases usually met with in veterinary practice.

An art, therefore, which has so much influence for good or evil, so far as the usefulness and comfort of the horse are concerned, surely deserves the serious study of all those who are interested in that animal. A good system, founded on the teachings of anatomy and physiology, and perfected by daily experience, must prove of immense benefit to horse and owner; while a bad system, conducted in ignorance or carlessness, cannot but bring about pain and speedy uselessness to the animal and loss to the proprietor.

ANATOMY OF THE HORSE'S FOOT.

One of the primary considerations for those who have the shoeing and management of the horse's foot, should be the acquisition of a knowledge of its structure and functions in health; not a profound knowledge, certainly, such as the scientific veterinarian requires,

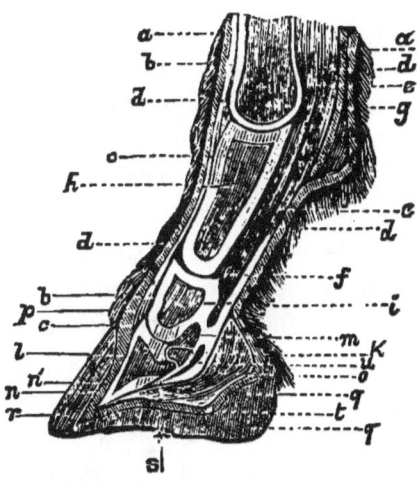

FIG. 1.—SECTION OF THE HORSE'S FOOT —a a, Skin of leg; b b b, extensor tendon of foot; c, its insertion into the foot-bone; d d, capsular ligament of joints; d' d', flexor tendon of foot inserted into sole of foot-bone (s); e e, flexor tendon of pastern inserted at f into the smal pastern bone, i; g, shank or large metacarpal bone; h, large pastern bone; k, navicular bone; l, foot or pedal bone; m, ligaments of navicular bone connected with deep flexor tendon; n, sensitive laminæ, dovetailing with horny laminæ, n'; o, plantar cushion; p, coronary cushion; q, horny frog; r, wall of hoof; t, sensitive membrane of frog and sole; u, the face of the navicular bone over which the flexor tendon plays—the seat of navicular disease.

but sufficient to enable them to understand the situation, relation, texture, and uses of the parts of the organ with which they have more particularly to deal. If the artisan does not possess this knowledge, is it possible that he can practice his handicraft to advantage, or minister effectually to the varied requirements of this organ? It

must be admitted that he cannot do so; and it is from neglect of this fundamental consideration that so much improper and vicious shoeing prevails, and that so many horses
are crippled and prematurely worn out. By the majority of
farriers the foot of the horse is looked upon as little, if anything, more than an insensible block of horn which they may
carve and mutilate with impunity and as suits their fancy,
and for which nothing more is necessary than the attachment, by an unreasonable number of nails, of a clumsy
mass of iron that may not only be unsuitable for its requirements, but positively injurious to it and the other parts of
the limb. The art of farriery in this country has never received a scientific development, but has ever been a mere
affair of routine and tradition. Such should not be the
case; and allusion is only made to this matter here in order
to urge most strenuously the necessity for farriers being
properly instructed in the elements of their art, and made
to comprehend as much as may be required of the construction and functions of the very important organ upon which
they are destined to exercise their skill.

The horse's foot may be said, for practical purposes, to be
intended not only as an organ of support and defence (or
offence), but also as that part of the limb in which the efforts
created elsewhere are concentrated, and as the instrument
through which propulsion and progression may be mainly
effected. It is also largely endowed, in a natural state,
with the sense of touch, which enables the animal to travel
with safety and confidence on rough as well as even, and on
soft as well as hard ground.

When we come to examine it in a methodical and careful
manner, we find that it has for its basis the last three bones
of the limb—the small pastern, navicular, and coffin or pedal
bone. The latter is more particularly the foundation of the
foot, and is the nucleus on which the hoof is moulded, and

which in shape it much resembles. At its highest point in front, the large extensor tendon of the foot is inserted, and in the middle of its lower face or sole is implanted the powerful tendon which bends or flexes the foot ; these tendons are the chief agents in progression. An elastic apparatus surrounds them and a portion of the pedal bone, and the whole is enveloped by a membrane that attaches the hoof in the closest possible manner to its outer surface. Into each of the wings or sides of the bone (for it is crescent-shaped, the horns extending backward on each side) is fixed a large plate of cartilage that rises above the hoof, where it may readily be felt, and which has important relations with its fellow on the opposite side, as well as with other elastic bodies admirably disposed to sustain weight, prevent jar, and insure that lightness and springiness which form so striking a feature in the horse's movements. The navicular bone is a narrow piece, placed transversely between the wings of the coffin bone, and is intended to throw the flexing tendon farther from the centre of motion, and thus increase its power ; the tendon plays over its posterior or lower face, and this disposition, together with the relations established between it and the pedal bone through their connecting ligaments, and the bend the tendon makes in passing over it, cause this part of the foot to be one particularly liable to disease, and one especially deserving of attentive study.

The elastic apparatus of the foot consists of (1) the lateral cartilages just mentioned ; (2), a prominent ring or cornice surrounding the upper border of the pedal bone usually known as the "coronary-substance," but which might be more aptly designated the "coronary cushion" ; this fits into a corresponding concavity in the inner and upper margin of wall of the hoof, and, besides acting as an elastic body or cushion, performs the important function of secreting this

wall or crust of the horny envelop; (3), a triangular body—
the plantar cushion, known to farriers as the "fatty" or
"sensitive frog" (to distinguish it from the horny frog
which immediately covers it), admirably disposed between the wings of the coffin bone, with a view to protect and sustain the flexor tendon during its efforts, as well
as to diminish concussion by its own resiliency and by the
connection it has with the elastic cartilages. From its position at the back part of the foot, and the importance of the
parts it covers, this portion of the elastic apparatus derives
much interest, and must not be overlooked by the farrier.

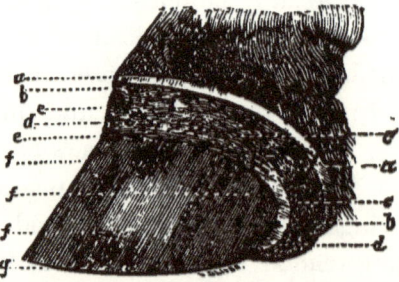

Fig. 2.—Horse's Foot divested of its Hoof.—*a a*, Perioplic ring; *b b*, perioplic
or coronary fissure; *c c c*, coronary cushion covered with villi; *d d*, white
zone; *f f f*, vascular laminæ terminating in villi, *g.*

Besides the elastic apparatus of the foot more immediately in connection with the pedal and navicular bones, we
have the wonderful arrangement of living membrane envel-
oping these parts, whose office appears to be the secretion
and attachment of the horny box we designate the "hoof;"
to it large quantities of blood are conveyed by the ultimate
ramifications of the arteries proceeding to the foot, and
from it, by a complex distribution of veins arising from
these ultimate arterial divisions, to the great venous trunks
that pass up the limb. The terminal twigs of the sensory
nerves of the foot are also freely and wisely distributed in

its substance in the form of exceedingly fine filaments, which endow the organ with a sufficient sense of touch to enable it to perform its varied functions with safety and precision. A peculiar and striking disposition of this membrane can be observed around the front and sides of the pedal bone, when the hoof has been removed by steeping the foot for some time in water. This disposition consists in the elevation of the membrane into parallel vertical leaves, which extend from the coronary cushion to the lower border of the bone, and to a certain distance within its wings. These leaves, which resemble in appearance those on the under side of a mushroom, are known as the "vascular" or "sensitive laminæ," and number between six and seven hundred. Their chief use seems to be to afford a wide and close attachment for the wall of the hoof, within which, through their agency, the pedal bone is, as it were, suspended; so that the relations between bone and hoof are not so rigid as if they were directly united to each other. These laminæ are exceedingly vascular and sensitive, and when they become inflamed through bad shoeing, excessive traveling, or other cause, the horse suffers the most excruciating pain, and in a large majority of cases the chronic inflammation that remains produces serious alterations in the structure and formation of the hoof, leading to more or less lameness and diminished utility.

Besides entering into the formation of these leaves, this membrane covers the other parts of the foot within the hoof, as a sock does the human foot, and endows it with a high degree of vitality and secretory power. It overspreads the coronary and plantar cushions, as well as the sole of the pedal bone, and its surface in these parts is thickly studded with myriads of tufts or "villi," which give it the appearance of the finest Genoa velvet. These minute processes vary in length from one-eighth to more than one-fourth of an inch, and are best observed when a foot, from which the hoof has just been removed by maceration, is suspended in clear water. Examined with the microscope, they are found to be merely prolongations from the face of the membrane, each composed of one or two minute arteries, which branch off into exceedingly fine net-work, and end in hair-like veins. A nervous filament has also been traced into the interior, so that these tufts are not only vascular, but also sensitive. They play an essential part in the formation of the hoof,

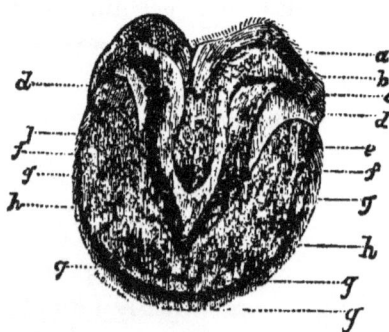

FIG. 3.—SENSITIVE SOLE OF HORSE'S FOOT.— *a*, Cartilaginous bulbs of the heels, covered by sensitive membrane; *b*, inflexion of the coronary cushion; *c*, middle cleft or lacuna; *d d*, plantar laminæ; *e*, limit between the coronary cushion and plantar laminæ; *f f*, branches of the plantar cushion; *g g g.g*, termination of the laminæ in villi; *h h*, sensitive membrane of sole covered with innumerable fine tufts or villi; *i*, prolongation of the coronary cushion into the lateral lacuna.

and their relations to that covering must not be neglected by the farrier in his treatment of it.

This is all that need be said at present with regard to the anatomy of the living parts of the horse's foot; we have referred to it merely to show that this organ is not a crude block of insensitive matter, but a most wonderfully-constructed apparatus, possessed of qualities which are not to be found in any other part of the body. In constructing the foot of this noble creature, Nature sought to do more than merely protect the extremely delicate and exquisitely sensitive structures contained within the hoof from injurious contact with the ground. This redoubtable difficulty is comparatively insignificant in comparison with the other portions of the task she set herself. It was necessary that the lower extremity of the limb of such a glorious creation as the horse, should be an organ endowed with the acutest sense of touch for the instantaneous perception of the consistence and inequalities of the ground over which it moved ; and, while it possessed this quality in a high degree, it was also indispensable that it should be gifted with the properties of resistance, pliability and lightness to the extent necessary for the support and progression of the body, in addition to the rigidity essential to impulsion, the elasticity and suppleness needful to avert reactions or jar, and the durability and rapidity of renovation demanded by incessant wear. Here we have a combination of requirements whose simultaneous existence in one organ might almost be deemed incompatible, so opposite do they appear ; insensibility with a delicate sense of touch ; resistance with lightness, rigidity with elasticity, suppleness with durability.

THE HOOF.

The "hoof" plays no small share in rendering the horse such a complete animal as it is ; and, as this is the portion of the foot which comes more immediately under the care and manipulative skill of the farrier, its study should be a little more detailed and minute, perhaps, than that of the internal structures. For convenience and simplicity in description, it has been divided into " wall " or " crust," " sole," " frog," and " coronary frog-band," or " periople." It is essential that the shoer should understand the structure, nature, and uses of these parts.

The *Wall* of the hoof is that oblique portion which covers the front and sides of the foot from the coronet to the

ground, and is suddenly inflected or bent inward at the
heels, toward the middle of the sole, to form the "bars,"
which are merely prolongations of its extremities ; it consti-
tutes the circumference or margin of the hoof, is the part of
the horny box that is intended more especially to come into
contact with the ground, and is that on which the iron de-
fense rests, and through which the farrier drives the nails
that attach it. The inner face of its upper edge is hollowed
out into a somewhat wide concavity, which receives, or
rather in which rests, the coronary cushion ; this concavity

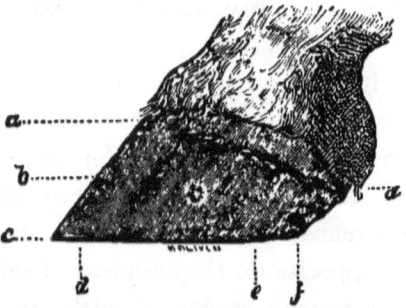

FIG. 4.—PROFILE OF A FIVE-YEAR-OLD FRONT HOOF THAT HAD NEVER BEEN SHOD ;
    EXTERNAL FACE.—Angle of wall at toe 51° ; *a a*, frog-band or periople ; *b*, wall;
    c, toe, between which and *d* is the "outside" or "inside" toe or "mammilla,"
    and between *e* and *f* the "outside" or "inside" heel.

is chiefly remarkable for being pierced everywhere by count-
less minute openings which penetrate the substance of the
wall to some depth ; each of these perforations receives one
of the "villi," or minute tufts of blood-vessels already mentioned as prolonged from the face of the membrane covering
the interior of the foot. Below this concavity, which receives
a large share of the horse's weight, the wall is of about equal
thickness from top to bottom ; on the whole of its inner
surface are ranged thin, narrow, vertical horny plates, in
number corresponding to the vascular laminæ, between
which they are so intimately received or dovetailed—a
horny leaf between every two vascular ones—that in the

living or fresh state it is almost impossible to disunite without tearing them. The inner face of the lower margin is united in a solid manner to the horny sole through the medium of a narrow band of soft, light-colored horn, situated between the two, and which we may call the "white line," or "zone."

The outer surface of the wall is generally smooth and shining in the natural healthy state.

The dimensions of the wall vary in different situations; in front it is deepest and thickest, but toward the quarters and heels it diminishes in height and becomes thinner; at its angles of inflection—the points of the heels—it is strong. Its structure is fibrous; the fibres pass directly parallel to each other from the coronet to the ground, each fibre being moulded on, as it is secreted by, one of the minute tufts of blood-vessels lodged in the cavity at the coronet. Microscopically, the wall is composed of minute cells, closely compressed, and arranged vertically around each fibre, and horizontally between the fibers. A point of much practical interest is to be found in the fact that the fibers on the surface or outside of the wall, are very dense, close, and hard—so dense, indeed, that the wall of an unmutilated hoof looks like whalebone; but toward the inner surface they become softer, more spongy, and easily cut.

The *Horny Sole* is contained within the lower margin of the wall, and is a concave plate covering the lower face of the pedal bone. In structure it is fibrous like the wall, the fibers passing in the same direction, and formed in the same manner by the tufts of vessels projected from the membrane which immediately covers the bone. These tufts penetrate the horn fibers to some depth, and, as in the wall, maintain them in a moist, supple condition, such as best fits them for their office.

The sole is thickest around its outer border, where it

joins the wall; thinnest in the centre, where it is most concave. A notable peculiarity in this part of the hoof, and
one which distinguishes it from the wall, is its tendency to
break off in flakes on the ground face when the fibers have
attained a certain length; the wall, on the contrary, con-
tinues to grow in length to an indefinite extent, and, unless
kept within reasonable dimensions by continual wear or the

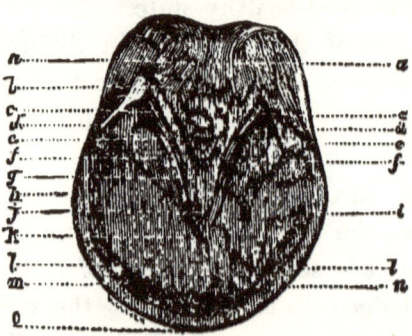

FIG. 5.—PLANTAR SURFACE OF LEFT FORE HOOF OF A FIVE-YEAR-OLD HORSE THAT
HAD NEVER BEEN SHOD—*a a*, glomes or heels of the frog; *b*, median lacuna or
"cleft" of the frog; *c c*, branches of the frog; *d d*, heels, "angles of inflexion,"
or "buttresses" of the wall of the hoof; *e e*, lateral lacunæ or spaces between
the frog and bars; *f f*, inflexions of the wall or "bars;" *g*, body of the frog;
h, outside quarter of the hoof; *i*, inside quarter of the hoof; *j*, point of the
frog; *k*, sole; *l l*, commissure, "white line," or line of junction between sole
and wall; *m, n*, mammilla; *o*, toe.

instruments of the farrier, would in time acquire an extraordinary distortion. The horn of the sole, for this reason, is
less dense and resisting than that of the wall, and is designed
more to support weight than to sustain wear.

The "*Horny Frog*" is an exact reduplication of that within the hoof, described as the *sensitive* or *fatty frog*. It is
triangular, or rather pyramidal in shape, and is situated at
the back part of the hoof within the bars; with its point or
apex extending forward to the centre of the sole, and its
base or thickest portion filling up the wide space left between the inflexions of the wall. In the middle of the pos-

terior part is a cleft, which in the healthy state should not be deep, but rather shallow and sound on its surface.

In structure, this body is also fibrous, the fibers passing in the same direction as those of the other portions of the hoof; but, instead of being quite rectilinear like them, they are wavy or flexuous in their course, and present some microscopical peculiarities which, though interesting to the comparative anatomist, need not be alluded to here. The fibers are finer than those of the sole and wall, and are composed of cells arranged in the same manner as elsewhere in the hoof; they are formed by the villi which thickly stud the face of the membrane covering the sensitive frog.

The substance of the horny frog is eminently elastic, and corresponds in the closest manner to the dense, elastic, epidermic pads on the soles of the feet of such animals as the camel, elephant, lion, bear, dog, cat, etc., and which are evidently designed for contact with the ground, the support and protection of the tendons that flex the foot, to facilitate the springy movements of these creatures, and for the prevention of jar and injury to the limbs.

In the horse's foot, the presence of this thick, compressible, and supple mass of horn at the back of the hoof, its being in a healthy, unmutilated condition, and permitted to reach the ground while the animal is standing or moving, are absolutely essential to the well-being of that organ, more especially should speed, in addition to weight-carrying, be exacted.

The frog, like the sole, exfoliates or becomes reduced in thickness at a certain stage of its growth; the flakes are more cohesive than those of the sole.

It must be remarked, however, that this exfoliation of the sole and frog only takes place when the more recently-formed horn beneath has acquired sufficient hardness and density to sustain contact with the ground, and exposure to the effects of heat, dryness, and moisture.

The "*Coronary Frog-Band*," or "*Periople*," is a continuation of the more superficial layer of the skin around the coronet and heels, in the form of a thin, light-colored band that descends to a variable depth on the outer surface of the wall, and at the back part of the hoof becomes consolidated with the frog, with which it is identical in structure and texture. It can be readily perceived in the hoof that has not been mutilated by the farrier's rasp, extending from the coronet, where the hair ceases, to some distance down the hoof; it is thickest at the commencement of the wall, and gradually thins away into the finest imaginable film as it approaches the lower circumferance of this part. When wet it swells and softens, and on being dried shrinks, sometimes cracks in its more dependent parts, or becomes scaly.

The fibres composing it are very fine and wavy, as in the frog; they likewise spring from villi which project from the true skin immediately above the "coronary cushion."

The use of this band would appear to be twofold: it connects the skin with the hoof, and thus makes the union of these two dissimilar textures more complete, its intermediate degree of density and its great elasticity admirably fitting it for this office; and it acts as a covering or protection to the wall at its upper part, where this is only in process of formation, and has not sufficient resistance to withstand the effects of exposure to the weather. The greatest thickness and density of the band correspond to the portion of the wall in which the villi or vascular tufts are lodged, and here the horn is soft, delicate, and readily acted upon in an injurious manner by external influences.

Thus far, then, we have rapidly glanced at the anatomy and uses of the various parts entering into the composition of the horse's hoof, and its horny box—the hoof. It may be necessary, before we pass to the consideration of the latter, as a whole, to allude to the structure and uses of that narrow strip of horn, whose presence every farrier or veterinary surgeon is cognizant of, but whose character and functions have been strangely left out of consideration by all anatomists hitherto. I refer to the "white line" or "zone," the slender intermediate band that runs around the margin of the sole, and connects that plate of horn so closely to the wall as to make their union particularly solid and complete. When preparing the border of the hoof for the reception of the shoe, this part is easily distinguished by its lighter color (in a dark hoof), and by its being softer and more elastic than either the sole or wall, between which it is situated. It would appear to be secreted by the villi which terminate the lower end of the vascular laminæ, and the horny leaves of the wall are also received into its substance—a circumstance that renders the junction of the two more thorough. I think there can be no doubt that the principal use of this elastic rim of horn, placed in such a situation, is to obviate the danger of fracture to which the inferior part of the hoof —particularly the sole—would be liable, if the junction between the hard and comparatively inelastic sole and wall was directly effected without the interposition of such a body.

It may be noted, that it is through this soft border of horn that gravel and foreign matters usually find their way to the sensitive parts of the foot, and there excite such an amount of irritation as to lead to the formation of matter, and cause much pain and lameness—an accident which the older farriers termed "graveling."

In viewing the horse's hoof as a whole, and in the unshod state, we find that it presents several salient characteristics, the consideration of which ought to dominate or serve as a guide in framing rules for the observance of farriers in the practice of their art. The first of these is the direction in which the wall grows in a healthy condition.

Viewed as it stands on a level surface, the hoof may be said to be somewhat conical in shape, its upper part being a little less than its base ; and although, geometrically, its shape may be described as the frustum of a cone, the base and summit of which have been cut by two oblique planes— the inferior converging abruptly behind toward the superior—yet the circumference of the hoof does not offer that regularity which this description might imply ; on the contrary, in a well-formed foot, we find that the outline of its inferior, or ground border, is notably more salient on the outer than the inner side, giving it that appearance which has been designated the " spread."

A cone being intersected by two planes oblique to its axis, and not parallel to each other, gives a good idea, neverthe-

Fig. 6.

less, of the obliquity which forms so marked a feature in the hoof. The degree of obliquity of the front part, or toe, and of the upper surface, varies with the amount of growth ; but where this has been counterbalanced by a proper degree of wear, it will be remarked that this obliquity corresponds to the inclination of the pastern-bones immediately above the hoof, when the horse is standing.

It will be obvious that this inclination also varies with the breeding of the animal and the conformation of the limbs, so that no definite degree can be assigned. But it must be pointed out, that giving the angle of 45°, as is done in almost every treatise on shoeing and the anatomy of the foot, is a grave error. Looked at in profile, a hoof with this degree of obliquity would at once be pronounced a deformity—the slope is too great (Fig. 6); and if the farrier were to attempt to bring every foot he shod to this standard, he would inflict serious injury, not only on the foot itself, but also on the back tendons and the joints of the limbs. Careful measurement will prove that the obliquity of the front of the hoof is rarely, if ever, in a well-shaped leg and foot, above 50°, and that it is, in the great majority of cases, nearer 56°. The sides or " quarters " of the wall are less inclined, though the outer is generally more so than the inner ; while the heels are still more vertical, and the inner may even incline slightly inward. Viewed in profile, the posterior face of the hoof will be observed to have the same degree of slope as the front face. In height, the heels are usually a little more than one-half that of the toe ; both heels are equal in height.

These features, as will be seen hereafter, are sufficiently important to be constantly remembered. The other characteristics are to be found on the lower or ground face of the hoof—the most important, so far as the farrier's art is concerned.

In a natural condition, the whole, or nearly the whole, of this face, comes into contact with the ground, each part participating more or less in sustaining the weight thrown upon the limb. On soft or uneven soil, the entire lower border of the wall—the sole, bars and frog—are subjected to contact. Nature intended them to meet the ground, and there to sustain the animal's weight, as well as the force of its impelling powers. But on hard or rocky land with a level surface, only the dense, tough crust and bars, the thick portion of the sole surrounded by them, and the elastic, retentive frog, meet the force of the weight and movement; and, in both cases, not only with impunity, but with advantage to the interior of the foot, as well as the limb. The horn on this face is, as has been said, dense, tough and springy to a degree varying with the parts of which it is composed; while its fibres are not only admirably disposed to support weight, secure a firm grasp of the ground, and aid the movements of the limbs, but are also an excellent medium for modifying concussion or jar to the sensitive and vascular structure in their vicinity.

The whole circumference of the wall meets the ground, and from the disposition of its fibres, the arrangement of the cells which enter into their composition, and its rigidity, it is admirably fitted to resist wear and sustain pressure. It projects more or less beyond the level of the sole, and the space measured between the white zone within it and its outer surface gives its exact thickness. This is a fact not without interest to the farrier in the operation of attaching the shoe by nails, as these have to be driven only through this dense horn—which in good hoofs cannot be said to much exceed half an inch in thickness—and in proportion to its thinness is the necessity for carefulness and address on his part, in order to guard against wounding or bruising the sensitive textures.

The sole is more or less concave from its junction with the wall; nevertheless, even on moderately firm ground, a portion of its circumference, which is generally the thickness of the wall, takes a share in relieving the latter of pressure. This is also a fact to be borne in mind. In soft ground, the whole of its lower surface is made to aid in sustaining the weight and prevent the foot sinking. But it must be noted that the pressure of the lower face of the pedal bone on the upper surface of the sole can never be very great, else the sensitive membrane between them would be seriously injured. This injury is prevented by the coronary, and, to a lesser extent, by the plantar cushion, which largely retard the descent of the bone on the floor of the horny box.

The frog, on both hard and soft ground, is an essential portion of the weight-bearing face. In the unshod, healthy foot it always projects beyond the level of the sole, and seldom below that of the wall at the heels; indeed, it is found, in the majority of hoofs, either on a level with the circumference of this part, or beyond it, so that its contact with the ground is assured. Hence its utility in obviating concussion,. supporting the tendons, and on slippery ground, in preventing falls. In pulling up a horse sharply in the gallop, or in descending a steep hill, the frog, together with the angular recess formed by the bar and wall at the heel of the hoof, are eminently serviceable in checking the tendency to slip; the animal instinctively plants the posterior portions of the foot exclusively on the ground.

Dark hoofs are generally the best; they owe their color to the presence of minute particles of black pigment, which contains a notable proportion of iron, and are somewhat resisting and indestructible.

A good hoof should have the wall unbroken, its outer face smooth and even; the angle at the front not less than 50°—the lower or ground face of the front hoof should be nearly circular in outline—the sole slightly concave at the circumference, deeper at the center; the border of the wall ought to be thick at the toe, gradually thinning towards the heels, but at the inflexion or commencement of the bar a strong mass of horn should be found; the bars should be free from fracture, and the frog moderately developed, firm and solid.

The hind foot should possess the same soundness of horn, though it differs from the fore hoof in being more oval in outline from the toe to the heels; the sole is also more concave, the frog smaller, and the heels not so high. The horn is usually less hard and resisting—a circumstance perhaps due to the hind feet being more frequently exposed to humidity in the stable than the fore ones.

GROWTH OF THE HOOF.

In any treatise on shoeing, the *growth* of the hoof cannot be left out of consideration, as on it the foot, in an unshod condition, depends for an efficient protection, while without this process the farrier's art would quickly be of no avail.

In its unarmed state, the hoof being exposed to continual wear on its lower surface, from contact with the ground on which the animal stands or moves, is unceasingly regenerated by the living tissues within. We have already referred to the special apparatus which is more immediately concerned in this work of regeneration, and pointed out that the wall with the laminæ on its inner face* is formed from the coronary cushion at the upper part of the foot; the sole from the living membrane covering the lower face of the pedal bone; and the frog from the plantar cushion. It has been also mentioned that this dead horny envelope, instead of being merely in juxtaposition with this exquisitely sensitive secretory membrane, is everywhere penetrated to a certain depth on its inner face (with the exception of the portion of the wall covered with the horny leaves) by multitudes of minute processes named villi, which are not only concerned in the growth of the horn-fibres, acting as moulds for them, and endowing the hoof with that degree of lightness, elasticity, and toughness, which are so necessary to its

---

* It is generally stated that the horny leaves are formed by the sensitive ones, with which they are in such close union. That this is an error, the microscope, physiology, and pathological experience, abundantly testify.

efficiency, but also make this insensitive case a most useful organ of touch.

The growth of the horn takes place by the deposition of new material from the secreting surface ; this deposition is effected at the commencement or root of the fibres; where the horn is yet soft, and its incessant operation causes these fibres to be mechanically extended or pushed downward toward the ground in a mass. Once formed they are submitted to no other change than that of becoming denser, harder, less elastic, and drier, as they recede farther from the surface from which they originated.

So regular is this growth generally in every part of the hoof that it would appear that the secreting membrane is endowed with an equal activity throughout.

But, though this equality in the amount of horn secreted over so wide a surface is an undoubted fact, yet it must not be forgotten that, under the influence of certain conditions, the growth or descent of the corneous material may be effected in an irregular manner, either through a particular portion of the secretory apparatus assuming a more energetic activity or being hindered more or less in its function.

For instance, the way in which the foot is planted on the ground has a most marked influence, not only on the amount of horn secreted, but also on that subjected to wear.

When the superincumbent weight is equally distributed over the lower face of the hoof, the foot may be said to be properly placed as a basis of support to the limb; but when, through mismanagement or defective form, this base is uneven—one side higher than the other, for example—the weight must fall on the lowest part to a greater degree than the highest; thus causing not only disturbance in the direction of the limb and its movements, but considerably modifying the growth of the horn. This growth is diminished at the part subjected to most pressure—in all probability from the smaller quantity of blood allowed to be circulated through the secretory surface; while to the side which is subjected to the least compression the blood is abundantly supplied, and the formation of horn is consequently augmented. This is a fact of much importance and practical interest in farriery, as it demonstrates that any irregularity in the distribution of the weight of the body on the foot has a prejudicial effect on the secreting apparatus of the organ, and, as a result, on the form of the hoof.

When the weight is evenly imposed on the foot, this apparatus, being uniformly compressed throughout its extent, receives everywhere an equal quantity of the horn-producing material.

It is the same with the *wear* of the hoof. A just disposition of the weight is a necessary condition of the regularity of wear. While the animal is standing on unshod hoofs the wear of horn is slight; it is in movement that it becomes increased, and this increase is generally in proportion to the speed, the weight carried, nature of the ground, and whether its surface be wet or dry. Each portion of the lower face of the hoof—wall, sole, bars and frog—should take its share of wear and strain; but it will be readily understood that this cannot be properly effected if the weight is thrown more upon one side than the other. That part which receives the largest share will be subjected to the greatest amount of loss from wear, and this, with the diminished secretion of horn, will tend to distort foot and limb still more.

In a well-formed leg and foot the degrees of resistance of the different parts of the hoof are so well apportioned to the amount of wear to be sustained, that all are equally reduced by contact with the ground, and the whole is maintained in a perfect condition as regards growth and wear.

The amount of growth, even in a well-proportioned foot, varies considerably in different animals, according to the activity prevailing in, or the development of, the secreting apparatus; and in this respect the operations of the farrier, as we will notice hereafter, are not without much influence.

It may be laid down as a rule that the horn grows more rapidly in warm, dry climates than in cold, wet ones; in healthy, energetic animals than in those which are soft and weakly; during exercise than in repose; in young than in old animals. Food, labor and shoeing also add their influence; while the seasons are to some extent concerned in the growth and shape of the hoof. In winter it widens, becomes softer and grows but little; in summer it is condensed, becomes more rigid, concave and resisting, is exposed to severer wear and grows more rapidly. This variation is a provision of nature to enable the hoof to adapt itself to the altered conditions it has to meet: hard horn to hard ground, soft horn to soft ground.

In this way we can account for the influence of locality upon the shape of the foot. On hard, dry ground, the hoof is dense, tenacious and small, with concave sole, and a little but firm frog; in marshy regions, it is large and spreading, the horn soft and easily destroyed by wear, the sole thin and flat, and the frog an immense spongy mass, which is badly fitted to receive pressure from slightly hardened soil. In a dry climate, we have an animal small, compact, wiry and vigorous, traveling on a surface which demands a tenacious hoof, and not one adapted to prevent sinking; in the marshy region we have a large, heavy, lymphatic creature, one of whose primary requirements is a foot designed to travel on a soft, yielding surface. Change the respective situations of these two horses, and Nature immediately begins to transform them and their feet. The light, excitable, vigorous horse, with its small vertical hoofs and concave soles, so admirably disposed to traverse rocky and slippery surfaces, is physically incompetent to exist on low-lying swamps; while the unwieldy animal, slow-paced and torpid, with a foot perfectly adapted to such a region—its ground face being so extensive and flat that it sinks but little, and the frog developed to such a degree as to resemble a plough-share in form, which gives it a grip of the soft, slippery ground—is but indifferently suited for traveling on a hard, rugged surface. In process of time, however, the small con-cave hoof expands and flattens, and the large flat one gradu-ally becomes concentrated, hardened and hollow, to suit the altered physical conditions in which they are placed.

The degree of health possessed by the horn-secreting ap-paratus at any time has also much to do with its activity in generating new material. When its blood-vessels become congested or contracted from some cause or other, its func-tion is in a proportionate degree suspended, and the hoof grows in an irregular manner, and may be altered in thick-ness, texture and quality.

In the ordinary conditions of town work and stable man-agement, I have observed that the wall of a healthy foot— its chief portion, so far as farriery is concerned—grows down from the coronet at the rate of about one-quarter of an inch per month, and that the entire wall of a medium-sized hoof has been regenerated in from nine to twelve months.

The process of growth can be greatly accelerated and ex-aggerated by irritating the surface which throws out the horn material. Thus a blister, hot iron, or any other irri-tant or stimulant applied to this part, will induce not only a more rapid formation, but one in which increased thick-ness is a marked feature.

SHOEING.

In the foregoing pages we have considered the foot of the horse in a natural condition, as perfectly adapted for the performance of most essential functions : as a basis of support while the animal is standing, and, in addition, as a powerful propelling instrument during progression.

We have also pointed out that the hoof which envelops it, like a huge finger-nail, is admirably constructed and endowed as an aid and protection to this organ, its utility mainly depending on the texture and arrangement of the horny matter of which it is composed, and the peculiar disposition of this in fibers of variable density, size, and elasticity.

But these qualities of the hoof, it was again remarked, are intimately dependent upon the manner in which the horn-secreting surface performed its office ; as if this becomes diminished, weakened, or unable to supply sufficient material to compensate for undue wear, the protecting case soon ceases to guard the living tissues within from injury.

In a natural state, when the equilibrium between growth and wear is destroyed, and the latter takes place in a rapid and unusual manner, the animal is compelled to rest until the worn hoof has recovered its proper thickness ; for acute pain results when the living parts are exposed, or when the wasted horn is insufficient to guard them against being bruised by the ground.

In an artificial condition, when the horse is employed on hard roads, broken ground, and in a humid climate, to carry and draw heavy loads at different degrees of velocity, and forced to stand on stony pavements during resting hours, his hoofs are unable to meet the many severe demands imposed upon them.

The wear more than counterbalances the growth ; and, therefore, it becomes an absolute necessity, if the animal is to be continuously and profitably utilized, that an artificial protection, sufficient to meet the exigencies of the case, be employed.

The lower border of the wall is, as we have mentioned, the part most deeply concerned in resisting wear and strain in the unshod state, as on it the stress chiefly falls; it is, consequently, the portion of the hoof that suffers most severely from undue wear, and that which alone requires protection.

This fact must have been brought prominently before the primitive shoers thousand of years ago, as the earliest specimens of shoes yet discovered are narrow, and in width do not much exceed the thickness of the wall. To guarantee this from wear was to increase the value of the horse a thousandfold, and the simply-wrought, narrow rim of iron, boldly and securely attached to the hoof by a few rudely-shaped nails, was sufficient for the purpose.

But having fastened on this light metallic armature, and allowed it to remain fixed to the hoof for a lengthened period, it would soon be discovered that the balance between growth and wear was again disturbed, but this time in favor of growth; for the wall being removed from contact with the ground, and the rate of growth continuing as in the unshod state, the hoof, instead of becoming diminished as before, now became abnormally overgrown and caused inconvenience. Then the shoe required to be taken off, and the superfluous growth either removed by instruments and the shoe replaced, or the animal made to travel without the iron defence until it was again needed when the hoof had become too much worn.

Such was horse-shoeing, in all probability, in early times, and such it is at the present day where utility is not sacrificed to stupid theories or foolish practices.

The evils attending the usual methods of shoeing are, as has been said, very serious and glaring; and the chief of these do not so much depend upon the faulty conformation of the shoe—though this is, in the majority of cases, not to be exempted from blame—as upon the treatment the hoof receives before and after the application of that article.

To illustrate these evils, and to show how unreasonable the modern art of farriery is, as well as how it should be practised, we will commence with the foot of the unshod colt, and, in the simplest words at our command, indicate the ordinary procedure in applying shoes to its hoofs for the first time, pointing out, at each step in the process, what is wrong and what is right, and giving reasons for the adoption of the principles which ought to guide the farrier in this most important operation.

PREPARING THE HOOF.

We will premise that the young horse about to have its hoofs armed for the first time is tolerably docile, and that its tranquility is not likely to be severely disturbed by the strange manipulations to which its limbs are to be subjected. For many months previously its attendants have had this ordeal in view, and in handling it have not forgotten to manipulate its legs and feet quietly and gently in something the same fashion that the farrier is likely to do—even going so far in the lesson as to tap lightly on its uplifted hoof, as if nailing on the shoe. The young creature is intelligent enough to perceive that in this no harm or punishment is intended, and it soon becomes familiar with the practice.

The farrier who shoes a young horse for the first or second time should be a patient, good-tempered man, and an adept in the management of horses and handling their limbs. If the operation is to be performed in a forge, there should be as little noise of hammers or glare of fires as possible—everything ought to be conducted quietly, steadily, and with kindness. Harsh treatment or unskilful handling should be severely reprehended, and all restraint or contention ought to be dispensed with—at any rate until gentleness and patience have been diligently employed and have failed. If accustomed to companions, it should have one or two horses beside it in the forge.

In describing the construction of the foot, we referred to the shape of a well-formed hoof. We will presume the animal before us—like nearly every unshod horse—has hoofs of this description.

The first step, usually, in the preparation of this part for the shoe, is to level and shorten the lower margin of the wall, pare the sole and frog, and open up the heels. These details may not be carried out so fully in the first shoeing as subsequently, but we will note them as they are commonly practised during the horse's lifetime.

Leveling the Wall is an important operation, which but few artisans rightly understand or care to do properly. It has been stated that unequal pressure on one side of the foot —one side of the wall being lower than the other—is not only injurious to the whole limb by the undue strain it imposes on the joints and ligaments, but that it tends to deform the hoof and modify the growth of the horn.

It is, therefore, most essential that both sides of the hoof be of equal depth, in addition to the whole lower margin of the wall being level; and to make them so, the rasp should be applied to this border in an oblique manner, across the ends of its fibres, to bring them to the same length.

A good idea of the necessary reduction to be effected on either side will be derived from an inspection of the limb from the knee or hock downward when placed firmly and straight upon the ground. Any deviation of the hoof to the inside or outside—most frequently it is the former—can be readily detected by looking at the leg and hoof in front.

The ground surface of the foot should be directly transverse to the direction of the pastern, and it is in maintain-

ing or restoring this relation, that care and skill are required. If the pastern is perpendicular to the shank-bone,
and the two sides of the lower margin of the foot are directly
transverse to the line passing down from these, then the
wall has only to be lowered equally on both sides, if it be
too high.

It must be remembered, in levelling both sides of the
lower surface of the hoof, that the difference of a few fractions of an inch between them will cause considerable, and
perhaps very hurtful. oscillations of the weight thrown on
the limb.

A properly-instructed farrier should be able, at a glance
across the upturned foot, to discover whether it is tolerably
level. In Fig. 7 I have shown what is meant by a properly-

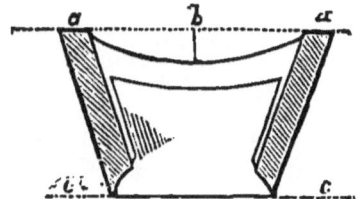

Fig. 7.

levelled hoof, the dotted line *a a* being directly transverse
to the vertical line *b*, and the distance from *a* to *c* of one
side being equal to that from *a* to *c* of the other.

Shortening the Wall.—Reducing the wall to proper dimensions is another important matter in connection with the
preparation of the foot for the shoe. We have seen that
the natural and moderate wear of the unshod hoof is com-
pensated for by the incessant downward growth of the horn,
and that this process of wear and regeneration maintains the
proper dimensions and just bearing of the foot. But on
the application of the shoe a barrier is at once opposed to
the wear, while the growth is not interfered with; conse-

quently, the hoof continually increases in length and obliquity—a change which causes derangement in the disposition of the weight on the lower part of the leg and foot, and other inconveniences.

In speaking of the growth of the horn, it was remarked that in health this took place in a regular manner over the whole surface. It seems rather contradictory, therefore, to assert that the hoof increases in obliquity—appears to grow faster at the toe than the heels—when, if this statement was correct, their increase in length should be always the same. In the unshod hoof this lengthening of the toe is

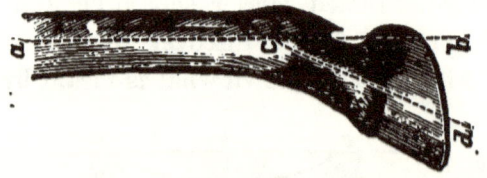

FIG. 8.

not observed; it only occurs in one that has been shod, and is to be accounted for by the fact that the shoe, not being nailed back so far as the heels, is, every time the foot falls on the ground, pressed against the horn at these parts, and so great is this downward friction or pressure that, after a time, not only is the hoof considerably worn, but the face of the shoe is also deeply channelled at corresponding points. Owing to the shoe being firmly fixed around the toe, there is no play at this part, and hence the apparent inequality in growth between the front and back of the hoof—a circumstance more observable in the fore than the hind foot, from the heels of the former being more under the centre of gravity, and so having a greater weight to sustain.

The pastern and foot form part of a lever that extends from the fetlock to the ground and supports the weight of the body. The strain comes perpendicularly from the shoulder.to the fetlock (Fig. 8, *a*, *c*); but thence to the ground it passes along the pastern and foot (*c*, *d*)—the extremity of the lever—and these are inclined more or less obliquely forward; hence the charge imposed on the limb has an incessant tendency to increase this obliquity by bringing the fetlock nearer the ground (*b*). To resist this tendency, however, we have the two flexor tendons and the powerful suspensory ligament at the back of the limb, which support this joint and maintain its angle.

But it will be readily understood that the longer and less upright this lever is, the greater is the strain and fatigue thrown upon the tendons and ligament. Though an oblique pastern may look graceful and make the horse's step more elastic and agreeable to the rider, yet, when the degree of obliquity exceeds that intended by nature, great risk is incurred of injury to the supporting apparatus. Hence the necessity for maintaining the hoof at its normal angle—a necessity, however, which can never be met except at the moment when the animal is newly shod; for no sooner is the equilibrium restored between the front and back of the hoof and the shoe fastened on than it begins to be disturbed again. This inconvenience is inevitable, from the very nature of the means we adopt to defend the foot from injury.

On the other hand, the suspensory apparatus is less severely taxed, as the lever is short and vertical; or, in other words, as the pastern and hoof are upright. But this, though relieving the tendons and ligament, throws the weight too directly on the bones; consequently the jar to these and the whole limb is great, and even dangerous, while the back parts of the foot are unduly strained to relieve them.

It must be, then, very evident that leveling and bringing the ground-face of the hoof to the necessary length—equal on both sides from toe to heel, and justly proportioned in depth at toe and heel—is no trifling matter, as the soundness

of the limb and ease in progression are concerned in the
operation.   Excessive length or obliquity of hoof strains
back tendons and ligament; a hoof long at the toe and low
at the heels (Fig. 9, *a*, *b*) increases the obliquity; on the
contrary, when the heels are high and the toe of the hoof
too short (Fig. 9, *c*, *d*), the bones suffer and the whole limb
experiences, more or less, the effects of concussion.

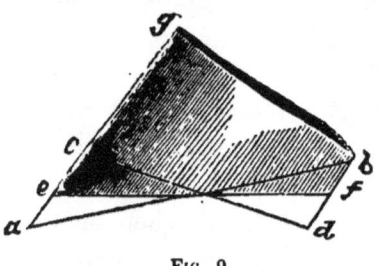

Fig. 9.

In both cases progression is fatiguing, imperfect and hurtful to an extent proportionate to the excess.

Another disadvantage in shoeing, arising from the tendency of the hoof to increase in length at the toe, and also
from its form, is the change in the position of the shoe itself.
The hoof being more or less conical in shape, with its base
opposed to the ground, it follows that, as it increases in
length, its lower circumference also widens in every direction.   The result is that the shoe, although at one time
accurately fitting the hoof, gradually becomes too narrow ;
at the same time, the increase in length at the toe carries
the iron plate forward, away from the heels.

This is one more of the inevitable evils of shoeing, but
which, nevertheless, the skillful workman may greatly pal-
liate.

The farrier equalizes both sides of the hoof by applying
his rasp in a sloping direction to the ground border or end
of the wall ; he also brings it to its natural angle with the

same instrument, by removing the necessary amount of horn from the margin of the hoof at the toe or heels; by reducing the former without interfering with the latter, the obliquity of the foot is diminished (as in Figs. 9, c, d, 10, a): while rasping down the heels and leaving the toe untouched increases it (Fig. 9, a, b).

In the great majority of cases, the heels, for the reason stated, require but little interference; the excess of growth is nearly always at the toe, and thus no absolute rule can be laid down as to the angle to which the hoof should be brought. The practiced eye can discern at once whether the angle is in conformity with the natural bearing of the limb,

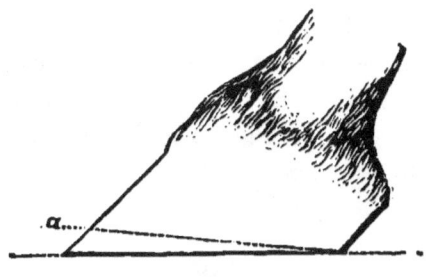

Fig. 10.

and will have no difficulty in adjusting it, should it not be so, provided there is sufficient horn to spare for this purpose.

We have previously shown that the inclination of the front of the hoof varies from 50° to 60°, and probably the mean between these two angles will be that usually observed. (Fig 9, g, e, f, is a hoof with about 52° of obliquity ; g, a, b, 45°; g, c, d, more than 60°.)

On ordinary occasions, causing the horse to stand on a level floor, and viewing the hoof in profile a few paces off, is sufficient to inform one of the angle; but to insure attention to this matter and prevent mistakes, I have contrived a little instrument for my farriers, which at once shows

them the degree of obliquity, and gives them an indication
as to the amount of horn to be removed from the toe or
heels.

In the operation of levelling and shortening the hoof, is
included the general reduction of the wall.

Provided the hoof, before it comes into the hands of the
farrier, has the proper inclination and is equal on both sides
of its ground face, but is nevertheless overgrown, the artisan has then only to remove the excess of growth without
disturbing the relations between the several regions of the
wall. Or should the hoof be overgrown, too oblique, too
upright, or unequal at the sides, then in remedying the one
defect he at the same time remedies all. The amount of
horn to be removed from the margin of the hoof will depend upon circumstances. It may be laid down as a rule,
however, that there being but little horn to remove at the
heels, these should only be rasped sufficiently to insure the
removal of all loose material incapable of supporting the

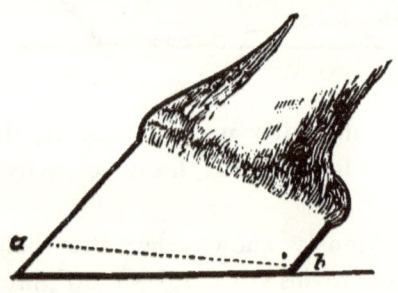

Fig. 11.

shoe; the quarters or sides of the hoof may require a freer
application of the rasp, but as the toe is reached, a larger
quantity must be removed, as in Fig. 11, *a, b*. The limit to
this removal at the front of the hoof must be when the wall
is almost or quite reduced to a level with the strong unpared sole. It must ever be borne in mind that, if the wall

does not stand beyond the level of the sole, it does not require reducing.

When the circumference of the hoof has at length been brought to a condition fit to receive the shoe, the rasp must finish its task by removing the sharp edge, and rounding it so as to leave a thick strong border not likely to chip. The unshod hoof nearly always exhibits this provision against fracture of the wall-fibres.

Paring the Sole.—After the necessary diminution and correction of the obliquity of the hoof, and the preparation of the bed for the shoe, the farrier usually proceeds to pare the sole. Indeed, while the colt is still at large, and before the time has arrived when its hoofs are to be shod with iron, the workman is frequently called in to *trim* the hoofs, and paring the lower surface is part of the operation.

This procedure is as barbarous as it is unreasonable, especially when carried to the extent that has been advised in books on horseshoeing, viz., to pare the sole until it springs to the pressure of the thumb. In the great majority of forges this most pernicious practice is carried out, either because the owner of the horse thinks it necessary, the groom or coachman that it makes the horse go better and the feet to look well, or the farrier that it is more workmanlike—though if he is pressed hard for any other reason he is unable to give one of a satisfactory character.

Like so many practices relating to the management of the horse, this paring of the sole is absurd in the extreme, and has not the most trifling recommendation to support it. Unfortunately for those who recommend, and also those who practice it, its evil effects are not immediately apparent; a horse with his soles denuded of their horn until the blood is oozing through them, may not at the moment manifest any great suffering, and may even go tolerably sound on a level pavement, though, if he chanced to put his foot on uneven ground or a sharp stone, his agony may be so acute as to cause him to fall.

The paring knife is skillfully used to remove all the surface horn down to that which has been most recently formed, or is in process of forming. So anxious is the groom or farrier that this, to them, most important operation should be carried out, that the soles are filled with cow dung, or some other filth, for some time previously, in order that the horn may be softened and rendered more amenable to mutilation. When this "stopping" has not been done, and particularly in hot, dry weather, the sole is often so hard that it cannot be touched by the knife, in which case a red-hot iron is applied to the surface to soften the horn, or hot ashes are used. Then the bars and soles are sliced away until nothing is left but the thinnest pellicle of their natural protection, through which not unfrequently the blood may be oozing. This is nothing else than downright cruelty, and should meet with the punishment it so well deserves.

To remove the excessive growth of the wall is an absolute necessity; but to denude the sole of its horn is wanton injury to the foot and cruelty to the animal. This is easily accounted for. The sole only increases its substance to a certain thickness—never too much—and then the excess is thrown off in flakes in a natural manner. In this way the sensitive parts are amply protected; the sole can sustain a share of the weight—especially around its margin in front, where it is strongest—and meet the ground, however rough and stony this may be, with perfect impunity. This is its function.

It has been mentioned that the horn is secreted from the living surface, and that myriads of beautiful vascular and sensitive tufts dependent from this surface, enter the horn-fibres to a certain depth, and play an important part in the formation of the sole. The newly-formed horn is soft and spongy, and incapable of resisting exposure to the air, but as it is pushed further away from this surface by successive deposits of fresh material, it becomes old horn, loses its moisture, and in doing so acquires hardness and rigidity sufficient to withstand external influences ; then it is subjected to wear, and if this be insufficient to reduce it sufficiently, it falls off in scales. But the process of exfoliation is not a rapid one ; the flakes remain attached to the solid horn beneath, more or less firmly, until it in turn commences to loosen on the surface, and yield new flakes, when the old ones separate. This natural diminution in the excess of horn of the sole is a most beneficial process for the hoof. Horn is a slow conductor of heat and cold, and when thick, retains moisture for a long period. These flakes, then, act as a natural "stopping" to the hoof, by accumulating and retaining moisture beneath, and this not only keeps the foot cool as it slowly evaporates, but ensures for the solid and growing horn its toughness, elasticity and proper development. In addition to this, every flake acts more or less as a spring in warding off bruises or other injuries to the sole ; and thus the floor of the horny box is protected from injury, externally and internally.

What occurs when the farrier, following out the routine of his craft, or obeying the injunctions of those as ignorant as himself, or so prejudiced as not to be able to reason, pares the sole until it springs to the pressure of his thumb? Why, the lower surface of the foot—that which is destined to come into contact with the ground, and to encounter its inequalities, and which more than any other part requires to be efficiently shielded—is at once ruthlessly denuded of its protection, and exposed to the most serious injury. The immature horn, stripped of its outer covering, immediately begins to experience the evil effects of external influences ;

it loses its moisture, dries, hardens, and shrivels up; it also occupies a smaller space, and in doing so, the sole becomes more concave, drawing after it the wall—for it must be remembered that the sole is a strong stay against contraction of the lower margin of the hoof—and the consequence is, that the foot gradually decreases in size, and the quarters and heels narrow. The animal goes "tender," even on smooth ground; but if he chance to put his mutilated sole on a stone, what pain must he experience! This tenderness on even ground or smoothly paved roads arises from the fact, that not only is the entire sensitive surface compressed, irritated, or inflamed by the hard, contracting envelope, and the unnatural exposure to sudden changes of heat and cold, but the little sensitive processes contained at the upper end of each of the horn-fibres are painfully crushed in their greatly diminished tubes, and instead of being organs of secretion and the most delicate touch, they are now scarcely more than instruments of torture to the unfortunate animal. Not only is pain or uneasiness experienced during progression, but even in the stable the horse whose soles have been so barbarously treated, exhibits tenderness in his feet by resting them, and if felt, a great increase of temperature will be perceived.

Owing to the secreting apparatus of the sole being deranged through this senseless paring, the formation of new horn takes place slowly, and it is not until a certain quantity has been provided to compensate in some degree for that removed, that the horse begins to stand easier, and travel better. Scarcely, however, has the restorative process advanced to this stage, than it is time for him to be reshod, when this part must again submit to be robbed of its horn.

The sole having been pared too thin and concave leaves the circumference of the hoof standing much higher than if it had been left intact, and apparently too long; so the wall must be still more reduced. This is done, and we now have the whole ground-face of the hoof so wasted and mutilated, that should the horse chance to lose a shoe soon after being shod, the impoverished foot cannot bear the rude contact of the ground for more than a few yards, and the poor creature is lame and useless.

The tenderness and lameness arising from this maltreatment are usually ascribed to everything but the right cause, and the most popular is concussion. To avert this and protect the defenceless sole, a most absurd shoe is required; and, still more absurd, the natural covering is attempted to be replaced by a plate of leather, interposed between the ground and the sole, and which is made to retain bundles of tow steeped in tar or some pernicious substance. It is scarcely necessary to say that this artificial covering is but a poor substitute for that which has been so foolishly, and with so much careful labor, cut away; indeed, in several respects the leather sole, even when only placed between the wall and the shoe, and not over the entire surface, is very objectionable.

Seeing, therefore, the natural provision existing in the sole of the hoof for its diminution in thickness, when necessary, and knowing that the intact sole is the best safeguard against injury and deterioration to this region, it must be laid down as a rule in farriery—and from which there must be no departure—that this part is not to be interfered with on any pretence, so long as the foot is in health; not even the flakes are to be disturbed.

By adhering to this rule, the horse can travel safely and with ease in all weathers and over any roads immediately after shoeing; the foot is maintained in a healthy condition; the sole can sustain its share of the weight, and thus relieve the wall of the hoof; and should a shoe happen to be lost, the animal can journey a long distance with but little injury to the organ.

Another of the many advantages derived from allowing the sole to remain in its natural condition, is that on a soft surface the hoof will not sink so deeply as one whose sole has been hollowed out by the farrier, neither is it so difficult to withdraw from the heavy soil.

Paring the Frog.—This part of the hoof is that which, in the opinion of the grooms and coachmen, most requires *cutting*, " to prevent its coming on the ground and laming the horse ;" and this reason, together with its softer texture, causes it to be made the sport of the farrier's relentless knife. It is artistically and thoroughly trimmed, the fine elastic horn being sliced away, sometimes even to the quick, and in its sadly reduced form it undergoes the same changes as have been observed in the pared sole. No wonder, then, that it cannot bear touching the ground any more than the sole. Strip the skin off the sole of a man's foot and cause him to travel over stony or pebbly roads ! Would he walk comfortably and soundly ?

The artistically-shaped frog soon wastes, becomes diseased, and at length appears as a ragged, foul-smelling shred of horn, almost imperceptible between the narrow, deformed, heels of the pared foot.

The function of the frog in the animal economy is one of great moment, and has already been indicated. It is eminently adapted for contact with the ground, and in this resides its most important office. To remove it from the ground and deprive it of its horn, is at once to destroy its utility and its structure, and withdraw from the foot one of its most essential components. The longer the frog is left untouched by the knife, and allowed to meet the ground, the more developed it becomes ; its horn grows so dense and resisting, yet without losing its special properties, that it

braves the crushing of the roughest roads without suffering
in the slightest degree ; it ensures the hoof retaining its
proper shape at the heels ; is a valuable supporter of the
limb and foot while the animal is standing or moving ; and
is an active agent, from its shape and texture, in preventing
slipping ; its reduction and removal from the ground, I am
perfectly convinced from long observation, have a tendency,
directly or indirectly, to induce that most painful, frequent,
and incurable malady—navicular disease, as well as other
affections of this organ.

The farrier should, therefore, leave the frog also untouched,
unless there be flakes which are useless—though this is extremely rare ; then these ought to be cut off. So particular
am I in this respect, however, and so well aware am I of
the fondness of the workman to cut into this part, that I
never allow any frogs to be interfered with unless I am
present. If any gravel has lodged beneath the flakes, at
the side, or in the cleft—which is most unfrequent—this is
removed by some blunt instrument.

To show the value of contact with the ground : when a
horse with a diseased frog is brought to me, I at once order
the hoof to be so prepared or shod that this part will immediately receive direct pressure—in a brief space the disease
disappears. Cases of what grooms call "thrush," of many
years' duration, and which had defied all kinds of favorite
dressings, have been cured, and the rotten, wasted frogs have
become sound and well developed in a few months.

Opening-up the Heels.—Having done everything possible
to ruin the sole and the frog, the farrier proceeds to complete his work by opening-up the heels. This operation is
quite as injurious—if it is not more so—than mutilating
the sole and frog ; it consists in making a deep cut into
the angle of the wall at the heel, where it becomes bent in_
ward to form the bar. In the unshod, natural state, or in

the unmutilated foot, this is a particularly strong portion of the hoof, and serves a very useful purpose, its utility being mainly owing to its strength. From its preventing contraction of the heels, it has been named the *arc boutant* or " buttress " of the foot by the French hippotomists.

When it is hacked away by the farrier's knife, the wall of the hoof is not only considerably weakened, but the hoof gradually contracts toward the heels.

Horse dealers and grooms are the chief patrons of " well-opened " heels, as they give the foot a false appearance by making it look wider in this region.

The fashion of paring the sole until it yields to the pressure of the thumb has been perpetuated through the ignorance of those who have had the management of horses, or the traditions and routine of the artisans who have more especially to attend to the requirements of the hoofs of these animals. But it must be observed that this paring, slicing away the frog and opening up the heels has been largely due, in later times, to the false notions propounded by some writers regarding the functions of the foot: such as the descent of the sole, the inability of the frog to sustain contact with the ground, and the expansion of the back parts of the hoof every time the weight was imposed upon it. It is scarcely necessary here to say more than that these notions are at least extremely exaggerated, and that the practices which were maintained to facilitate these supposed functions have been productive of an immense amount of suffering and loss of animal life.

It should be ever most strenuously insisted upon that the whole lower face of the hoof, except the border of the wall, must be left in a state of nature. The horn of the sole, frog and bars has an important duty to fulfill ; it is the natural protection to this part of the hoof, and no protection of iron, leather or other material is half so efficacious ; in addition, it is a capital agent in sustaining weight and in keeping the whole foot healthy and perfect in form.

THE SHOE.

The Ordinary Shoe.—The hoof having been prepared by the farrier, according to his fancy, for the reception of the metal plate which is to garnish it, here again we find that ignorance prevails and is productive of inconvenience and injury. "Improved principles" demand that a particular-shaped shoe be applied; no matter whether the animal be for saddle, harness or draught purposes, it must have a shoe

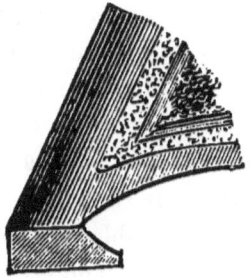

Fig. 12.

that rests only on the margin of the hoof—on the wall. Therefore, except a narrow border to correspond with this margin, the upper or foot-face of the shoe is beveled away, so as to leave a wide space between it and the sole, and throw all the weight and strain on the outer parts of the foot (Fig. 11); in addition to which disadvantage, this space is admirably contrived to lodge stones, gravel, hardened mud or snow, and in heavy ground it increases the suction immensely. But, as will be easily understood from the manner in which the under-surface of the foot has been treated, this beveling is rendered an absolute necessity if the horse is to be preserved from immediate lameness. The sole has been pared so thin that, so far from its being able to withstand a tolerably large amount of pressure around its margin—particularly toward the toe—it must be most carefully preserved, not only from contact with the shoe, but also with the ground. This necessitates a wide surface of metal, which increases the weight of the shoe, making it clumsier to wear, and affords a large under or ground surface for slipping. And even with a shoe of such dimensions the creature cannot travel at ease on stony roads, as the least pressure of a stone on the tender sole causes him to limp; and if the stone lodges in the space between shoe and sole, serious injury is likely to be done.

Weight.—In addition to the beveling and the width, the shoe in ordinary use has several other glaring defects. One of these is generally its excessive weight; it contains an amount of iron far greater than is necessary to protect the hoof from the effects of wear. One reason alleged for the employment of these cumbrous masses of iron attached to the ends of a horse's limbs is that they prevent concussion to the foot. This any reasonable person will at once perceive is a manifest absurdity. The hoof, by its lightness, its texture, and the wonderful arrangement of its component parts, is well adapted to avert concussion. An inelastic, heavy lump of iron firmly attached to it, and coming into forcible collision with the ground at every step, must surely be more likely to increase this concussion than diminish it.

There can be no difficulty, I imagine, in estimating the injury inflicted by unnecessarily heavy shoes. Nature formed the lower extremity of the limb with a view to lightness, no less than to other important ends. The hoof-bone is quite porous and open in texture, to diminish its ponderosity without detracting from its size or stability; while the hoof itself is, as we have just noticed, remarkable for the manner in which its material is arranged with a special intention to confer light-footedness upon the animal. The reason for this diminution in weight, while it is coincident with increase in bulk, is to be found in the fact that the muscles principally concerned in moving the limb — swinging, straightening, and bending it backward and forward—are all situated above the knee or hock. The moving power is at one end of a comparatively long lever with two arms, while the weight to be moved is at the other extremity. The arm of the lever to which the power is applied is very short, so that though rapidity is gained, more power is lost, and it is palpable that every additional ounce added to the foot must be nearly, if not more than equal to a pound at the shoulder.

In shoeing, this important consideration has been strangely overlooked ; and yet we cannot forget that it has a great influence on the wear of, not only the shoe, but also the muscles, tendons, ligaments and joints, and even, indirectly, of the entire animal. " If, at the termination of a day's work," says an eminent French veterinary professor, " we calculate the weight represented by the mass of iron in the heavy shoes a horse is condemned to carry at each step, we shall arrive at a formidable array of figures, and in this way be able to estimate the amount of force uselessly expended by the animal in raising the shoes that overload his feet. The calculation I have made possesses an eloquence that dispenses with very long commentaries. Suppose that the weight of a shoe is two pounds, it is not excessive to admit that a horse trots at the rate of one step every second, or sixty steps a minute. In a minute, then, the limb of a horse whose foot carries two pounds makes efforts sufficient to raise a weight of one hundred and twenty pounds. For the four limbs, this weight in a minute is represented by $120 \times 4 = 480$ pounds ; for the four feet during an hour, the weight is 28,800 pounds ; and for four hours, the mean duration of a day's work in the French omnibuses, the total

amount of weight raised has reached the enormous figure of
115,200 pounds. But the movement communicated to
these 115,200 pounds represents an expenditure of the
power employed by the motor without any useful result;
and as the motor is a living one, this expenditure of strength
represents an exhaustion, or, if you like it better, a degree
of fatigue proportioned to the effort necessary for its mani-
festation."

This question of weight is one of no small moment to
the well-being and utility of the horse, and therefore demands particular attention. Nature, in constructing the
animal machine, and enduing it with adequate power to sustain the ordinary requirements of organization, and even to
meet certain extraordinary demands, could scarcely have
been expected to provide the large additional amount of energy necessary to swing several ounces, or even pounds, attached to the lower extremity of the limb. A horse shod
with a two-pound shoe to each foot, traveling at the rate of
sixty steps in a minute for a period of four hours, as has
been stated above, carries nearly fifty-two tons. This
weight, too, as has been stated, is most disadvantageously
placed at the end of the long arm of the lever. It must be
remembered, also, that a two-pound shoe is a very moderate affair when compared with many that are worn every
day in town and country, even by horses employed in fast
work.

Not only does an unnecessarily heavy shoe fatigue and
wear out the limbs sooner than a light one, but the fatigue
it induces causes it to be less durable, in proportion to the
quantity of iron. This is accounted for by the manner in
which the fatigued limbs drag their heavy load along the
surface of the ground. Heavy shoes also require more and
larger nails to attach them securely to the hoof, and this in

itself is an evil of no trifling magnitude, as we shall see presently.

The shoe, besides being heavy, may offer other serious defects. It may be very uneven on its upper bearing surface—that on which the hoof rests; it may have too many clips, and these not well formed or situated; its ground surface may be unequal; or the holes for the nails may be badly placed, and improperly stamped.

An uneven upper surface is apt to produce lameness, from the undue pressure it occasions on limited parts of the hoof, and through these to the corresponding living textures; or it may cause the wall of the hoof to split, etc.

Nails badly placed and improperly stamped are a prolific source of injury to the foot, and the same may be said of mal-formed or wrongly-situated clips; and much evil results from the ground-face of the shoe being higher at one part than another. This inequality is in nearly every case due to the presence of what are termed "calkins" at the extremities of the branches of the shoe; or to one side of the plate being thicker than the other.

Calkins.—Calkins are injurious to the limb in proportion to their height. When smallest they are an evil, as they have a tendency, in raising the back part of the foot higher than the front, to alter the natural direction of the limb, and throw undue strain on the fore part. Intended to prevent slipping, their use in this respect is but temporary, unless they are made high and thick; when their unfavorable influence on the limb and foot is increased. Added to this, from their throwing so much of the weight and strain on the front of the foot, the shoe is more rapidly worn away at the toe; so its thickness there must be greater, and the shoe in consequence heavier, or the animal will have to be more frequently shod. From their only lasting for a limited period, the horse, at first inclined to rely on them to preserve his footing on slippery roads, becomes timid and unsafe when they are worn down to the surface of the shoe. By their form, and their projecting so much beyond the level of the plate, they jar the limb; expose it to twists and treads sometimes of a grave character; induce shortening of the flexor tendons; and until they have been considerably reduced, interfere with the animal's action. They are also liable to cause the shoe to be torn off, by getting caught between paving-stones; while they produce severe lacerations, should the horse wearing them happen to kick another animal. This is more particularly observed among army horses which have calkins on their hind shoes—and especially when in camp or picketed. They also throw more strain upon the nails and the hoof itself. Neither must it be forgotten that they remove the frog from contact with the ground.

One side of the shoe being higher than the other produces the same results as follow when the hoof is unequal in this respect. The hind limb is more exposed to this evil than the fore one, from calkins being most frequently added to the hind shoes, and from the fashion of having the inner branch thickened, but not sufficient to compensate for the height of the calkin on the outer heel. This inequality is productive of injury to the fetlock and hock joints, and is doubtless not unfrequently the cause of that formidable disease of the latter—spavin.

But even if the farrier has reason to apply shoes whose ground-surface is not studded with calkins or any other kind of "catch," he, in nearly every case of ordinary wear, puts on one which has the whole of this surface perfectly plane, and not relieved throughout its length or width by any thing, except perhaps the groove around its outer circumference, in which the nail-holes are placed. This wide, smooth surface is evidently adapted to facilitate slipping on smooth pavements, or even on grass or clay land.

Size.—Besides constructing the shoe of a faulty shape, a very common practice is to apply one smaller than the actual contour of the ground-surface of the hoof. This is a grave error, and in all probability arises from the desire to make the horse's foot look neat, and to produce fine work; just as the maker of shoes for the human foot thinks it the perfection of workmanship to squeeze it into the smallest possible space. In the horse, however, small shoes are more fruitful of lameness and chronic deformity than even the worst-shaped cramped coverings can be for the human organ, as the horse is compelled to wear his tight plates day and night, and must accomplish all kinds of severe labor in them; while man can relieve himself of his torturing, uncomfortable boots for at least some hours out of the twenty-four.

We shall allude to the evils of this stupid practice hereafter; in the meantime it may be sufficient to point out, that in selecting and applying a shoe smaller than the circumference of the hoof, we are depriving the foot and limb of a portion of their stability and weight-bearing surface. The limb is, in reality, a column of support for the body, and the hoof is the base of this column. This base is very much wider than any other portion, and only commences at the foot, which gradually widens toward the ground, so as to make it still more expanded and efficient. To diminish this is to frustrate Nature's mode of affording security and ease to the limb, and consequently to do it harm.

The above are only some of the more prominent evils attendant on the present method of constructing and shaping the horse's shoe; others, such as making it of bad material, altogether unlike the outline of the hoof, etc., we will glance at presently. We have only now to consider what has been for very many years the aim of those who, overlooking the real injury done to the foot by the barbarous fashion of paring and rasping, imagined the chief, if not the sole, cause of lameness and inefficiency arose from the faulty character of the protection applied to it, and have sought to avert these by devising various kinds of shoes, or other methods of arming the hoof.

It is scarcely necessary to say, that from their neglecting, or being unconscious of the harm that resulted from the malpractices already indicated, their so-called improvements have been impotent for good, and have soon been consigned to forgetfulness.

Objects to be Attained.—We have stated what were the objects to be attained when shoeing was first introduced. To prevent undue wear of the horn, and at the same time to secure a good foothold for the horse, appear to have been all that was considered essential in the infancy of the art of farriery. And it must be conceded that, even now, these are the primary advantages to be achieved in constructing a horse-shoe, no matter what kind of task the horse that wears it may be required to accomplish.

There can scarcely be a doubt that any thing more simple and efficient, and at the same time less expensive, than a well-devised iron shoe, cannot at present be produced; nor can the comparatively safe and ready method of attaching it by nails be superseded by any other means that we are acquainted with. All tentatives in this direction have failed, either because of their inefficiency or greater expense.

Simplicity, cheapness, durability, and perfect adaptability to various requirements, are the essentials to be obtained in horse-shoes; and if one or more of these is absent in any particular pattern, it can never be generally adopted, and is certain to have but brief success.

The effects of applying an iron defence to the horse's foot, and securing it to the hoof by means of nails, are no doubt a source of injury to that organ; and even with every care a few of them are unavoidable; but they are increased in number and heightened in intensity when the shoe is badly constructed and attached; whereas, by the exercise of a little common-sense and observation, those which are not to be avoided may be mitigated.

The foot, as has been observed, is a perfect organ, formed in harmony with the other parts of the limbs to meet every requirement in bearing weight and aiding movement.

The hoof, as an integral portion of the foot, possesses these qualities to a high degree, and, but for its inability to withstand incessant wear, would need no assistance from man, except perhaps a little trimming when it became over-grown or irregular. Its lower margin—hard, narrow, and projecting slightly beyond the sole—is well adapted to support weight, withstand wear, and retain a hold of the ground; the concave sole, in addition to its assisting the margin to support weight and wear, also lends its aid in securing a foothold by its hollow surface; while the angle of the wall at each heel—the "buttress"—would appear to be specially designed to afford a most effective check to the sliding forward of the foot as the animal suddenly pulls up when moving at a fast pace on level ground, or attempts to stop or diminish his descent on a slippery declivity.

Those who study the functions of the animal body, and who have to restore these when deranged, well know that in their attempts to keep them in a normal condition or to bring them back to a healthy state, they must attend to the laws which govern these functions, and follow the indications of nature. Therefore I have asked myself if it is possible to construct a shoe which, while cheaply and easily manufactured by any ordinary farrier, will answer the same ends as the lower surface of the foot does in a natural state, at the same time protecting and supporting it, without interfering to any appreciable extent with the healthy functions

of the organ. We have seen that the ordinary shoe is extremely imperfect, if it is not diametrically opposite to what
we should consider as calculated to protect the foot, secure
a good foothold, and interfere but little with its functions.
Instead of supporting the sole at its strongest part, and thus
relieving the wall from much of the strain, it rests on the
wall alone; this is contrary to natural indications.   The
wide space between sole and shoe affords lodgment to foreign
bodies which, when the sole is artistically mutilated, may
do grievous harm, and it also increases suction in soft
ground; the hoof shows nothing of this kind.   Then, again:
the ground-face of the shoe is a wide and smooth plane
which, instead of preventing slipping, conduces to it; or
thickened portions project above this face, which disturb
the balance and injure the limb, while they are only of very
temporary and questionable service in insuring a firm footing.

In the unshod hoof we see nothing of this, and we are
brought to the conclusion, which daily experience amply
confirms, that in addition to the ordinary management of
the hoof being utterly erroneous, the shoe usually applied
to it is very far from what it ought to be.

Pattern of Shoe Recommended.—If the sole of the hoof
has not been mutilated by the knife, it does not require to
be covered by the shoe, as Nature has furnished an infinitely better protection.   Wide-surface shoes can therefore
be at once dispensed with, and a narrow shoe, made of the
very best and toughest iron, adapted for traveling on slippery roads, and for aiding foot and limb, and sufficient to
withstand wear for four or five weeks, is all that is required.
We will therefore conclude that the upper or foot surface
should be the whole width of the shoe, and plane—not bevelled—for we have seen that the sole was destined, particularly at this junction with the wall in front, to sustain

weight. We also know that it is advantageous to the whole foot and limb to allow the sole as wide and general a bearing as possible; so that one part may relieve the other—the sole coming to the aid of the wall, and the frog interposing to share the fatigue imposed upon both, as well as to relieve the strain on the hinder parts of the foot, flexor tendons and limb, and keep a firm grasp of the ground by its elastic and adhesive properties.

The shoe applied to the foot, then, should have its hoof surface flat, in order that it may sustain the wall and as much of this strong portion of the sole as its width permits. This is contrary to the usual practice, which only allows the wall to rest on a narrow surface, and bevels off the remainder of the shoe to prevent contact with the sole. Many years' experience of this plane foot-surfaced shoe in various regions of the globe, and on feet of every kind and quality, have proved the soundness of this view. The foot is brought as near to a state of nature when the greater part of its plantar surface supports the weight of the body, as man can hope to achieve while submitting the horse to an artificial existence.

A light thin shoe is always preferable to a heavy thick one; as the narrowness of the metal insures a good foothold—in this respect imitating the wall—while its thinness brings the sole, frog and bars in closer approximation to the ground.

It is impossible to devise a shoe that will successfully meet every requirement. The heavy draught-horse, doomed to bring into play every muscle in endeavoring to move and drag along an enormous load, must have his feet differently armed to the hunter or race-horse, with which speed is the chief requisite. Taking into account the different character of the horny textures, it is none the less true, however, that the same rule holds good in all with regard to the sole and frog-sustaining weight, though in the slow-moving animal it is of less importance, perhaps, than in the lighter and more fleet one. The massive draught-horse requires toe and heel projections or "catches" on the ground-surface of the shoes, to economize his locomotive powers and to aid his powerful efforts; though his hoofs none the less require the observance of those conservative principles which have been so strongly insisted upon, but which are so very seldom applied.

To give the greatest amount of strength and foothold to the shoes of the heavy draught-horse, with the least amount of weight, should be an object always kept in view in making them. But, with this animal, the principal object is the preservation of the wall of the hoof in order that it may remain sound and strong for the retention of the nails; to assist in effecting this, the sole and frog must be preserved intact.

The form of the shoe in all cases should in outline resemble the shape of the ground-surface of the hoof. It has been decided that its upper surface must be flat from the outer to the inner margin. For horses other than those of heavy draught, its width will of course vary; but it is an advantage to have it as narrow as is compatible, in relation to its thickness, with the amount of wear required from it.

The ground-face of the shoe is the next point for consideration. This should always be, if possible, parallel with its upper face; that is, the shoe ought to be plane on both surfaces, and of the same thickness on both sides, not only in the fore but also the hind shoes. This guarantees the foot and limb being kept in a natural position. What are termed "calkins" on one or both heels are very objectionable, for the simple reason that, as has been stated, they raise the back part of the foot higher than the front, and throw the limb forward; unless the hoof meets the ground in its natural direction, some portion of the leg or foot will be certain to suffer. Therefore, whatever device may be employed to prevent slipping and secure a hold on the ground should not interfere with the natural direction of the limb or foot. If calkins are deemed necessary, then the front part of the shoe ought to be raised to a corresponding height either by thickening its substance or adding a toe-piece. In the majority of cases, however, the use of these projections is problematical, and it is certain that hundreds of horses travel as safely without them as with them. In many of our large towns and cities they are but little employed, and with advantage to the legs and feet. For many years I have not allowed a calkin to be worn on the shoes of any of the horses in my charge, and no complaints of slipping or insecure footing have ever been made, nor have any reports of horses falling down either on slippery turf or the smooth surface of paved streets, from the absence of calkins, ever reached me. Having studied the subject of farriery practically for several years, in the large cities of Glasgow and Manchester before entering the army, and having during fifteen years' service been attached to those branches in which light or riding-horses and heavy or draught-horses are employed, my opportunities for observation have been extensive. These opportunities have led me to form the opinion just given as to the value of calkins. While stationed with my regiment in Edinburgh in 1864–65, I obtained permission to dispense with calkins on the hind-shoes (they are not worn on the fore-shoes of cavalry-horses), and though the orderly and other duties were somewhat heavy on the streets of that city—which are perhaps the most slippery in Britain—no accident occurred.

For more than three years I have been stationed in a large garrison town in the south of England with nearly three hundred horses—most of which are draught—in my

charge. The greater portion of these animals are employed
several hours every day conveying heavy loads up and down
very badly-made and excessively-steep roads ; no calkins or
toe-pieces are worn, no slipping is ever observed, while the
sprains and injuries arising from the use of calkins are unknown.

This immunity I attribute not alone to the absence of
these projections, but to the care always taken to keep the
hoofs healthy, properly adjusted, and strong, with the frogs
resting as much as possible on the ground.

In attempting to prevent slipping, and to afford a firm
hold of the ground, without having recourse to calkins, a
great object is to diminish the wide surface of metal of the
shoe, without interfering, as little as possible, with its resistance to wear. The simplest method of doing this is
to merely change the bevel on the foot-surface of the ordinary shoe to its ground-surface—making what is now concave, flat, and what is now the flat, slippery ground-surface,
concave. The effect is almost magical in the security it
gives the animal during progression, and is best exemplified
in the case of the hunter, which is usually shod with shoes
of this description. Here, again, we are only imitating
Nature by copying the concavity of the sole. There can be
no doubt whatever as to the advantages to be gained by
using such shoes. The sole is pretty well supported as well
as the whole of the wall, by the wider surface of the
metal above, while the narrow surface toward the ground
affords security of tread.

For general purposes this is an excellent form of shoe, but
to make it still more efficient I devised a modification of it
some years ago, which is an exact reproduction in iron of the
ground-surface of this part of the hoof; it has been employed on the road and in the field with most satisfactory
results both on the fore and hind feet.

In this shoe (Fig. 13), instead of the bevel on the ground-surface gradually becomes shallower as it approaches the heels, as in the ordinary hunting shoe, it becomes deeper, until, within an inch or two of the extremity of the branch, it has cut down through the thickness of the inner border ; it then abruptly ceases, leaving a sharp catch on each side, that, like the inflexion of the wall at this part (Fig. 5, *d d*), affords

Fig. 13.

an excellent grip, which moreover lasts until the shoe is quite worn out. With a modification of this kind, three important objects are secured : 1, The plane upper surface, resting flat and solidly on the crust and unpared sole, leaves no space in which foreign bodies—as clay, stones, or gravel—may lodge, and in heavy ground suction is lessened. 2. The metal is only removed from the parts where it can be best spared, and where there is least wear ; consequently the shoe is lightened without being weakened. 3. The level border and extremities of the branches afford an equal bearing for the foot, while the gradually deepening bevel, with its sudden check, secures a permanent and powerful catching point like that at the angle of the wall.

The shoe is easily made by any farrier, differing, as it does, so little from the ordinary hunting-shoe, and the shape is the same for the fore as the hind shoe, except that the former is, of course, more circular than the latter, to correspond with the shape of the hoof.

To make its fabrication as simple, speedy, and easy as the ordinary shoe, I have made it in two moulds or "cresses," which fit into the anvil. These moulds are of iron faced with steel; one (Fig. 14) has two wide, slightly curved transverse grooves cut on its surface, the one side of each being shallower than the other; in these each branch of the shoe is moulded. The other cress (Fig. 15) has also two indentations so formed as to cut the check or "sunk calkin." With these moulds, the shoe is as easily and quickly made as the common one, and requires but little finishing. The moulds may be of three sizes, to suit different-sized feet and different kinds of work, and can be forged by any ordinary blacksmith or farrier.

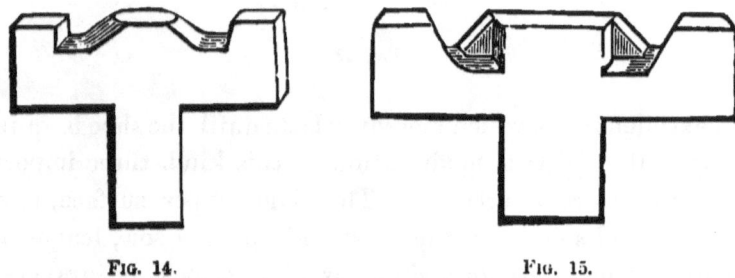

FIG. 14.   FIG. 15.

This shoe has been somewhat extensively tried by carriage and saddle horses, and with the very best results. For hunting or cavalry purposes it is excellent, particularly on slippery grass-land, the sharp point of the catch biting the surface of the ground most effectively.

Clips.—For carriage and saddle-horses and hunters, each fore and hind shoe should have a clip drawn up at the middle of the toe, except in special cases, as when the horse overreaches, or, from being required to jump, or any other cause, is likely to strike any part of the back of the forelegs; in which case, the hind-shoes require to have a clip at each side of the toe—none in the middle—the hoof in front being allowed to project beyond the shoe. The latter should have all sharp edges carefully removed at this part, particularly in the case of hunters.

Clips, when judiciously placed, are of service in retaining the shoe, and so permitting the number of nails to be diminished; but, as a rule, they should be as few as possible, as they are sometimes a source of injury to the hoof, particularly if they are situated in too close proximity to the nails.

Varieties of Shoes.—Various forms of shoes have been from time to time proposed with a view to prevent slipping, but only those which have had their ground-surface grooved, beveled, or "toothed," have met with any success. In recent times, an American shoe—the "Goodenough"—has had wonderful qualities claimed for it in this respect. It differs but little from the common hunting shoe. It has several trivial projections cut on the outer margin of its lower surface, which may prevent slipping so long as they last; but in a very short time they are worn away, and then it has nothing to recommend it beyond the ordinary hunting shoe. The shoe is made by machinery.

Mr. Gray, of the Mowbray Works, Sheffield, has introduced machine-made shoes faced with steel, and grooved into two or more sharp ridges on their ground surface. When fitted, these shoes are tempered; consequently they are harder than iron, should wear for a longer period, and may thus be made lighter. If their hardness does not cause them to be more slippery on smooth pavement, when the ridges have become somewhat worn, than the iron shoe, they should be an improvement, and prove cheaper than those commonly in use.

More recently, grooved and surface-cut rolled iron bars

have been introduced with some success for the manufacture of horse-shoes.

Material.—Machine-made horse-shoes have, unfortunately, never hitherto proved successful, from the material of which they are manufactured proving either too soft—when they were too rapidly worn out—or too hard, when they had a tendency either to break or induce slipping.

We have remarked how important it is that the shoes worn by horses should be as light as possible. It is generally a good plan, if a horse wears his shoes more at one part than another, so that they do not last a sufficient time, to weld in a small piece of steel at that place, instead of thickening the shoe and making it heavier. The latter method, which is that generally adopted to save time, most frequently defeats its purpose—the increased weight causing the animal to drag its feet heavily along the ground instead of lifting them freely.

Lightness and durability can only be attained by employing the best material.

Nail-holes.—The form of the shoe having been decided upon, the position and shape of the nail-holes, as well as their number, have next to be considered.

The shoe ought to be attached by nails to those parts of the wall where the horn is strongest and toughest. In the fore-foot, these parts are in front and along the sides to the quarters; there the horn becomes narrow and thin, and the nails find less support, and are nearer to the living textures; this is more particularly the case toward the heels, especially the inner one. In the hind-foot, the wall is generally strong toward the quarters and heel. These facts at once give us an indication as to the best position for the nail-holes. In the fore-foot, nails can be driven through the wall around the toe as far as the inside quarter, and a little nearer the heel on the outside. In the hind-foot, they may be driven around the toe, and even up to the heels with impunity.

The form of the nail-holes is a matter of secondary importance. The "fullering," or groove around the border of the English shoe, though artistic-looking, is a mistake; it is a waste of labor and of but little, if any, service. What is termed the "stamped shoe," is in every way preferable. The square or somewhat oval cavity, wide at the top and tapering toward the bottom, gives a secure and solid lodgment to the nail-head; which of course should fit the cavity accurately; it does not weaken the shoe, is easily made, can be placed nearer the outer or inner margin of the plate as required, and when filled with the nail is as capable of resisting wear as any other part of the shoe. It is usually better to have the nail-holes stamped "coarse" (that is, at some distance from the outer margin of the shoe) at points corresponding to those parts of the hoof where the wall is strongest; and "finer," where the horn is thin and its fibres short.

They should not, as a rule, incline outward or inward, but be so perforated that the nail-point can take a strong or weak hold of the wall, according to circumstances. If the hoof be strong, with plenty of wall at its lower margin, then the holes may be stamped *coarse*, in order to take a short but solid hold of it, by driving the nail obliquely outward (as in Fig. 16, *a*).

The number of nail-holes through which nails are to be driven should be as few as possible. Every nail penetrating the wall of the foot, no matter how skillfully it may be placed, may be looked upon as a source of injury to it, by splitting asunder or breaking its fibres. On the form and weight of the shoe will greatly depend the number of nails required to retain it. With that I have described as used in hunting, or as modified by me, and which rests firmly on wall and sole, as well as being as light as is compatible with a certain period of wear, but few nails are needed. The ordinary heavy shoe, on the contrary, is not only damaging to the foot, because it rests on such a narrow basis, but also because its weight and instability necessitates its being attached by a large number of long thick nails, which do great harm to the hoof.

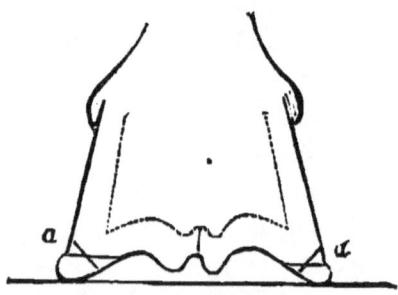

FIG. 16.

With care in fitting a properly constructed shoe, and skill in placing the nails firmly in sound horn, the usual number may be considerably reduced; so that instead of seven to ten being required, it will be found that from four to six are equally serviceable, and even these may be of diminished size. For shoes worn by medium-sized draught-horses, I seldom allow more than six nails in the fore and seven in the hind feet; more frequently the former are secured by five nails—three in the outside and two in the inside branch of the shoe, and the latter by three on each side.

The fewer the number of nail-holes, the greater is the necessity for distributing them wide apart; indeed, it is a grave blunder to cluster the nails closely together in the hoof, as they break and weaken the horn, and attach the shoe much less securely than if they were spread over a wider surface. Calkins demand the employment of additional nails, from their liability to become fixed between stones, and also from the strain they occasion.

It must always be remembered that the retention of a shoe for a sufficient period does not so much depend upon the number of nails attaching it, as upon their disposition and upon its exact fitting and solid bearing on the wall and sole of the hoof. It should also be borne in mind that where there is a clip there ought to be no nail ; lameness is not unfrequently produced by a tightly-adjusted clip making so much pressure upon the nail and horn within it as to cause pain and inflammation.

We have alluded to the various patterns of shoes in use, and pointed out their defects and requirements. As, in preparing the hoof, general principles were laid down which are applicable to every kind of animal—from the race-horse to the mammoth draught-beast employed in our large manufacturing cities—so in the shape of the shoe and its essential characteristics general principles must everywhere prevail. Where speed is demanded, as in the race-horse, hunter, etc., lightness and security of foothold on soft or slippery land are the chief *desiderata ;* with coach and other draught animals of less speed, and which are principally used on paved roads, heavier shoes are needed to sustain wear, and they must also afford security ; but while, with the racer, hunter, and other animals nearly always moving over soft soil, calkins may be resorted to without much detriment to the limb and foot, as they sink into the ground, on the shoes of horses working on hard roads they are objectionable for the reasons stated ; if they are resorted to, their injurious action should be averted by employing a toe-piece of the same height.

For the race-horse the narrowest iron rim is sufficient,

provided it is strong enough not to twist or bend. The present form of shoe is not objectionable.

For hunters, hacks, and harness horses, a shoe of the modified pattern I have described is well adapted; even the ordinary hunting pattern, but without the calkin on the hind-shoe, is infinitely preferable to that used for hacks and harness horses.

Another excellent form of shoe, introduced by Staff Veterinary Surgeon Thacker, and which has been in use for some time in Woolwich on riding and harness horses, deserves to be mentioned here. It is broader in the cover at the toe than the heels (Fig. 17); at the toe it is slightly curved upward, to remove it from the greater amount of wear occurring at this part, and also as a safeguard against horses' stumbling. This curve also acts as a clip to prevent the shoe moving backward. The foot-surface is quite flat, and

FIG. 17.

rests on the sole and wall (Fig. 17). The ground-surface (Fig. 18) is bevelled somewhat like the hunting or modified shoe I have described, with the intention of protecting the heads of the nails from too much wear, and offering no line or cavity whereby a stone can lodge or become wedged. The cover or "web" of the shoe is gradually brought very narrow at the heels, its outer rim corresponding exactly with the crust, and the ends of the branches terminating at the heels of the foot, thus offering protection to the crust only, and without presenting any surface to be trodden upon or allowing the least suction in heavy ground.

Fig. 18.

The nail-holes are in the centre of the *web*, and are directed outward, by which the nails pass obliquely across the fibres of the wall and secure a good hold, without approaching the sensitive parts too closely. Three-fourths of an inch is supposed to be the height necessary to drive the nails.

There are two small clips—one on each side of the curvature at the toe—and these not only support the diminished number of nails, but require that the farrier fit the shoe to the circumference of the foot. The smallest-sized nails should be invariably used, and fitted into each nail-hole before applying the shoe—the shoe to be light and made of good material. This pattern, like the modified shoe I have proposed, is suitable for either fore or hind feet.

It may be mentioned that, with the exception of the two side-clips at the toe, this shoe is nearly identical in shape with that recommended by Colonel Fitzwygram in his excellent work on shoeing.

APPLYING THE SHOE.

The foot having been duly prepared, and the form of shoe decided upon, the next step is to apply the shoe to the hoof, and retain it there by nails.

In ordinary practice the wall of the foot has been only partially diminished, the remainder of the task being left until the shoe has to be fitted. This causes the farrier to have a very imperfect idea of the proper shape or size of the hoof, and he therefore prepares a shoe which he guesses is *about* the size, though in nearly every case it is too small; and, moulding it according to his fancy, *he proceeds to adjust the foot to it.* This is done by cutting more or less deeply into the wall at the toe, to make the shoe appear long enough by embedding the clip deeply in its substance, or "letting it back," as it is termed. The consequence is, that when the shoe has been nailed on, the basis of support of the limb is abnormally diminished, a large portion of the wall of the hoof—its strongest portion—projects beyond the shoe in front and at the sides, and this is afterward carefully removed by the rasp, to the great injury of the most essential portion of the hoof. In every respect, the foot is made to fit the shape of the shoe, and as this is generally prepared with a view only to neatness or the traditions of routine, the organ suffers, to please the fancy or fashion of the un-reasoning artisan.

By our method, the horn having been reduced to proper dimensions, the shoe is now made to exactly fit the hoof, and to follow the outline of its lower face. The part of the hoof intended to be protected by the iron rim has been made as level as possible by the rasp, aided a very little, perhaps, by the knife; the surface of the shoe destined to rest on this horny bed has also been made perfectly level and smooth, particularly at the clip or clips, and it is to be correctly fitted. The farrier should so mould the shoe that it be an exact reproduction in outline of the circumference of the hoof. To make it appear so when applied, it may be necessary to remove a little of the wall at the part corresponding to the clip, merely to make the fit more accurate and not allow any portion of the shoe to project unduly beyond the horn.

The length of the shoe will vary with the uses to which the horse is put. For racing, hunting, and other purposes in which the hind limbs are carried forward to an extreme degree in propelling the body, the branches of the fore-shoe must on no account extend beyond the inflexion of the wall, otherwise the shoe is liable to be torn off by the hind-foot, and the horse thrown down. The end of the branch should also be carefully rounded off and bevelled (as in Fig. 13), so as to leave nothing whatever by which the hind-shoe might catch it.

With harness and draught-horses this extreme care in shortening and bevelling the heels is not so necessary; indeed, in the heavier and slower-paced animals, it is frequently advantageous to allow the shoes to be rather longer at the heels than the hoof itself.

As a rule, then, the shoe ought to be wide enough at the toe, quarters and heels, to support the entire thickness of the wall, but yet not so wide or long as to endanger the opposite limbs by striking them, or run the chance of being torn off by the other feet treading upon it; and it should not interfere with the frog, or prevent that organ from playing its part in the physiology of the foot.

The adjustment of the shoe to the exact circumference of the hoof is usually effected at the same time as the fitting together of the two surfaces of iron and horn which are to remain in contact. To render both accurate, the horse should always be shod at a forge. A hammer and anvil are necessary to mould the heated shoe to the requisite shape; and it is almost, if not quite, impossible to obtain a perfectly true and solid adaptation of the upper face of the shoe to the horn on which it is to rest, within any reasonable time, unless it be fitted to the hoof in a hot state.

Hot and Cold Fitting.—For very many years the two systems of fitting horseshoes in a cold and a heated condition to the hoofs have been extensively and severely tested, and the result has been that cold fitting is, as a rule, only resorted to when circumstances prevent the adoption of the other method, or when the owner of a horse, imagining that the hot shoe injures the foot, incurs the risks attending a bad fit to guard against his imaginary evil.

It is needless, in a brief essay like the present, to enter into a relation of the observations and experiments which have established the undoubted and great superiority of what is termed "hot" to "cold" fitting. These will be found noticed at some length in a work recently published by me, entitled "Horseshoes and Horseshoeing." It may be sufficient to state that the evils supposed to result from fitting the shoes hot to the hoofs are purely chimerical. It is true, when the sole is excessively mutilated should the farrier keep the heated shoe too long in contact with it, injury would doubtless follow, but this accident is so exceedingly rare as to be scarcely ever known, even in forges where shoeing is performed in the most objectionable manner. The ill effects imagined to arise from hot shoeing can easily be traced to the operation of other causes, not the least of which is the fashion of paring the lower face of the foot.

The chief objections to cold shoeing are the want of solidity, the foot being made to fit the shoe, and the process being more difficult and expensive.

The defective solidity is patent to every one who has had

any experience in the matter. It is impossible to level the ends of the horn-fibres so accurately that they will all rest evenly on the surface of the iron; so those which are most prominent soon giving way to pressure, the bed of the shoe is altered, and this, becoming loose, is either lost, or we have projecting clenches. And even should the fibres be made perfectly level, wet softens them, causing them to become pulpy and shorter, by which means the seat of the shoe is impaired and the nails lose their firm hold of the wall. Ample experience on active service, as well as that gathered at home during peace, has demonstrated the instability resulting from cold fitting.

Owing to the increased trouble and loss of time incurred by this method in attempts to make the shoe fit somewhat accurately, but few farriers can afford or are willing to resort to it. Hence, when it is practised, if the shoe is at all like the foot, it is put on, and rasp and knife insure the hoof being made to fit it. This proceeding is very injurious.

In hot fitting we have none of these objections. The shoe is very readily adapted to the foot; it is more equally applied, and rests solidly on the hoof, so that the nails are not broken or displaced by the shoe becoming loose; in fine, there is a more intimate contact between the iron and the surface of the horn. The very fact of burning or fusing the ends of the fibres insures a solid, durable bed which cannot be obtained otherwise, as this destroys the spongy absorbent properties of the horn and renders it eminently calculated to withstand the influence of moisture. The effects produced on horn by the hot iron have been compared to those of fire on pieces of wood whose ends have been superficially carbonized before being buried in the ground. Every one knows that this operation contributes to the preservation of the wood by preserving it from the action of humidity.

Horn is a very slow conductor of heat, and it requires a

very prolonged application of the hot shoe to affect the hoof
to any considerable depth. Three minutes' burning of the
lower face of the sole has been found necessary to produce
any indication of increase of temperature by the thermome-
ter on its upper surface. It is never required that the shoe
should be applied longer than a few seconds.

The hot shoe, in fusing the horn with which it comes in
contact, imprints itself like a seal in melted sealing-wax,
and in this way the two surfaces of foot and shoe exactly
coincide; while no matter how expert the workman may be
in using his tools to level the horn in a cold state, he can
never do it so quickly or so completely as may be done by
making an impression with the heated shoe, and consequently establishing between the lower margin of the hoof
and the shoe an exact coaptation.

It may be added that, when the surface of the horn has
been softened by the action of caloric, the nails enter it more
readily, the clips and inequalities are more easily embedded,
and when it recovers its habitual consistency after cooling,
the union between it and the metallic parts which are in
contact becomes all the more intimate because of the slight
contraction that follows the expansion produced by the
heat. Under these conditions, the horn contracts on the
shanks of the nails, and retains them most securely.

All the highest veterinary authoritities who have studied
the subject are unanimous in recommending hot fitting in
preference to cold; the latter is only justifiable when it is
impossible to adopt the former. The ret-hot shoe at once
disposes of those inequalities which cannot be discovered, or
removed by tools; and it shows the workman at a glance
the bearing of the shoe on the hoof, as well as the imprint
of the nail-holes. Without being reheated, any alteration
can be readily and at once effected in moulding the shoe to
the shape of the two.

The whole surface of the shoe intended to be in contact with the horn should be distinctly impressed on the contour of the hoof, so as to insure the closest and most accurate intimacy between the two; and this carbonized surface should **not** be interfered with on any account, except by the rasp, which is only to be employed in removing any sharpness or inequality on the extreme edge of the wall that may have been caused in fitting.

It is necessary to bear in mind that the shoe should be fitted at a *red* heat. Its application then need only be very brief, and it is far more effective in producing a solid, level surface; it ought not to be applied at a *black* heat. Should the margin of the hoof not be sufficiently levelled by the rasp before the application of the hot shoe, a slight contact of the latter will show the inequalities, and these may then be removed by rasp or knife. On no occasion ought the shoe to remain longer on the hoof than is necessary to produce a solid, perfectly level surface.

The Nails.—The shoe having been made to fit the hoof exactly, is cooled and finished with the file. It is then ready to be attached to the hoof by nails. These should not be unnecessarily large, as is too often the case, but well proportioned to the size of the shoe. The heads should only be sufficient to fill the nail-holes when subjected to two or three smart blows of the hammer, and the shanks thin. It is scarcely necessary to add that the nails, like the shoe, should always be made of the best iron.

Driving the Nails.—In driving the nails into the hoof, every one should be made to pass through sound horn. It is a mistake to place them where the wall is broken or perforated by previous nails, as this only makes bad worse; and care should be taken to direct each nail so accurately that it may make its exit at the desired point in the face of the wall at once. Careless or unskillful driving of the nails necessitates their being withdrawn several times before they are properly implanted, and as each nail, however carefully it may be placed in the wall at the first attempt, is a source of injury by splitting asunder and perforating the fibres, it follows that when several attempts have to be made the injury is proportionately increased.

A short thick hold of the wall is better than a long thin one. If possible, no more horn should be included within the grasp of the nail than is likely to be removed at the following shoeing. By this means the wall is constantly maintained sound.

A foot allowed to grow strong in the manner I have described, will suffer no inconvenience in having the nails driven tightly into the shoe and hoof after they have been placed in the wall.

Where the hoof is thin, as at the quarters and heels of the fore-foot, smaller and more slender nails must be used, and these must be less tightly driven. The toe nails should be first hammered home firmly, then the quarter and heel nails lightly. Every nail should form a part of the shoe, and the head should barely project above it; when all are solidly disposed, they must be tightly "drawn up" at the ends (the points having been twisted off previously) by means of the hammer and pincers, using the same graduated degree of force as in driving them home.

Conclusion of the Operation.—Nothing then remains to be done but to bend down or "clench" the portion of nail so drawn up on the face of the wall. This should be accomplished by shortening the fragment to a proper length by the rasp, so as to leave just enough to turn over; the rasp also removes the small barb of horn raised in drawing up the nail, but without making a notch, and then the clench is laid down evenly. No more rasping or cutting should be allowed on any pretext whatever.

Rasping.—Very different to this treatment is that practised in nearly every forge, where the front of the hoof is rasped most unmercifully as high as the coronet. Indeed, in the majority of books on farriery it is recommended that, though the wall ought not to be rasped above the clenches, this must be done below them ; evidently ignorant of the fact that nearly as much, if not more, harm is done by this operation below than above these rivets.

Those who study what I have said concerning the structure of the wall of the hoof will readily enough understand the amount of injury inflicted on the foot by this rasping.

Over the whole external face of this part there appears to be spread a fine translucent horn, which looks like a varnish, whose office in all probability is to prevent undue drying of the hoof and consequent brittleness. Immediately beneath this are the dense resisting fibres of the wall, which are intended to resist wear, and are best adapted to support a shoe, through the medium of the nails ; in fact, they are the fibres which ought to perform this duty, as beneath them, toward the inside of the wall, the horn rapidly becomes soft and spongy, and more like the pith of a rush.

In consequence of the farrier having neglected to remove a sufficient amount of horn from the lower margin of the wall, when preparing the foot for the shoe, or having nailed on a plate too small for its natural circumference, a large piece of the solid material projects beyond the shoe, particularly in front and at the sides. This is torn away by the rasp, after the clenches have been laid down ; and when this has been done what do we see? The wall of the foot, instead of coming down from the coronet to the shoe in all its integrity and evenness of slope, as soon as it reaches the clenches is chopped abruptly downward, giving the foot a stump or club-like appearance, and greatly diminishing the extent of its bearing surface. The greatest evil, however, is the loss of the strong, tough horn, whose presence is so necessary to protect the lower margin of the hoof and afford support and hold to the nails.

In consequence of its removal, these have nothing to retain them but the thin pellicle of soft horn remaining, and this being so weak, and exposed to influences it was never intended to encounter, quickly dries up, shrivels, becomes brittle, and cracks or breaks away in flakes. Then we have a hoof deprived of its horn, and in as unnatural a condition as can well be imagined; it has been so barbarously mutilated as to require the greatest care next shoeing to place the nails in a shred of sound horn; the operation of rasping and curtailment being repeated each time increases the evil, and should a shoe chance to come off on the road—an accident, it may be inferred, extremely likely to happen—great damage will be done to the pared sole, and the thin, brittle, slit-up wall, and in all probability, after a few yards traveling, the animal will be lamed.

The morbid desire to make fine work of shoeing, when the horse was first shod, ends in the greatest amount of skill and labor being required to continue it, and keep the animal to some extent fit for service, though with deformed feet, seriously damaged horn, and perhaps great suffering.

The truth of this can be verified by a casual glance at the hoofs of almost every horse that passes us in town or country, though perhaps it is most conspicuous in town-shod horses.

One of the most serious results of this excessive mutilation of the lower part of the wall is the production of a chronic form of laminitis, marked by slight subsidence half-way down the front of the foot, and to a less degree at the side, with an abrupt, rounded protrusion of the part that is always exposed to rasping.

This deformity, which causes pain and altered gait in the

majority of cases, arises from the irritation caused to the sensitive parts within by the removal of their natural protection, but more particularly from the fact that the nails, to retain the shoe, must be driven through a sufficient amount of the soft horn, and this brings them so near the living parts that they press upon them to such a degree as to set up an acute or subacute inflammation that leads to this deformity and its attendant lameness.

Cases of this description will be found to be by no means uncommon among the horses in our streets, and for many years I have been able to trace the evil effects of the practice from their commencement until the animal was a hopeless cripple.

When the coachman, groom, or farrier's fancy causes the rasp to be carried above the clenches to the top of the hoof, then of course the injury is greatly aggravated.

The thin, semi-translucent horn that extends in a somewhat wide, whitish-colored band around the upper part of the foot, is chiefly intended by Nature, I think, to protect the fibres of the wall from the effects of external physical influences, such as heat and dryness, while they are being secreted, or so immature as to be incapable of resisting these influences—for it will be remembered that the wall is formed at the coronet, and this covering guarantees not only the integrity of the newly-made horn-tubes, but also maintains the secreting vessels that enter them in a healthy condition, and competent to supply fresh material for wear.

The destruction of this band, and the rasping of the fibres beneath it, is detrimental to the healthy secretion of the wall-fibres, and leads to the same result that paring the sole was shown to do—shrinking of the horn-tubes containing the tufts of vessels, wasting of these, a diminished supply of horny material in consequence, and a thin, brittle wall that scarcely appears to grow down at all in depth or

thickness, and barely allows a shoe to be attached to it.
Sand-crack, and other diseased conditions of this part of the
hoof, are mainly due to this cause.

After applying the shoe in the manner we have described,
and laying down the clenches evenly on the wall of the hoof,
no more requires to be done, unless, perhaps, it be to round
a little more the edge of the narrow shreds of horn that
may project on each side of the clip, and thus prevent their
liability to split. The angle of the face of the hoof should
never be interfered with after the shoe is nailed on, but
should be the same from top to bottom as in the natural
state. This is a matter of great importance. Too much
stress cannot be laid upon the preservation of the horn of
the hoof in its integrity. No amount of rasping or artifi?
cial treatment can give the hoof the beautiful polish it has
in its natural state.

Laying down Clips.—At this stage, it is usual to apply
the clip or clips more exactly and evenly to the hoof before
completing the operation of shoeing; and even this apparently trifling matter demands care. With gradually de-
creasing blows of the shoeing-hammer, each clip should be
applied close to the hoof, commencing at the bottom, where
it springs from the shoe, and ascending to its point. Clips
should never be driven tight into the hoof. This is injurious, and may induce disease.

When, in due course, the period arrives for re-shoeing—
usually in a month or five weeks—the hoofs require to be
reduced to their normal dimensions ; the rules we have laid
down for guidance are to be followed out in the most
scrupulous manner. The old shoe is to be *gently* removed
from the foot by carefully cutting away the clenches with
the buffer; the pincers are then to be inserted toward the
heel, between the hoof and shoe, and the latter prized steadily *upward from* and *across* the foot. When by this means

the nails have been sufficiently sprung, they may be withdrawn one by one. Particular care must be taken that no
clenches or broken nails remain in the hoof, as these are
likely to turn the points of the succeeding nails into the
living parts of the foot.

Such, then, on the one hand, is shoeing as it is usually
practiced, to the great injury of the horse ; and, on the
other hand, shoeing as it ought to be performed, so as to
maintain the comfort and efficiency of this noble and invaluable animal.

It will be observed that no claim is here made to any
wonderful novelty or discovery in the way of a shoe that
will answer every purpose, and keep every horse wearing it
in a state of health. Such an invention must be left to
those whose practical experience is of the most limited character, and who fancy that the evils of shoeing are concentrated in the metal plate alone. It may be sufficient to
say, in this place, that, so far as the comfort, utility, and
well-being of the horse are concerned, the preservation of
the foot in health by abstaining from mutilating and de-
forming it with knife and rasp, is of the highest importance.
If this be done, the shoe most appropriate for certain purposes demands some attention, but is really a matter of
minor consideration.

Preserve the hoof intact and strong, and the animal will
travel long and soundly in a very uncouth foot armature;
pare and rasp it according to " improved principles," and the
most labored, expensive, and artistic device in the form of a
shoe will not prevent discomfort, unsoundness, disease, and
premature uselessness.

At an early period of my professional career, I was much
dissatisfied with the results of shoeing as it is practised in
ordinary forges, and with the unreasonableness of the fashion
of depriving the foot of its natural and most efficient pro-

tection, and was soon led to perceive that a vast majority of
the horses so treated soon became deformed and lame in
their feet; while some of the diseases occurring higher up in
the limbs were likewise due to this cause.

The rational method here inculcated was then adopted,
and now for very many years the only preparation the foot
has received for the shoe has been leveling the wall, in conformity with the direction of the limb and foot, and removing as much of its margin as will restore it to its natural
length, leaving the sole, frog, bars, and heels in all their
integrity. Such has been the treatment of the hoofs of the
horses under my care in various parts of the world, and in
far more trying circumstances at times, so far as shoeing is
concerned, than are likely to occur in the regular work of
towns; and so strong were the hoofs, as a rule, such solid
blocks of horn did they appear, that when a shoe was, by
some rare chance, lost on a journey, there was no danger
whatever to be apprehended from marching the horse ten,
twenty, or even thirty miles, without it. Horses have never
been pricked in nailing, and foot diseases, it may be said,
have been all but unknown. The roughest roads and the
sharpest stones can be traveled over with impunity. Nearly
every hoof might be taken as a model, and be pronounced
as perfect as before the animal was shod, many years previously.

This abstinence from paring and rasping, it will be seen,
very materially lessens the time and labor required in the
ordinary method ; indeed, nothing can be simpler than the
conservative principle of shoeing, and this simplicity can be
effectively carried into practice with one-half the instruction
and toil required for the popular mode.

Other methods of shoeing have been devised from time to
time, and may be briefly referred to here.

To diminish the weight and permit a portion of the posterior part of the foot to come in direct contact with the ground along with the frog, a three-quarter shoe is often applied—the portion of iron extending from the inside quarter to the point of the heel being cut off, and the shoe at this part thinned a little. The horn left unprotected is never interfered with. This is an excellent shoe for saddle and carriage, and even draught horses, which may be employed on the worst roads while wearing it. For feet that have suffered very much from the effects of rasping and paring, and which are liable to have bruised heels (or corns), its use is attended with the greatest benefit.

The same may be said of "tips" or half-shoes. An unreasonable prejudice appears to exist against the use of these light, short plates; but, if they are applied in appropriate cases, there can be no doubt whatever that they are entitled to a far larger share of attention than they have yet received. Their very limited employment hitherto may have arisen from the imperfect manner in which they have been used. They protect those parts of the wall most exposed to damage by wear, extending around the toe and reaching no farther than the quarters; while the heels and frog, when left unpared and unrasped, are strong enough to meet all demands made upon them, at the same time they are not deprived of their physiological functions.

In addition to these considerations, the diminution in the weight of the shoe is a matter of some importance. Of course, the three-quarter shoe and tip are only required for the fore-feet; the hind-feet shoes, so long as they are level, are not over heavy, and do not wound the opposite limbs, may be of the ordinary pattern. On this difference between the management of the fore and hind foot we cannot too much insist. The fore foot is particularly disposed to disease and injury; the hind-foot is wonderfully exempt. So much is this the case, indeed, that the proper management

of the first is all important, while the other requires but little attention.　The reason of this is due to the fact that the
horizontal body, and long, heavy neck and head of the horse,
cause the largest proportion of the weight to fall upon the
front pair of supporting columns, and, through them, upon
the feet: the fore-limbs are those most concerned in supporting weight, the hind ones in propelling the body forward.　Hence the necessity for allowing as much of the lower
face of the fore-foot as possible to come in contact with the
ground ; and hence the prevalence of disease in it when improper shoeing limits its points of contact to the narrowest
dimensions.

Various Methods of Shoeing.—Another form of shoe
is that commonly known as the "bar shoe"—a ring or an-
nular plate of metal which increases the surface of contact
by resting, to a large extent, on the frog, and allowing that
important body to participate in weight-bearing; in this way
it also relieves the heels when these are weak or injured.　It
is a very useful shoe, but the additional weight given to it
by the bar, and the extra strain on the nails retaining it to
the hoof, are drawbacks.

To apply a shoe in such a manner as to allow the frog to
receive a due amount of pressure has always been the aim of
those who have made the horse's foot an object of careful
study.　Even with the ordinary shoe, if it be not too thick
nor garnished with calkins, the frog, if unmutilated, in the
large majority of cases will rest upon the ground for nearly
the whole of its length, and sustain beneficial wear.　Nearly
every one of the horses at present in my charge, though
shod with the army regulation shoe—a very defective model
—have their frogs in this condition ; while all the private
horses wearing the modified shoe I have described, exhibit
the frog resting for the whole of its length and breadth on
the ground.

But this object, with others of importance, is perfectly attained in what has been designated the "periplantar shoe and method of shoeing," introduced by Veterinary Surgeon Charlier, of Paris. Leave the hoof entirely in a natural condition, so far as frog, sole and wall are concerned, and imbed a narrow rim of iron, no thicker than the wall, around the lower circumference of the foot—that exposed to wear—like the iron heel of a man's boot, and we obtain an idea of what the periplantar method of shoeing really is.

The principle of this method of shoeing is, physiologically, perfectly correct. Knowing that the horse's foot is admirably constructed to perform certain definite functions, and that the hoof in ordinary condition is designed to act as the medium through which the most important of these are carried out, but that its circumference is liable to be broken away and worn when rudely exposed, we have only to substitute for a certain portion of this perishable horn an equivalent portion of more durable metal, and the hoof is secured from damage by wear, while its natural functions remain unimpaired.

This novel method of shoeing has attracted so much attention, and has in many instances proved so beneficial and worthy of adoption, so far as my experience goes, that I venture to describe, as briefly as possible, the way in which it is carried into execution in the forge.

The sole and frog, as well as the bars, are left unpared. The crust or wall is bevelled off at the edge by the rasp, and by means of a special knife with a movable guide * a groove is made along this bevelled edge to receive the shoe. This groove is made a little shallower than the thickness of the sole, and slightly narrower than the thickness of the

---

* A knife of this kind which I invented, is manufactured and sold by Messrs. Arnold & Son, Instrument Makers, West Smithfield, London.

wall, not extending beyond the white line separating the sole from the wall (Fig. 19).

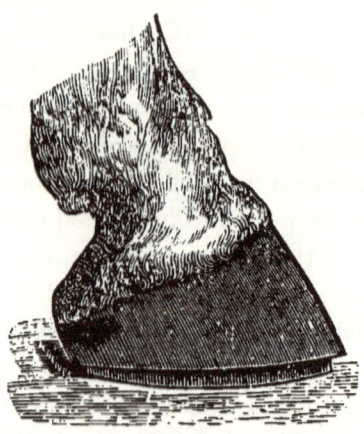

FIG. 19.

Into this groove is fitted the shoe. This is a narrow, but somewhat deep band of iron (or, as now, a mixture of iron and steel), narrower at the top than the bottom, and forged in such a manner that its front surface follows the slope of the foot. It is perforated by from four to six oval nail-holes of small size, and if necessary may be provided with a clip at the toe. Its upper inner edge is rounded by the file, to prevent it pressing too much against the angle of the sole, and the ends of the branches are narrow and bevelled off toward the ground (Fig. 20).

The nails are very small, and have a conical head and neck (Fig. 21). They must be of the best quality.

It is best to fit the shoe in a hot state, as it must have a level bed and follow exactly the outline of the wall. After it has been fitted, it is advisable to remove, by a small drawing-knife, a little of the horn from the angle of the groove in the hoof, to correspond with the rounded inner edge of the shoe. This insures a proper amount of space between the latter and the soft horn at the margin of the pedal bone.

In strong hoofs the shoe is almost entirely buried in the groove; but in those which have the soles flat or convex, with low heels, it is not safe to imbed it so deeply.

The application of the hot shoe in fitting should not extend beyond a very few seconds.

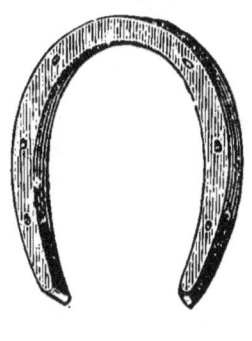 

FIG. 20.　　　　　　　　　FIG. 21.

The shoe is nailed to the hoof in the ordinary manner (Fig. 22). For saddle and light carriage-horses, I have usually found four nails—two on each side—for each shoe sufficient. These should be placed wide apart at the toe and rather close to the heel (Fig. 23, *a*, *b*). Every nail must be driven in sound horn, otherwise the shoe, being so narrow, may get the branch bent out, and nothing more is needed than to lay the clenches down evenly on the wall. No rasping is required. When the shoe is attached to the foot, we then perceive that a portion of the sole and bars, and the whole of the frog, meet the ground as in the unshod state (Fig. 23).

The great advantages of this method of shoeing consist in its simplicity, when farriers have been made to understand it ; its placing the hoof in a natural condition, so far as its ground-face is concerned ; the small number and size of the

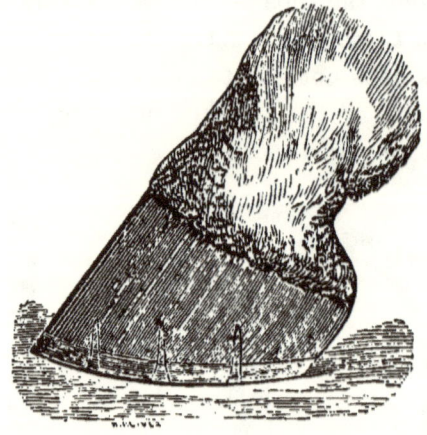

Fig. 22.

nails required to retain it ; the lightness of the shoe, and the security it gives to the horse in progression.

Since its introduction by M. Charlier, I have tried this

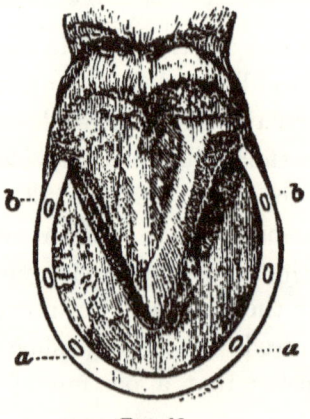

Fig. 23.

method on a large number of horses of various sizes, and which have been employed for hunting, road, carriage, and draught, and am perfectly satisfied that it is a valuable accessory mode of defending and preserving the hoofs, and remedying their diseases or defects. It cannot be applied indiscriminately to every foot, and to make the groove in the hoof and fit the shoe accurately, requires some care. When the horn and metal are combined in this way, it is somewhat astonishing for how long a period a very light rim will sustain wear even on hard roads.

I have not tried the shoe on the hind-feet, because I do not think it so well adapted for them ; as before mentioned, the front-feet only demand all our attention.

WINTER SHOEING.

In such a variable climate as ours, it is not an easy matter to provide economically and successfully for the occurrence of frost and snow during the winter months, so far as shoeing is concerned. Some winters are so mild that there is no necessity for making any difference in the shoe, while others are so severe, and the roads are covered with ice for such a long period, that special appliances must be resorted to if the services of horses are to be made at all available.

To be generally useful, these appliances must be cheap and simple.

The quickest, cheapest, but at the same time least durable of these, is the "frost-nail." This is nothing more than the ordinary horse-shoe nail, with its head flattened gradually to a thin edge. Two or three of the nails are withdrawn from each side of the shoe, and replaced by the frost-nails. The heads may be flattened in different directions, according to circumstances. Sometimes the heads are of steel, when of course they are more lasting. For short journeys, frost-nails are useful and easily available ; but as they only last for a brief period, and as their frequent renewal injures the hoof to some extent, they are only to be

used when the services of the horse are not likely to be in
great demand for any length of time, or when the frost
promises to be very transient. They are best adapted for
saddle and carriage-horses. To prevent injury to the hoof,
and at the same time to obtain all the advantages of frost-
nails, I have often, in the winter season, had extra holes
punched in the shoes—one at the extremity of each heel,
and one on each side of the toe. These nail-holes were large,
and were stamped so obliquely outward that the frost-nails,
when the occasion required them, could be passed through
them and lapped firmly over the edge of the shoe without
interfering with the hoof. They may be made altogether of
soft steel, the heads alone being tempered. I have found
this plan most convenient and effective, as the hoof and shoe
are not disturbed, and the nails can be renewed as often as
may be necessary.

The usual plan is to remove the shoes from the hoofs and
give them sharpened calkins, and it may be toe-pieces also
sharp. This is not a good fashion if it has to be often repeated, as the hoofs are damaged by the frequent nailing,
the horses are apt to be lamed, and the shoes to become
loose. It is for the time being, however, very effective.
When the calks and toe-pieces are only made of iron, and if
the ground be not covered with a sufficient layer of snow to
protect them to some extent, they soon become blunted, and
the shoes then require to be taken off and the process repeated. To remedy this, if time permits, it is an excellent
plan to weld in the calkin, or toe-piece, or, on the face of
the shoe, a piece of steel (Figs. 24, 25 a), which, when sharpened and tempered, lasts a very considerable time.

In sharpening the calkins, regard must be had to their
situation—that on the outside heel may be flattened across
the branch of the shoe (Fig. 26), but that on the inside
must be drawn as much as possible from the outer margin

of the branch (Fig. 27), in order to avoid treads and wounds to the opposite foot.

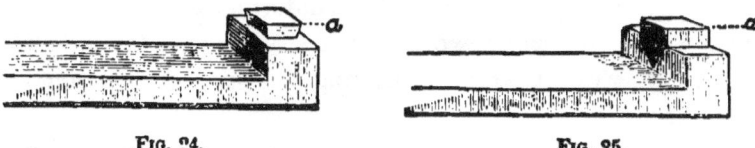

FIG. 24.   FIG. 25.

As a rule, it is better that toe-pieces of the same height as the calkins be used on all shoes, to keep the foot and limb from being injured.

The Canadian shoe, made of steel, concave on the ground-surface, with the concavity forming a sharp edge on the

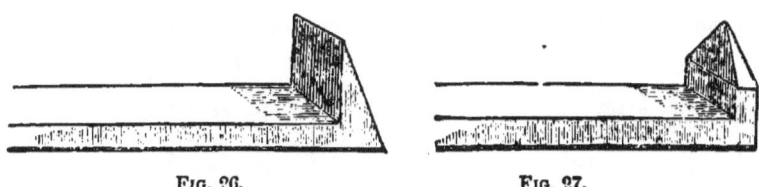

FIG. 26.   FIG. 27.

margin, is very useful when there is a thick layer of ice with snow.

But perhaps the most useful and expeditious method of making the horse useful on ice-covered roads is by the adoption of the screw studs. For these, each new shoe, at the commencement of the winter, has a circular hole punched at the heels and another at the toe. This is screwed, and into it is fitted, for ordinary wear, a flat-headed stud (Fig. 28), which is turned in with a wrench. These studs last for some time, and preserve the shoe from wear. When worn nearly to the level of the shoe, they are removed and replaced by new ones. Should frost set in suddenly, the flat-headed studs have only to be removed by the groom when the horse is required, and sharp steel ones substituted. This, can be done in a few minutes.

The usual shape of the sharp stud is that of a wedge, the screwed portion being much smaller than that projecting beyond the shoe. This is a faulty conformation, which leads to the stud frequently working itself loose and falling out, or breaking off at the neck, leaving the screwed portion in the shoe.

For some years, I have remedied this defect by employing steel frost-studs of a conical or pyramidal shape, and having the portion screwed into the shoe as thick as that projecting from it (Fig. 29). This pattern is not at all liable to turn round and fall out on meeting the ground; while, being the same thickness throughout, there is no check at the screw to weaken the stud; consequently, it does not break if carefully forged and tempered.

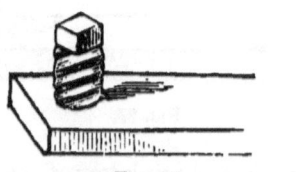

FIG. 28.

FIG. 29.

Of all the appliances designed to enable horses to travel safely on ice, without taking them to the forge, or requiring the services of the farrier, none have stood the test of trial so satisfactorily as this screw stud. I have experimented with all the recent inventions, but have found them either too complicated or expensive — not fit for severe work, or else only adapted for shoes of one pattern.

SHOEING OF DEFECTIVE LIMBS.

Shoeing is a powerful auxiliary in the hands of a competent farrier for remedying the natural defects which are not unfrequently observed in the position of the limbs and feet of horses; while with the scientific veterinary surgeon it is no less a most potent aid in curing or palliating certain maladies or deformities of a special character.

Perhaps the most frequent defects the farrier has to contend with, are turning out or turning in the toe of the foot; both of which are not only unsightly, but are productive of more or less injury to the limb from the unequal manner in which some of its parts have then to sustain the weight of the body.

To rectify the leg or foot when the toe turns outward, the hoof should be levelled as before described, the margin of the wall at the outside toe and back nearly to the quarter being well reduced and rounded. The clip is to be drawn up nearer to the inside than the middle of the toe; the shoe to be fitted close to the outside and quarter, but the inside, from the quarter to the heel, should be more full than usual. In the course of several shoeings, by this reduction of the wall at the outside of the hoof and the fitting of the shoe, a most noticeable improvement will be effected.

When the toe is turned inward, precisely the reverse treatment must be followed; the inside toe must be reduced, the clip of the shoe formed nearer the outside toe, and the shoe itself fitted close at the inside toe, but wide at the outside. In both cases the shoes ought to be of the same thickness throughout.

"Cutting," or striking and wounding the inner side of the leg with the opposite foot, is sometimes a cause of much annoyance. It may be due to weakness, fatigue, or to a sudden change in the manner of shoeing; in which cases it is only temporary. But it may also arise from malformed limbs or faulty action, and these defects may be so exaggerated as to be scarcely, if at all, remedied by shoeing alone.

The usual part of the hoof with which the horse strikes the opposite limb, is the inside toe or quarter. Whichever of these regions it may be, the hoof must continue to be levelled at right angles to the direction of the pastern, and a shoe equally thick throughout applied, the only difference between it and the ordinary shoe being the removal of a portion of the iron from the margin at a point corresponding to the portion that causes the injury to the opposite limb ; or the shoe, instead of being narrowed in the branch at this part, may be straightened, so as to lie within the hoof. No nails are to be inserted here ; they may be placed in front of, and behind the striking portion—at the toe and heel. The hoof, after the application of the shoe, may then be reduced at the quarter with the rasp, to diminish its convexity, and thus avert " cutting " or striking.

The periplantar method of shoeing is well adapted for horses that " cut."

Some horses have the awkward habit of lying like a cow with one or both fore-legs doubled up at the knee, and the elbow resting on the heel of the foot. Should the ordinary shoes be worn, it almost inevitably follows that the ends of the branches pressing upon the elbows will cause the formation of a large, unsightly tumor, which may in time become an abcess or ulcerate. The prevention of this is in the hands of the farrier, who has only to shorten and smoothly round the extremities of the shoe, so as to keep them within the hoof. Most frequently it is the inside heel, in which case a three-quarter shoe at once remedies the evil.

GENERAL MANAGEMENT OF THE HORSE'S FOOT.

After what has been said with regard to the management of the horse's foot in shoeing, there is but little to add concerning its general treatment ; as shoeing influences more or less, for good or for evil, the general condition of that organ, and renders its ordinary management either a matter of much or trifling moment.

When it has been robbed of its horn by the farrier, and brought to such an artificial and abnormal state as we have indicated, then its preservation in anything like a healthy or efficient condition is a matter of no small difficulty, and appears sometimes to demand very curious and often by no means reasonable practices on the part of the groom.

The most common are: applying to the face of the wall tar, oil, fish-oil, or advertised mixtures of various kinds to make the horn grow, prevent brittleness, cure diseases, etc.; and to the sole plates of leather, bolsters of tow steeped in tar, filthy applications of cow-dung, mud or clay, and other matters.

It is scarcely necessary to say that to the unpared and un-rasped hoof these are not only unnecessary, but some of them even positively hurtful. Oil, for instance, not only renders the wall brittle, but loosens the nails; while cow-dung, from the ammonia it contains, destroys the frogs.

The unmutilated hoof is easily kept in health. All it re-quires is keeping cool, and moistening occasionally with cold water during hot weather or after severe exertion. When a journey has been long continued and severe, the horse should not be immediately put into a stable, but ought to be walked gently about until the circulation of blood in the feet has had time to accommodate itself to the altered con-ditions of rest. By this means laminitis (inflammation of the feet) is averted.

In washing the hoofs a water-brush should not be employed, but a soft sponge, with a view to prevent the translucent horn on the front of the wall being destroyed.

The sides and clefts of the frog may be cleaned out occasionally with a blunt picker, though if sound this is scarcely required.

Nothing more is needed, so far as the every-day stable management of the foot is concerned, except to caution the groom against cutting away the hair immediately above the coronet, as this acts like a thatch in preserving the frog-band at its commencement from the effects of perspiration and moisture.

Much harm is done to horses' legs and feet by the some-what cruel custom of keeping them, while in the stable, constantly tied up in one position in stalls with sloping floors. This fashion is not only entirely opposed to the animal's natural habits—for the horse loves to move about and change his attitude—but the limbs and feet, more especially the front ones, are, instead of being rested, greatly fatigued; and this brings about alterations which may be none the less serious because they are not immediate in their effects.

A loose box, even if no larger than a stall, with a level floor, is infinitely preferable, and by all means to be commended to those who place some value on the soundness of body, eyesight, and limbs of their horses, as well as on their comfort.

STREETS AND ROADS.

The roads over which horses travel have also much influence for good or evil on the condition of the feet and legs. In the majority of the towns and cities in Great Britain, it would most certainly appear that considerations for the safety, comfort, or efficiency of the thousands of horses in daily use were altogether lost sight of or neglected in constructing the public thoroughfares.

Masses of the hardest and closest-grained stone are laid down in most streets in such a fashion that they seem as if purposely designed to afford an insecure foothold, and prevent the horse's strength being profitably utilized. These paved streets—always a source of danger to the animals—while hindering them from employing their force to the best advantage, are also particularly injurious to the legs and feet, from the incessant efforts made to maintain a footing. More especially is this the case in wet weather, when they are covered with greasy mud, and in summer when their dry, smooth surface becomes *leaded*. It is needless to say, that no kind of metal defence to the hoof will for many days insure a firm foot-hold on such roads; and nothing but a metal defence has ever been found suitable to the horse's foot.

Every device has been tried to meet the demands for traveling with safety on such paved streets, and none have proved successful. Nor is it at all likely that future inventions will meet these demands; the basaltic or granitic surface, perfectly smooth, and offering a most insecure surface for fixing the foot during movement, is not at all adapted for horse traffic.

From the durability of these roads, they may be, to those who have to pay for their construction and maintenance, more economical than others on which horses can journey with ease and without risk of falling down; but they are far from being economical to those whose carriages and wagons traverse them. A portion of the horse's motive power is devoted to maintaining his foothold, and the fear induced by this insecurity operates against what remains being applied as profitably as it ought to be. So that less is gained in the economy of construction and durability, and in the easier traction of vehicles, than is lost in the injury done to the horse's extremities, and the waste of power required to maintain the equilibrium.

Even more injurious to feet and limbs is the barbarous, slovenly, and stupid method prevailing in this country of repairing macadamized roads—or what are intended for them —by depositing a heap of angular stones in a loose, rugged layer of uncertain depth, and compelling horses and carriages to travel over them until they are imbedded in a very irregular manner in the soil beneath them. Such a practice is not only extremely short-sighted on the part of those who make or repair roads in this manner—as these roads can neither be durable nor very serviceable—but also deserves the severest censure as most cruel and destructive to horses. Not only is the labor in drawing a carriage over such a surface immensely increased, and the horse's strength thereby expended, but the unstable footing afforded by the loose masses of stone throws a great strain in every direction upon the legs and feet, and not unfrequently the animal is thrown down, and gets seriously injured or blemished for life.

If the hoofs chance to be pared and rasped according to the groom or farrier's "improved principles," then the consequences are greatly aggravated.

Legislation should be appealed to, to put an end to such a disgraceful method of road-making or mending, which is only worthy of the most uncivilized country.

The best mode of constructing and repairing our public thoroughfares and highways, with a view not only to economy, but to the safety and comfort of horses, is a matter that deserves serious attention.

Taken in connection with our subject, it is one that cannot be overlooked. We may preserve and defend the horse's foot to the best of our ability in our forges and stables, but if the roads over which he travels are not adapted to his employment, our exertions on his behalf can only be partially successful.

INSTRUCTION OF FARRIERS.

The foregoing instructions relative to shoeing are, in substance, those which I have been in the habit, for several
years, of laying before the farriers in the different regiments
in which I have served, and with an amount of success
which amply rewarded me for the trouble I took to see that
they were carried into practice. Not only have my own
duties been considerably lightened in the greatly diminished
number of lame and unserviceable horses, but the labors of
the farriers have been considerably abbreviated and simplified, and by their being able to understand the reasons for
acting as I desired, their intelligence was awakened, and
they took an interest in carrying out my views.

In our army this is not always the case. The subject of
farriery is often looked upon much as it is in civil life—as a
matter that concerns the farrier only, and tradition and
routine extensively prevail. In saying this, however, I do
not intend for a moment to insinuate that the army veterinary surgeons are averse to giving their attention to a most
important, though it may appear a minor, part of their duty.
On the contrary, many of them do so, and with the greatest
advantage to the service; but there is not the same encouragement offered either to veterinary surgeons or farriers in
this respect as there is in Continental armies. In the
French army, for instance, there are schools and professors
of farriery, the most notable of these being at the cavalry
school of Saumur. In these, the farriers are regularly
trained to a uniform and approved system before being
posted to different regiments, and direct encouragement is
given to these men by the institution of competitions, in
which the most successful are rewarded by medals and gifts
of money.

But not only does the French Government bestow some

care in the advancement of farriery in the army; it also stim-ulates competition and improvement among the civilian far-riers. So late as the 28th, 29th, and 30th of April last (1870) there was a *concours* of "maréchalerie" at Valence, divided into two sections—a civil and military, presided over by two special juries composed of eminent veterinary surgeons and professors.

At this *concours* not only were models of shoes and shod hoofs exhibited, but the farriers—civil and military—were tested in the various operations of farriery on the spot, by shoeing saddle, carriage, and draught-horses, draught and pack-mules, and oxen. A large number of gold, silver, and bronze medals, as well as a considerable sum of money, were given away.

These *concours* cannot but effect much good, by attracting attention to this very important subject, and encouraging good workmen.

In Belgium there are also *concours*, and, if I remember aright, farriers who attend them receive instruction from properly-qualified veterinary surgeons, who are authorized to grant certificates of proficiency.

In both countries, as well as in Germany, the students at the veterinary schools are taught the principles and practice of shoeing, and this instruction is of great value to them in after-life.

It is scarcely necessary to say that in this country noth-ing of the kind is attempted.

The Government does nothing to improve or encourage veterinary science in any way; hence the low state of this important branch of medicine and rural economy in Brit-ain, and hence the enormous losses she has sustained for so many years. Hence, also, the degraded and barbarous con-dition of farriery, even in our cities and towns. With the exception of, on very rare occasions, the distribution of a prize or two at some local agricultural show to farriers, who imagine that paring and rasping, and a fantastically-wrought piece of iron, constitute the *acme* of shoeing, the subject is thought unworthy of notice. Even at the veterinary schools, during my matriculation, it was dismissed in a brief lecture of an hour, and then pathological shoeing was chiefly referred to. Nothing of the principles or practice was ever taught.

When the Veterinary Colleges are so indifferent to a matter so closely related to the comfort and efficiency of the horse, we cannot wonder that veterinary surgeons, as a rule, and farriers, take but little interest in shoeing.

The remedy for this, of course, should be, in the first place, applied to the teaching-schools. The anatomy and physiology of the horse's foot, its management in health and disease, and the principles and practice of shoeing, ought to be thoroughly inculcated.

It would be most advantageous if, when this course was adopted, farriers could be prevailed upon to attend, and, after due examination as to their competency to practice their art in a rational manner, they were to receive certificates of proficiency as in Belgium—these certificates carrying with them similar advantages to those that the diploma of surgery confers upon the surgeon.

In default of this, veterinary surgeons properly qualified for the duty, and possessing the necessary convenience and opportunity, might be induced to receive and instruct apprentices in farriery, granting them authorized certificates when judged to be fit to practice the art.

Agricultural meetings should also be made the means of instructing farriers in shoeing, and of stimulating competition in the districts in which they are held. Of course it is a *sine quâ non* that the instructors and judges should themselves understand the subject thoroughly.

These are the only means by which, I believe, the art of farriery can be improved in this country, where nearly all improvement is left to private enterprise. A profound knowledge of the anatomy and physiology of the horse's foot is not absolutely necessary to the farrier. What I have sketched out on these subjects in this essay, I have generally found sufficient to enable my farriers to comprehend the character of the organ they were called upon to protect and preserve, and this much was easily taught them in a short time. I have always had more difficulty in making them unlearn their unreasonable practices than acquiring those which were novel, though easier; and my chief antagonists in all improvements have been the ignorant grooms and coachmen—the lovers of well-pared and rasped hoofs, oiled or blacked like a boot; hot stables; physic; bearing-reins; blinkers; cruppers; powerful bits; and everything, in fact, unnatural and injurious to the horse.

Notwithstanding that we have given a long and valuable essay on the shoeing of horses, and have had something to say about them going barefooted, we still have something more to say on this subject.

There is more damage done to horses from shoeing than by letting them go without shoes ; and we would have the reader to understand that we are speaking from experience, and not theory. We have handled hundreds of wild horses, of all ages, that never had a shoe on their feet, and we never have seen one lame, because the sole, frog and wall sustained a certain portion of the weight ; but when the shoe is put on in the old way, having it bear on the wall only, the sole and frog are not allowed to come in contact with the ground, so that they have no labor to perform, and will soon become dormant and diseased.

If a horse that has been shod for years in this way loses his shoe, and is compelled to walk on the frog and sole, he will get lame very soon, from the fact that the portion of his foot that has been idle many years is brought into use. The wall is diseased also to a considerable extent, and will break off easily, thus letting the sensitive laminæ of the foot come in contact with the ground, causing instant lameness. We will give you an illustration : Suppose you should place your arm in a sling and tie it to your body for six months, without using it at all, and then take it out, attempting to use it. Do you suppose you could use it like the one that has been in exercise all the time ? Most assuredly not.

By the same principle, it will disable the horse to have his weight come on the sole and frog of his foot after being idle for years, by being shod in the manner we have mentioned. The frog that is kept off the ground by this method of shoeing, without ever having the pressure that nature intended should come on it, will become unable to sustain the horse's weight when the shoe is taken off.

So while we would advise the abolition of shoeing as far as possible, we have too much knowledge of the horse's foot to advise it in every case. There are some horses that have been shod so long that their feet are in such a horrible condition that it would not do at all. But there is no danger of driving or working a colt, even on hard roads, without shoes, provided the wear of the wall of the foot is not greater than the growth.

I have driven colts over hard roads and pavements for many months at a time, and they never gave any evidence of lameness. But if those colts had been shod for a year or two, in the faulty manner described, and then had their shoes taken off, they would have become lame in a very short time.

If the colt must be shod, we would advise the use of the shoe illustrated on the first page of the essay on horse-shoeing. If this shoe is properly adjusted and fitted, we are satisfied the foot will never become diseased from shoeing, because it comes nearer to nature, and it is impossible to *improve* on nature.

We will now have a word to say to the farrier or smith : When horses are brought to them that are mischievous and bad to shoe, and they have to break the horse to stand quiet as well as to fit the shoes, we would advise them to charge the owner for breaking the horse as well as for shoeing, for we consider it an imposition on the blacksmith to bring him such horses to be shod. Time is money to the blacksmith as well as to the owner of the horse. However, if it is necessary to break the horse to stand quiet while being shod, it is only a matter of a few minutes to break him.

Fix him in the same position and handle him all over and

about the legs with the pole, as directed in the lesson for breaking the colt. When he submits to being handled all over with the pole, and before untying his head from his tail, pick up his leg, and if he should kick, give him a little more whirling round, which will make him giddy and will finally conquer him.

When traveling through Pennsylvania, I came across a horse that was considered impossible to shoe while standing on his feet.

The only way this horse could be shod was by throwing him down and strapping him. All the known methods of subduing the horse had been resorted to, in a vain endeavor to quiet and subdue him so he could be shod. I was approached by the owner and asked if I could break him to be shod. I answered "Yes." He then offered to pay me $25 to break him so two shoes could be placed on his hind feet. This happened just before the hour for the assembling of my class.

Immediately after my class met, I asked several of them if they thought the owner of this horse would pay me the amount he had promised, in case I succeeded in the undertaking, to which they replied, " We think he will."

Then I invited the owner to bring in his horse, which he did, and in less than fifteen minutes the blacksmith had one shoe on, at which the owner remarked:

" There's twelve dollars and a half gone to the devil."

I don't know whether he meant I was the devil, or whether he thought he was foolish for making me the proposition to pay $25 for putting on two shoes. I soon had the other shoe on and he paid me the $25, for which I thanked him and proceeded with the lesson.

We have found many horses fully as hard to shoe as the one we have mentioned, but never have we been as well paid as we were for this particular one, which was at the rate of $50 a set, and second-hand shoes at that !

Our experience with blacksmiths during our travels has been that most of them oppose any new ideas that may be advanced concerning the paring and preparing of the horse's foot for the application of the shoe, especially if not in accordance with the manner in which they have been taught; they also oppose the use of any shoe that is foreign to their ideas, and we expect many good blacksmiths and numerous horsemen will oppose some of the ideas advanced in this book. The reader will bear in mind, that at one time it was the belief, both among the scientific and the uninformed, that the earth was flat, and that the sun rose in the morning, passing over the earth during the day and under it at night, making its appearance again next morning in the East, thus causing us to have night and day. This was unquestionably Joshua's idea when he commanded the sun to stand still.

When Galileo advanced the idea, in the year 1633, that the earth was round, and that it revolved on its own axis every twenty-four hours, and thus gave us the night and the day, and not the sun passing over the earth, he was obliged to read his recantation in the church of Santa Maria Sopra Minerva, and then received his sentence. He was condemned, as "vehemently suspected of heresy," to incarceration at the pleasure of the tribunal, and by way of penance, was enjoined to recite once a week the seven Penitential Psalms. Finally, he was given some freedom, but eventually died after spending the last eight years of his life in the strict retirement which was the prescribed condition of his comparative freedom.

But in these enlightened days every one, both the scientific and the unscientific, believe as did Galileo, that the earth is round and revolves on its own axis, and is not stationary while the sun passes over it. Nevertheless, people still continue to condemn all new theories and methods they do not understand; consequently we anticipate no little criticism on some of the ideas presented in this work.

Course to be pursued in Purchasing a Horse.

First—Examine the eyes, in the stable, then in the light ; if they are in any degree defective, reject. Second—Examine the teeth to determine the age. Third—Examine the poll, or crown of the head, and the withers, or top of the shoulders, as the former is the seat of poll-evil, and the latter that of fistula. Fourth—Examine the front feet, and if the frog has fallen, or settled down between the heels of the shoe, and the heels are contracted, reject him ; as he, if not already lame, is liable to become so at any moment.

Next observe the knees and ankles of the horse you desire to purchase, and if cocked, you may be sure that it is the result of the displacement of the internal organs of the foot, a consequence of neglect of the form of the foot, and injudicious shoeing. If these defects are still incipient, and the owner will make a liberal deduction in the price on this account, you may venture to purchase, as this may readily be corrected by the use of a shoe that will expand the hoof. Fifth—Examine for interfering, from the ankle to the knees, and if it proves that he cuts the knee, or the leg between the knee and the ankle, or the latter badly, reject.

"Speedy cuts" of the knee and leg are most serious in their effects.

Many trotting horses, which would be of great value were it not for this single defect, are by it rendered valueless.

Six—Carefully examine the hoofs for cracks, as jockeys have acquired great skill in concealing them.

If cracks are observable in any degree, reject.

Also, both look and feel for ringbones, which are callouses on the bones of the pastern near the foot. If apparent, reject.

Seven—Examine the hind feet for the same defects of the foot and ankle that we have named in connection with the front foot. Then proceed to the hock, which is the seat of curb, and both bone and blood spavins.

The former is a bony enlargement of the posterior and lower portion of the hock-joint ; the second, a bony excrescence on the lower, inner, and rather anterior portion of the hock, and the latter is a soft enlargement of the synovial membrane on the inner and upper portion of the back. They are either of them sufficient reason for rejecting.

PROMISCUOUS RECIPES.

Sore Tongue,

Is relieved by washing with strong alum-water.

Liquid Blister.

Take 1 pint alcohol, ½ pint turpentine, 4 oz. ammonia, 4 oz. oil origanum, 1 oz. naptha. Apply this with sponge every three hours until you feel the skin thicken.

Blistering Paste.

Take 4 oz. pulverized cantharides, 2 oz. turpentine, 2 oz. English rosin, 2 oz. beeswax; melt all together over a slow fire until dissolved. Rub it on well with the fingers.

Cough Powder.

Ginger, fenugreek, licorice, blood-root, equal parts. Half proportion lobelia and camphor may be added.

Dose—Tablespoonful twice a day. For Heaves, add more camphor.

Cough Cure.

Resin	2 oz.
Bloodroot	1 oz.
Tartar Emetic	1 oz.
Ginger	2 oz.
Salts of Tartar	2 oz.

Mix and give teaspoonful three times a day in the feed.

Cough Remedy.

Put all the tar into alcohol it will cut, and add one-third quantity tincture belladonna.

Dose: From one to two teaspoonfuls once or twice a day. It is a splendid remedy.

Laxative Alterative Balls.

Soft Soap.................................4 oz.
Common Moss.........................24 oz.
Aloes.....................................4 oz.
Dose : 1 oz.

Diuretic Alterative Balls.

Resin...................................2 oz.
Licorice Powder.......................½ oz.
Castile Soap.........................6 drams.
Dried Common Soda...................1 oz.
Barbadoes Tar.................to form 6 balls.
Give one daily.

Tonic Ball (Vegetable Tonic).

Opium. ....½ dram.
Ginger............. ....1½ dram.
Peruvian Bark ....1 oz.
Oil of Caraway...... ....20 drops.
Treacle to form a ball.

Cooling and Diuretic Drink.

One ounce of nitre dissolved in a pail of water.

Aromatic Powder.

Licorice................................2 oz.
Ginger.................................2 oz.
Caraway ....6 oz.
Pimento...............................4 oz.
Mix.   Dose : 6 to 8 drams.

Cordial and Anodyne Ball.

Camphor..............................2 drams.
Ginger...............................1½ drams.
Castile Soap ....3 drams.
Venice Turpentine...................6 drams.
Make into 1 ball.

Diabetes Remedy.

Ginger	2 drams.
Oak Bark, p	1 oz.
Opium	1 dram.
Decoction of Oak Bark	1 pint.

Tonic Diuretic Ball.

Nitre	$\frac{1}{2}$ oz.
Sulphate of Iron	2 drams.
Gentian	1 dram.
Resin	$\frac{1}{2}$ oz.
Ginger	$\frac{1}{2}$ drams.

Mix with molasses.

Fever Balls.

Ginger	3 drams.
Emetic Tartar	$\frac{1}{2}$ dram.
Nitre	2 drams.
Camphor	$\frac{1}{2}$ dram.

Mix in ball.

Diuretic Balls.

Make the following into six balls, and give one every morning or every other morning :

Camphor	3 drams.
Oil of Juniper	3 drams.
Resin	3 oz.
Nitre	3 oz.
White Soap	8 oz.

Another—

Equal parts of Resin, Soap and Nitre, beaten together into a mass.

Dose: 1 oz. to $1\frac{1}{2}$ oz.

Mixed Balls, Cordial Astringent Balls.

Catechu, 1 dram; opium, 10 grains.   To wash horses before or after a journey.

For the Appetite.

Take equal parts of aloes, bayberries, assafœtida and saffron; make into a mass with extract of gentian.   Dose, 1 oz.

Cordial Balls.

No. 1—Gentian and ginger, equal parts.
     Treacle to form a mass.
     Dose—1 oz. to 1½ oz.

No. 2—Caraway and ginger.............each 4 ℔s.
     Palm-oil.............................4½ ℔s.
     Gentian................................1 ℔.
Beat together.   Dose—1 oz. to 1½ oz.

Anodyne Ball.

Camphor..........................1 dram.
Anise-seed...........................½ oz.
Opium.......................½ to 1 dram.
Soften with Ext. of Liquorice.

Anodyne Drenches.

No. 1—One dram opium, dissolved, ½ pint water; add one quart starch gruel.

No. 2—Mix sweet spirits of nitre, 1½ oz., with tincture of opium, 1 oz., ess. peppermint, 1 dram, and water, 1 pint.

A Splendid Liniment.

Oil wormword........................1 oz.
Oil sassafras ....1 oz.
Oil origanum.........................1 oz.
Oil juniper..........................1 oz.

Oil spruce.............................1 oz.
Oil chloroform.........................1 oz.
Aqua..................................1 oz.
Ammonia.. ....1 oz.
Tr. iodine.............................½ oz.
Alcohol..............................2 pints.
Gum camphor.........................2 oz.

The above liniment can be used for any sprain-swelling of the legs of a horse.

Condition Powders.

Cream of tartar ....16 oz.
Powdered gentian root.................8 oz.
Sulphur...............................32 oz.
Saltpetre.............................4 oz.
Powdered rosin.......................16 oz.
Black antimony.......................4 oz.
Powdered ginger......................12 oz.
Powdered elm-bark....................16 oz.
Powdered fenugreek seed...............17 oz.
Powdered aniseseed....................8 oz.

Two to six tablespoonfuls to be given morning and evening. A general alterative for hide-bound, etc.

Condition Powders.

Sulphur...............................10 ℔.
Saltpetre.............................10 ℔.
Powdered fenugreek Seed ....5 ℔.
    "   Licorice Root...................5 ℔.
    "   Anise Seed....................5 ℔.
Cream Tartar.........................2 ℔.
Pulverized Squills.....................1 ℔.
Tartar Emetic.........................1 oz.

Dose—1 to 3 tablespoonfuls 3 times a day.
An excellent remedy when there is cough and fever.

Hoof Ointment for Cows and Horses, to Soften and Heal Hoofs and Cows' Teats.

Beef Suet	½ ℔.
Beeswax	¼ ℔.
Honey	¼ ℔.
Fine Tar	1 pint.
Whale Oil	1 pint.

This ointment has been used extensively throughout the United States, with uniform success.

Recipe to Soften the Horse's Foot.

Apply a poultice of 2 qts. linseed meal, 2 qts. rye meal, 1 pt. salt, ½ pt. tar.

Cooling Lotion.

One pt. of vinegar, 1 pt. alcohol, 1 pt. water, and ½ pt. of salt.

The Use of the Hook.

The hook used for cleaning the soles of the feet is a common appendage of the stables in many districts, especially in New York and New England, and nowhere have we found feet in such a horrid condition. The sole of the foot of the wild horse, as also those of the domesticated in the pasture, we generally find well stuffed with soil, filling all the depressions in it, and no one ever saw any evil effects from this natural stuffing.

But little sagacity is requisite to enable us to learn a most valuable lesson, by observing the natural cause and effect of natural stuffing on the feet. If we had a stud of a thousand horses, we would not allow a *foot-hook* in the stable. Snow-balls should be jarred out of the feet, but natural clay packing is useful; hence it should not be removed. Anything that excludes the air from the foot of the horse is useful, and it is to this effect that we attribute such unprecedented success in the use of our hoof preparation.

HOW TO TEACH HORSES TRICKS.

, We will next illustrate the methods of teaching the horse to lie down, etc., as practiced by circus-men for hundreds of years. This method is the same as used by Denton, Offett, Rarey, and others engaged in the business of taming horses. They all gained a great reputation as horse-tamers in consequence of these supposed new methods. We will first explain how to apply the straps.

Take a good strong strap, about fifteen or eighteen inches long, such as used for a breeching-strap, with a slip-loop on it. Put the strap around the pastern-joint on the near fore leg, and buckle his foot to the arm as shown in the cut, then place a strong girth around his body.   Fasten a small strap around the off fore-foot—run it between the horse's body and the girth (see cut).   Take hold of your bridle-rein with your left hand, and the strap that is fastened to the off foot with the right hand ; give him a push with your right shoulder, at the same time pulling up the off foot, holding the strap with the right hand firmly ; this will bring him on his knees.   Hold him steadily, and in a few moments he will lie down ; pull his head around to the off side so as to bring the horse down on his near side [see cut], and when he comes

down on his side, bring his head up to his off shoulder and hold him in this way until he gives up, and treat him kindly. Then unbuckle the strap from the near foot and say "get up."   Of course he will not understand what this means. Urge him a little, so he will understand what you mean. Make him lay down again, repeating the operation of getting him up and down a number of times, or until he will lie down readily when you pull on the strap.   To dispense with the strap on the off foot, take a small whip and touch him on the off foot before you pull on the strap, and as he moves his foot pull up on the strap.   In a short time he will come down on his knees without pulling on the strap, by touching him with the whip on the front leg below the knee, and in this way you can dispense with the strap on the off foot altogether.

When you touch the horse with the whip on the front leg he will get down on his knees; should he attempt to get up, tap him on the front leg and he will soon learn to lie down at the motion of the whip. Do not work on him too long at one lesson.

You should select a nice, soft place in which to put him through this exercise, or his knee-caps may become sore. Pads are useful for the protection of his knees.

After your horse has been taught to lie down, you can begin to teach him to sit up, by putting a good strong strap around his neck; at that part where the collar is placed have two strong straps, made with rings on them. Buckle the straps around his hind legs, at the fetlock joint. Have them covered with sheep-skin, with the wool next to his hide, to prevent his ankles from being galled.

Avoid using anything that has a tendency to hurt or scar him. Then take a stout rope, double it and fasten the doubled end to the strap around his neck; take the two ends and run them through the rings in the strap on the hind legs, bringing them back to the strap on the neck. Draw his feet forward; take hold of the bridle-rein; step back and say to him "sit up." When he puts his front feet forward he cannot get his hind legs in the right position to get all the way up, consequently he remains in a sitting posture. Steady him while in this position with the reins.

Rub and caress him a few minutes while in this position. Then untie the ropes that are fastened to the strap around his neck.

These ropes should be tied in a knot that will enable you to loosen them both at the same moment. Repeat these instructions with your horse a few times, and he will soon learn to *lie down* and *sit up* at command.

Now proceed to teach the horse to follow you all around the training-yard. This you can do by taking a stage or four-horse whip, long enough to reach him at any part of the yard, saying to him, " *come here.*"

He will not understand the meaning of your words, and to help him to understand, keep snapping him with the whip well down on his hind legs, until he turns his head toward you. This he will do in his endeavor to get away from the whip. When he has turned his head toward you, hold out your left hand ; step slowly toward him, and should he wheel around, snap your whip at him as before until he faces and approaches you.

Repeat this a few times, and he will follow you all over the place.

This is the true principle of teaching all dumb brutes— treat them roughly when they disobey and kindly when obedient. Reward your horse with something he likes when he does as you wish him to, and remember always to use but one command to signify a certain act.

By this whip-training you can not only make your tame and gentle horse come to you, but also the wild, unbroken colt or horse. This is a good plan to teach any horse to come to you when you want him.

Your horse is now trained to come to you when called; to lie down; sit up, and to follow you about the yard. Next proceed to teach him to pick up your glove, whip, hat, or anything you wish.

There are two ways to accomplish this: one is, to take a small sack containing oats or corn, and throw it down in front of him. He will get it in between his teeth and commence to get out the oats or corn. When he picks it up, take the sack from him and again throw it down before him, and when he again picks it up, take it away from him, and repeat this treatment for some time.

Every time you throw down the sack, say to him, *"Pick it up, sir!"*

In the course of a little time he will get so he will pick up anything at your word of command.

Another way is to prick him with a pin on the off side. This you can do by taking a position on the near side, and reaching over with the right hand, holding the pin and handkerchief in it, and, in trying to remove the pin, he will get hold of the handkerchief.

Every time he takes the cloth or handkerchief from your hand pet and encourage him to do it again. He will soon take it from any place you may put it.

To Teach the Horse to Make a Bow.

To teach the horse to answer in the affirmative, take a pin in your right hand, stand on his near side, a little forward of the shoulder, and prick him slightly on the breast. He will naturally put his head down to bite off whatever causes the pricking, and when he does this, take your hand away and treat him kindly.

He will soon learn that when you touch him on the breast you want him to lower his head and make a bow. Every time you prick him with the pin on the breast, as you see him putting down his head, move the toe of your right foot forward and he will soon put his head down every time you move your right foot.

This will not be noticed by the spectators, and will make your horse appear wonderfully smart and intelligent, by bowing or answering questions, either in the affirmative or negative, every time you wish him.

To Teach the Horse to Shake his Head when Required.

To get your horse to answer in the negative, stand on his

near side, prick him with the pin on his neck a little above
the withers; as soon as he moves his head in the least, take
your hand away and treat him kindly as before. After repeating this a few times he will shake his head every time
you touch him on the neck.

Then you can take a pin and fasten it in the butt end of
your whip-handle, and touch him lightly on the neck with
the pin. Every time he shakes his head take away the
whip and pet him. By this treatment he will in a little
while get so he will answer any question you may ask him.

To illustrate the system of taking advantage of the horse,
we will give the following example :

You have now taught your horse to answer questions in
the affirmative and negative. Take your whip in your right
hand and say to your horse :

" Do you like this whip ?"

Then raise it up and touch him lightly on the neck, being
careful not to raise the whip before you ask the question, or
he will shake his head before you get through with the
question ; but always ask the question before you make any
motion. And when you make the motion, he will shake his
head. Then ask him :

" Do you like your oats ?"

And make a motion with your foot, by which sign he will
know you want him to bow, or answer in the affirmative.
By the horse doing these things well and promptly, he will
appear like a very intelligent animal.

When traveling in the South, on one occasion, I took a
horse into the woods to train him to get on a large stump
that stood in a clearing.

While engaged with the horse, a colored boy came along,
and stood some distance away watching me handle the horse.

I disliked to have the boy watching me, so I said to the
horse in a loud tone :

"Do you see that colored boy standing over there?" The horse bowed, signifying that he did. I then asked him if he thought he could catch the boy, and he replied by bowing that he could. Then I said to him :

"If he does not leave, will you go and bring him to me?" The horse answered in the affirmative.

This was too much for the boy, who immediately took to his heels and ran for dear life, probably thinking that the horse would surely catch him, as he had answered all questions relative to himself.

At another time, while in Acamack County, Va., I went out one morning to see how my horse Tom was being cared for, as I suspected that he was not fed as I wished. On entering the stable I said :

"Did you have a plenty of corn this morning?" and he quickly shook his head as much as to say "No."

The colored stable-boy stood near and heard me question the horse. He looked first at the horse then at me, and said :

"Look here, massa, dat ar horse ain't telling de truff."

"Well," I replied, "you give him about four cars of corn, and if he refuses to eat them, I will know he did not tell the truth, but I have never known that horse to tell a lie."

The boy went off, and soon returned with four cars of corn, which he gave to the horse. Of course, he began eating the corn, at which the boy remarked :

"Dat ar hoss am de smartest what dis 'fisticated young nigger eber seed in he life."

Now, as you have taught your horse to lie down, sit up, come to you when you call him, pick up any designated article, answer questions, follow you about, etc., you are prepared to go on and teach him other tricks, by the experience and methods employed for the above-mentioned tricks.

There is hardly a limit to which these performances can be carried. You can say to your horse : " Will you take the handkerchief from your front foot," and at the same time make a sign to him with your foot and he will bow.

Then tie the handkerchief on his front foot, in such a way as to be easily pulled off by the horse, leaving a corner of it handy for him to get hold of, and so on, until he will get the pocket-handkerchief from any place you may leave it.

Now, get a large box or platform, and get him up on it with his forward feet. First get one of his feet on, then get him to step up with the other—doing this a few times—after which he will get up at the command.

Next, make him get up on the box with all four feet, and gradually lessen the size of the box until he will get on a box not more than two feet across. Have the box larger on the bottom than at the top, so it will not upset and frighten him.

Then begin to teach him to walk around with his front feet on the box or pedestal and his hind feet on the ground; then make him get upon the box and get down with his front feet, keeping his hind feet on the box, and make him walk around the box on his front feet; then you can put the handkerchief up on a pole, making him climb up on the box with his front feet and reach to where the handkerchief is and bring it down.

Next, you can make him shoot a pistol by putting the handkerchief on the trigger. At first you should be careful not to frighten him by the report of the pistol. You can teach a horse almost anything you wish.

Begin now to teach him to paw by touching him lightly on the near forward leg with a pin. Then make a pile of dirt in front of him and get him to paw it down. You can then take your handkerchief and bury it in the pile of dirt;

then ask him if he could find the handkerchief if you should hide it, and give him the sign to make a bow, and he will bow, signifying yes. Have some one cover his eyes while you hide the handkerchief in the pile of dirt or sawdust. When his eyes are uncovered, let him run around the ring a few times, and when you stop him, see that he stops where he can paw the dirt covering the handkerchief. As soon as he sees the handkerchief he will pick it up.

Then you can change these tricks to suit your notion. At first you make signs to him and use a different word for each trick, and as you find the horse will do it without the motion, you can dispense with the sign and use the word only. When you first made him lie down you had to strap his feet up, but in a short time he would lie down by simply touching him on the front legs, and after awhile he would do it by only saying, "lie down, sir," or by the tap of a bell. Observe the street-car horse. He stops for one tap of the bell, and starts for two. The Fire Department horses go to their places by the tap of the bell; and if you wish you can have your horse perform by taps of the bell.

In this way you drop the sign as soon as you can. People who do not understand how a horse is taught, think because he performs these tricks that he has more sense than other horses. You can take any old plug and teach him to perform tricks.

When men are selecting a horse to train they generally get one of fine appearance and high-spirited, as they are the best for the purpose.

The first trick horse I had was a runaway horse I bought for almost nothing. The fourth one, "White Hawk," was a four-year-old colt, and very stylish, that had never been worked. I paid four hundred dollars for him. I kept him for one year, and then sold him to Mr. Skinner, of Ohio, for one thousand dollars; he is now traveling with a circus.

He would lie down, roll over and back again, walk on his knees, shoot a pistol, take the handkerchief off of either foot you would tie it to, or off of his back, and find it when hidden in the ring; pick up your hat, glove or whip and hand it to you, or any other person you might direct him to.

In fact, you could drill him like a soldier. He would advance, retreat, wheel to the right or left, gallop, trot, walk, perform on the pedestal and put his front foot on my head (as represented on the cover of this book).

By following closely the instructions here presented for the training of trick horses, you can teach a horse to perform all the tricks mentioned, and many more, such as ringing a bell, untying knots, holding your overcoat for you in his teeth, and helping you to put it on. Let some one tie your hands and have your horse untie them, or any other trick that will amuse, such as kissing you, shaking hands, answering a thousand questions. And if you wish, you can train two, and have them teeter on a plank, dance on a platform, waltz, jump through hoops of fire, and you can also teach them so that one will stop for the word that will make the other go, and go for the word that will stop him, and have one to lie down when you say get up, and get up when you say lie down. In this way you can make two horses perform at the same time, or have it appear that one of your horses is very stubborn, and in this way you can spend many hours with your horses. Be patient, persevering and good natured. Never allow yourself to get angry with your horse. If you find you are getting out of humor stop and rest for one or two hours, and it will be better for you and much better for your horse.

H. SAMPLE'S HORSES AND DOG "WILLIAM."

MANAGEMENT OF THE DOG.

The dog is the most domestic of all animals, and is a very agreeable companion and willing servant to man. If he is abused and ill-treated, he will be likely to become a nuisance. He is so close a companion of mankind, that it becomes a very important duty of his master to understand how to train and educate him properly. If he is well and skillfully trained he will reflect great credit upon his master, and become an agreeable member of his household as well as a useful assistant. There are various kinds of dogs and various methods of training them; of course I will not undertake in this work (being devoted principally to the horse), to describe more than a few of the varieties of dogs—those only that are best known—and neither can I devote much space to their training, only giving the rules by which a person with patience, perseverance, firmness and kindness can train the dog to perform various useful and pleasing tricks. We will give a sufficient number to lead the operator to the teaching of many more. Of course the dog is as varied in his dispositions and temperaments as there are different kinds of dogs.

I will here mention, by way of illustration, that the bloodhound will follow the trail of man or beast for miles, over all kinds of ground and almost under all circumstances, even many hours after the object of his search has taken his departure, and successfully find him by the scent alone. His sense of smell is so highly developed, naturally, that he requires no training whatever to teach him to accomplish this, for he is simply following the natural instinct of his nature. But it will take considerable training to bring him under proper subjection, as his nature and disposition incline him to rebel against anything that savors of curbing or controlling his impetuous and obstinate inclinations. For this reason, the ·Cuban slaveholders preferred to cross this breed of dog with the English mastiff, thereby securing an animal that possessed the fine nose of the bloodhound and the controllable disposition of the mastiff.

The Bloodhound.

The notice of the poetical and pictorial artist has been frequently attracted to the majestic head of this dog, and there is no doubt he is deserving of it. He excels the whole animal creation from this point of view, as the greyhound surpasses them in elegance of outline and grace of movement.

It is somewhat remarkable that two members of the ca-

nine race should be possessed to this full extent of these two
attributes so different in themselves.   In consequence of
this hound being used to track deer and sheep-stealers by
the scent of the blood dropped on the track, the prefix
" blood " has been given to this hound.   He was employed
to follow the body-scent of men and animals on account of
his fine nose, and in this manner he was formerly employed
to capture runaway slaves; but becoming almost unmanageable when he overtook them, the English mastiff, or a
cross between this mastiff and bloodhound, generally was
preferred on account of his greater amenity to the control
and discipline of his master.   The reason we specially mention the bloodhound is, that he being an uncommon animal,
and seldom seen in this country, and being possessed of such
a noble head and remarkable powers, we consider him well
worthy the prominence given him in this work.

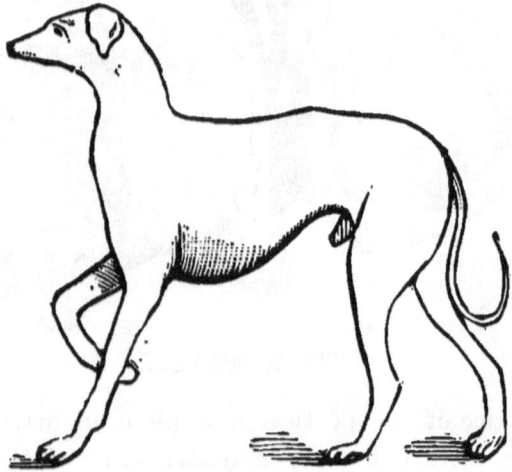

The Greyhound.

This dog naturally differs from the bloodhound; the bloodhound follows his game by his wonderful sense of smell,
while the greyhound depends solely on his sight and re-

markable speed. While in San Jose, Cal., a particular and highly-esteemed friend, Mr. Frank McKiernan, presented me with a fine young greyhound, which I valued highly: When at Livermore I thought I would take the pup out for a little run. Suddenly a hare jumped up, and to my great astonishment she sprang after him at full speed, although she had never seen one before. She chased it so close that she caused him to turn four times within half a mile. It will be seen that the hound was obeying the laws of her nature in giving pursuit to the hare, as she had received no training whatever. My dog, William, well-known over the greater part of the United States, was a splendid trick-dog of the bull-terrier type, but his natural inclination was to fight. He would attack a dog four times his size, and oftentimes would attack his master when closely pushed. I will mention William's tricks, and how to teach a dog to perform them, further on.

The Setter.

The setter is a handsome, bright, and highly-valued animal for all the purposes of finding and setting small game, as well as for recovering birds, etc., after being shot. He is also susceptible of being trained to do an immense number of tricks, such as returning to a store and selecting a letter left by his master among many others, or finding your pow-der-flask, picking up your pocketbook, if dropped accident-ally, going to the house and bringing you any desired gar-ment, etc. This dog requires no training to find and set birds in the fields and bush, as he does this work naturally. Good setters have been known to bring as high as $500.

The Mastiff.

The mastiff, in appearance, resembles the bull-dog about the head, but with the ears dependent; the upper lip falls over the lower jaw; the end of the tail turns up, and fre-quently the fifth toe of the hind foot is more or less devel-oped; the nostrils are separated by a deep groove; his coun-tenance is grave and somewhat sullen, and his deep-toned bark can be heard at any hour of his watchfulness. He is much taller than the bull-dog, but not so deep in the chest. His head is large, compared with the size of his body. It is generally believed that the mastiff is an original breed pe-culiar to the British Islands. He is generally used as a watch-dog, and his large proportions make quite an impres-sion on a stranger, especially during the still hours of night. It is with the greatest vigilance that he watches the property and abode of his master, never neglecting his duty. Nothing will induce him to forsake his watchfulness over anything placed in his charge to guard.   His attachment to his master, and great appreciation of kindness and favors bestowed on him, is fully as great as shown by the most diminutive canine, notwithstanding his great size, commanding appearance and faithful watchfulness over his master's abode.   The natural instinct of this dog is unmistakably that of a faithful watch-dog, and he requires little or no training for this purpose.

The Poodle.

From what particular breed the poodle descended is unknown, yet all his peculiarities of form, size, and suscep-tibility to training have been remarkably well retained. He was originally a water-dog, as is amply shown by his natural propensities while in a domesticated state, and he is the easiest trained and educated of any other dog.   As sporting dogs they are not recognized to any extent.   His great attachment to his master, the great number of useful tricks which he can be trained to perform, make him the most companionable of all dogs.

It is customary to strip the poodle of his natural long curly hair from the portion of the body back of his shoulders, leaving parts of his head and forward parts as nature intended, as shown in the cut; the contrast between the parts of his body may give a pretty effect, but is liable to be the cause of bringing rheumatism, to which disease this dog is very liable.

Smooth Rat-Terrier.

This dog has a convex forehead; pointed muzzle; prominent eye; short fur; moderate-sized ears, half erect. He is a most useful dog about the house and farm, having no superior as a destroyer of rats, weazels, polecats, etc., for which service he requires no training, his natural propensities guiding him in his work. There are the rough and smooth terriers; the rough dog probably obtained his shaggy coat from the cur, and the smooth terrier may derive his from the hound. Was it not for this very useful dog many a granary and barn would be the scene of an immense loss of grain by rats. The terrier is quick and active, and easy to train for the performance of many novel and interesting tricks.

Collie, or Shepherd Dog.

This animal is used for the purpose of watching, returning stray sheep to the flock, heading off, guiding and driving sheep, as well as protecting them from wild animals and dogs. He is also a faithful house watch-dog, of good disposition. He is used extensively by the ranchers throughout California and Oregon. The hair on this dog is long and inclined to be shaggy, his snout sharp, body full and well-rounded, legs of moderate length ; tail has fine brush, similar to that of a fox. He is capable of standing an unusual amount of exposure to wind, rain, snow and cold, his fine long hair providing him ample protection.

Among those dogs most readily trained to perform tricks are the French poodle, water spaniel, setter and pointer. In fact, any common cur such as we have illustrated on page 255 can be taught to perform many interesting and amusing tricks, as will be shown farther on in this work.

Training the Shepherd Dog.

After you have selected the kind of a dog you desire to train—one from six months to a year old—take him into some large room or lot with a high fence, being careful that there is nothing to interfere with your work, or any place for the dog to crawl through and out of the room or lot. Take your dog into the place prepared for his training. It is preferable to get an animal unaccustomed to being played with by boys and also one unused to the words of command made use of to other dogs.

The first thing to teach him is his name and to obey
promptly, when you call him by name and order him to
come to or go from you. He must at first be taught to mind
by the use of a single word, and when accustomed to the
use of a single word as *here* (emphasizing here), teach him
to obey by the use of two or more words, such as " come
here," "lay down," etc. There are many ways of teaching the
dog, as well as other animals, but our methods for teaching
him will be very simple and effectual, being applicable to
every case. If we teach the dog by coaxing, he will come
only when he feels disposed to, and is liable to disobey at a
time when we are extremely anxious to have him obey our
commands, therefore we resort to other means than by coaxing. Most writers claim that it will take the dog three or
four days to learn his name by their methods—we propose
by our method to teach him in ten or fifteen minutes. Place
a strong strap or collar about his neck — there is a
patent collar for this particular purpose, but is unnecessary,
as the above-mentioned strap or collar will answer all requirements and inflict no cruelties on the animal. Attach
a cord to the collar, long enough to reach across the room or
enclosure ; take hold of it about six or eight feet from the
dog, and say " Here," or any other word you propose using
when you want him to come to you. A German, French-
man, Italian, or, in fact, a person of any nationality, will,
of course, use whatever word suits his language, and whatever word he may use, it is evident the dog will not understand it ; so jerk on the cord sharply, using whatever word
you intend using to have him come to you. This will have
a tendency to hurt the dog a little at first. Then move a
little from him and repeat the word and the jerking—
always using the word first, followed quickly by pulling on
the line. As soon as the dog shows any signs of coming
toward you in answer to your commands, approach, and

by caressing him, encourage his obedience in the future. After fondling and kindly treating him for a little while, step away from him further than before, and repeat the operation until he will come to you from any part of the room or enclosure, at the word of command—" Here ! " When you get him to come to you, say " do " in place of saying " that will do." This lesson will occupy about thirty or forty minutes, and will be sufficient for the first time.

On the conclusion of the lesson, romp and play with him, so that it will not appear like a long lesson. During the training of the dog, allow no one to approach or speak to him, and never permit him to be fed by any one but yourself. When the dog has had a good rest, begin again as before with the cord and collar, saying to him, " Come," at the same time pulling him with the cord toward you, should he fail to obey. If he comes at your word of command, kindly treat and encourage him. Then you can begin to teach him to go from you, at the word " go." This you can do by leaving the room door open, or by getting a piece of meat and throwing it from you, and encouraging him to go after it. When he understands how to *go*, then teach him to *halt*, by holding him with the cord when he is going after the meat or toward the door. In fact, this dog wants to be taught obedience only, and his natural instinct will teach him to drive and care for the sheep.

To teach the dog to take hold of anything, first get a piece of stout cloth or rope, and get him to take hold of it, at the same time using the word " Hold ;" and when he has held it long enough, say to him, " Do," in place of "That will do," and repeat this performance until he will readily and willingly take hold and let go of the rope when ordered to do so

When he has accomplished these things properly, procure a gentle cow and encourage the dog to hold on to her tail until you give him the word to let go; and then you may take him along, accompanied by other dogs, to drive the cattle, encouraging him to drive them. At the same time do not send him after cattle unused to dogs, or they may turn and frighten him. After doing this a few times, take a well-broke dog along that has been taught to drive, and let your new dog have a chance to see the old dog work. The young dog will require very little encouragement to learn to drive and work with sheep and cattle. After having learned to come, go, take hold, let go, etc., his natural propensities will direct his future efforts.

TEACHING THE DOG TRICKS.

Many amusing tricks may be taught the dog, that will make him appear very intelligent. As I have before said, much depends on the breed; a dog of the poodle family may be taught to perform one set of tricks, while one of the bloodhound, terrier or greyhound family may be taught to perform things entirely at variance with those of the poodle. When selecting a dog to train, I always get one that is considered very difficult to train—a mongrel or common cur. If we select a well-bred dog, that is considered very intelligent, we could claim but very little credit for having such a dog perform interesting tricks; therefore, I would advise the selection of the former kind for a trick-dog, by which course the trainer will receive greater credit than the dog for his clever performances.

The reader must bear in mind the necessity of giving the dog *primary* lessons before undertaking to instruct him in the lessons pertaining to the *grammar* department' of his course 'of instructions, or, in other words, teach him the simplest first, then the more difficult tricks. My celebrated dog William was trained to drink when he was not thirsty and to 'eat when not hungry. He was a cross between the

bull-dog and terrier, and did not have the appearance of a
dog susceptible of a high degree of education, yet he was
trained to perform numerous difficult and interesting
tricks.

Having first taught your dog to obey every command
promptly, proceed to teach him to sit up. This you
can do by placing him in a corner in a sitting position, and

Common Cur.

should he attempt to come down, tap him lightly on the
chin, and say, "Sit up!" Keep him in this position for a
little while, and should he come down again, straighten him
up, saying to him, "Sit up!" After he has sat in this position a little while, say to him, "Do," meaning that will do.
The object in placing him in the corner is to furnish support at first, that he may not fall over. After he has learned

to sit up well in the corner, sit him up against the wall and try the same thing; this will require more patience, as he can easily fall over to either side. When he has learned this well, take him from the wall to the middle of the floor, and set him up; but as he has no support whatever, it will require more time and patience before he can accomplish the feat. When he sits up on the floor without support, then proceed to teach him to stand up. This you can do by taking hold of his front feet with both hands and straightening him up, at the same time saying, " Up !" Then replace him in the sitting position. Repeat this until he will stand up readily at the word " Up !" and sit down at the word " Down !" The trainer must bear in mind that this is not all to be accomplished in a single lesson, but requires several. Do not prolong the lessons until the dog becomes tired and inattentive. Next proceed to teach him to walk on his hind feet. This you can do by taking hold of his forward feet with both your hands and walking him forward and backward on the floor, at the same time saying to him, "Forward !" or "Back !" according to the way you require him to go. After he understands what you want him to do, holding on to him with your hands, you can then encourage him to do it without holding on to him, by having him a little hungry, and inducing him with a piece of meat to rise up and walk after it, backward and forward. Next proceed to teach him to jump over things. The best way to get him to do this is to get a small bar or pole, six or eight feet long, placing one end of it on a box about a foot high, and the other on the floor ; then place the cord on his neck, the same as in training him to come to you, and get on one side of the bar, with the dog on the other, saying, " Jump," at the same time pulling on the cord to induce him to do so. You might also have a small switch in your hand as a " persuader," using the switch at the same time you pull on the cord.   After jumping over the pole readily, following you over every time, induce him to jump over the bar closer and closer to the box, at which point the bar is highest from the ground.   Every time he jumps over fondle him, and by kindness show him that he has done what you required of him.   Now you can increase the height of the box to two feet, and repeat the lesson as before, until he will jump over a bar at any reasonable height.

In giving these lessons never use the word "jump" more than once, and then enforce your order.   By this method the dog will soon find out that he is never punished except when he disobeys, and receives kind treatment and reward, with food, for prompt obedience.   This prepares him to jump on the box, chair or stool.   You can now take the bar away and make him jump upon the box.   When he jumps up encourage him by kindness, then say :

"Jump *down.*"

If he does as ordered, proceed as before.   Repeat this until he will readily do it at the words "jump up," or " down."

The dog is now prepared to receive a higher and more difficult branch of his education.

Get a barrel to begin with ; prop it so as to have it solid ; then stand at one end and teach the dog to jump on the barrel, and down, as you did when exercising him with the box, chair or stool.   Have the cord on the dog's neck, holding it with your left hand, all this time, so as to compel him to take the position you desire.   Then walk half way around the barrel, obliging the dog to keep his head to your left hand and his tail to your right.   Get him to do this perfectly, before allowing him to attempt anything new—to prevent his being confused.

For each act you require of the dog, use a different word of command and do not repeat it, but insist on prompt obedience at the *first* command, and never neglect to kindly use him on the conclusion of a well performed lesson. After he has accomplished this part of the lesson, take the props from the sides of the barrel so it will roll ; compel your dog to get upon it, standing across the middle, with his sides toward the barrel ends ; pull gently on the cord—this will start the barrel to roll slowly toward you, as you always stand facing the dog. The movement of the barrel necessitates the dog's changing and lifting his feet to balance himself as it rolls along. Never permit him to squat down, but keep in an upright position while going through this exercise. Having gone on in this manner across the room, walk around to the other side of the barrel, compelling the dog to "about face" and begin to pull gently again on the cord, causing the barrel to roll toward you. When he does this well without your pulling on the cord, take him down and give him a good rest.

Next, order your dog up on the barrel, again obliging him to roll it first one way and then the other. When he does this to your satisfaction, walk around to the end of the barrel and making him face you, with his head toward one end of the barrel, hold it, and say to him " *Stop!* " helping him at first, so he will not fall. Then go to the side of the barrel, the dog turning his head toward you, with his sides parallel with the ends of the barrel, and order him forward. He will start to moving his feet, of course, thus causing the barrel to roll forward. After he moves forward, reverse and stop the barrel satisfactorily, then teach him to steady the barrel, while he stands with his head toward the end.

When he has learned the above portions of his lessons, block the barrel again, and proceed to teach him to lie down, sit up, and stand up on the barrel.

When he has been taught well to stand erect on the floor,

you can then make him stand up on the box, and next on the barrel, and he will soon get the idea of standing up well on the barrel.

After your dog has been advanced to this high degree of education, you can proceed to teach him to pick up and lay things down at your word of command.

There are two ways to teach him to do these things. One would be to take a ball, or something he is used to playing with, getting him to run after it and bring it to you, making him drop it at your feet by putting your fingers in his mouth and pressing on the inside, at the same time saying "let go."

Another way would be to place the object inside of his mouth, and compel him to hold it there until told to let go. The best way is to get a piece of meat, or anything he is fond of, and of a size to prevent his swallowing it. When you have succeeded in teaching him this, you can substitute some other object in place of the ball or meat—for instance, a slipper or handkerchief.

Teach him to pick up and bring to you any desired object, always being particular to call it by name, so that he will become familiar with the sound as well as the sight of the object. Begin first with a single object, such as a boot, or hat. Step up close to it, making the dog take hold and pick it up, then step away, and calling it by name command him to bring it to you and place it at your feet.

If he does it all right pet him. By teaching your animal this one trick thoroughly, with a single object, he will soon be enabled to distinguish the names of several things placed in a row. When he can bring you any article asked for among a number of others, then substitute the *color* of the articles in place of their names, so when you order him to bring a slipper say to him "bring me the *green* slipper," placing great stress on the word which represents the color.

By this course of training it will appear as though the dog could readily distinguish colors, when in reality you have only substituted the name of the color of the object in place of its name ; for example, if the slipper is green, say to him to bring you the *green* slipper, or the *black* slipper, or the *blue* slipper, and so on, until you can teach him to bring you a slipper of any prominent color you may name.

By this course of treatment the dog will become able to distinguish one color from another, no matter what the object may be, whether it is a slipper, hat, paper, handkerchief or anything else.

There is a great deal of deception practiced in the exhibition of performing animals, by the skill of the trainer in directing their movements.

Remember, the trainer does the most of the tricks by his movements, for, after the dog has been trained to pick up things, he can do numerous tricks, such as telling the time by looking at your watch. Be careful you see the watch yourself, or the dog cannot perform the trick. You place on the floor cards with the numbers 1, 2, 3, 4, 5, 6, 7, 8, 9, 0. Every number you wish him to pick up, step in front of the number. If it is not the one that you want, say to your dog : "Go on, sir, and tell me the time." If he picks up the right one, say : "Bring it here, sir !" Then ask him how much 3 and 6 are, and make him pick up the card No. 9. Then ask him how many days there are in a week. Give him the sign to pick up No. 7. Ask him how many days he likes to work, and make him pick up the cypher, and so on. You can see how numerous you can make his tricks.

By having several dogs trained, each one in his line, and have them sit on a stool and perform in turn, will make a very interesting exhibition. Have the greyhound display his wonderful powers for leaping. When you require him to do this, have a pad for him to jump on, so as not to injure him as he alights. Have the setter perform tricks that require a fine nose; the spaniel or poodle for the water tricks; the bull terrier for those kind of tricks that require courage.

Bull Terrier.

If you want to make your dog sneeze, get a little snuff and put it on his nose. Say "Sneeze, sir!" In a short time he will sneeze if you point your finger at him.

In the foregoing we have given instructions for training dogs to perform many amusing tricks; the natural ingenuity of the experimenter will enable him to extend the list indefinitely.

DISEASES OF THE DOG.

Distemper.

Distemper is a feverish disease, marked by a rapid loss of strength and flesh in proportion to the severity of the attack. It may occur more than once in the same individual, and at any period of life. It is generally met with in the puppy, and in the majority of cases the dog is afterwards exempt. The cause of the disease consists in the poisoned state of the blood, which may be produced either by contagion or by putrid emanations from filthy and overcrowded kennels. It is from the efforts of nature to throw off this poison that the various symptoms are produced by which we know the disease. The symptoms differ in accordance with the difference of constitution of the animal, also to the state of surroundings, air, etc. Distemper is either simple or attended by complications in the chest, head, belly, etc. Although they are all essentially the same disease, the variations may be described as : 1st. Mild distemper. 2d. Head distemper. 3d. Chest distemper. 4th. Belly distemper. 5th. Malignant distemper.

In almost all cases of mild distemper, the following symptoms show themselves, with the additional symptoms peculiar to each. The first noticeable thing is a general dullness, especially in the eyes, accompanied by a loss of appetite and a dislike for exercise and play. A short cough soon appears, attended by a disposition to sneeze, and the dog appears as though he hardly knew which to do first, cough or sneeze. While the dog is quiet in his kennel, the cough and sneezing are seldom heard, but when brought out into the air, from the kennel, especially after he begins to run about and play, the mucous membrane is irritated and the cough begins, either by itself or alternately with sneezing. There is slight thirst, generally a warm, dry nose, a disordered state of the bowels, which may be either confined or relaxed, and a scanty secretion of highly colored urine. In a few days the dog loses flesh and strength, to a great extent, and then gradually recovers.

Head Distemper begins the same as in the mild form, and if there is any cough or sneezing it is very slight, sometimes being imperceptible. It will be noticed that the whites of the eyes are covered with blood-vessels loaded with dark blood, and strong light appears to give pain. Very often this kind of distemper is accompanied by a fit of short duration, at the beginning of the trouble, and leaves the dog in a state of torpor from which he can with difficulty be aroused. If the brain is not relieved, the fits recur at short intervals, the stupor increases, until the dog becomes insensible and dies in violent convulsions. Chest distemper is an extension downward into the chest of the irritation which causes the cough. It there generally sets up that kind of inflammation known as *bronchitis*, together with which, however, there is often inflammation of the substance of the lungs (pneumonia), or even of the external surface (pleurisy). Distemper of the belly is often caused by mismanagement, brought on by either the abuse of violent drugs or neglect for some time previous of the secretions. In the former case, the bowels become very much relaxed at the expiration of ten days from the commencement of a case of *mild distemper*, with constant diarrhœa, soon followed by the passage of large quantities of blood. When this comes from the small intestines it may be quite black and pitchy, or when from the lower bowels it is red and florid.

Generally these symptoms appear as the result of calomel, or other violent medicine; sometimes they appear of themselves. When the bowels have become confined from neglect, while, at the same time, the secretion of bile has been checked, a very dangerous symptom, named "the yellows," shows itself, the name being given in consequence of the skin and white of the eyes being of a yellow color from the presence of bile. When this occurs without distemper, it is not so fatal; but when it comes on during an attack of this disease, it almost invariably proves fatal. Malignant distemper may come on at first, the animal being, as it were, at once knocked down by the severity of the poison. At times it shows itself within a week or ten days after the first symptoms appear. It may follow either of the four kinds already described, being marked by an aggravated form of the symptoms of each. There are additional evidences of the poisoned state of the blood which present themselves in the four stages into which this disease has been divided. These stages are: 1st, *incubation*, during which the disease is hatching or brewing; 2d, *reaction*, when nature is working to throw off the poison; 3d, *prostration*, following these efforts; and, 4th, *convalescence*, wherein the constitution recovers its usual powers.

In well marked cases of malignant distemper the four stages average about a week or ten days each, and as the treatment for each varies considerably, it is important to ascertain their existence. The period of incubation may be known by the symptoms common to mild distemper, as well as to other kinds. In the malignant form the secretions are disordered, the strength is lost more rapidly, and the appetite is almost gone. During the reaction the pulse becomes hard and quick, the breathing is much hurried, and is often much quicker than the pulse, without the existence of any inflammation. It is important to notice this, as, when such is the case, any lowering measures are improper. On the other hand, the pulse may be very high and strong, and the breathing labored, which, together with other unmistakable symptoms, require energetic and lowering treatment. At this time, also, are developed those dangerous affections of the brain, bowels, or liver, to which I have before alluded. When this stage of *prostration* sets in the whole system is thoroughly prostrated, the dog is so weak that he is unable to stand, his strength is almost entirely gone, so that he must be drenched to keep him alive. The tongue, gums and teeth are coated with a black fur, and his breath is highly offensive. At this time an eruption of the skin shows itself, sometimes consisting in mere purple spots, in others of small bladders filled with yellow matter, but most frequently of bladders varying in size from a pea to half the size of a hen's egg, containing matter more or less stained with purple blood, and sometimes blood alone.

On the skin of the belly, and inside of the thighs, this eruption is thickest, but sometimes extends to the whole body. It is considered a favorable sign, taken by itself, though it generally attends severe cases. Health gradually returns in the convalescence from malignant distemper, but great care should be taken, or a relapse is apt to follow, and is often fatal. In distinguishing the various forms of distemper from the diseases that most resemble them, it is necessary to bear in mind the peculiarity of distemper. In its malignant form, especially, is the rapid tendency to loss of strength and flesh which accompanies it. A common cold or cough is attended with slight fever, languor and loss of appetite, yet it may go on for some days without the dog losing much flesh, and with but small loss of strength. So with ordinary diarrhœa—it requires a very severe attack to reduce a dog anything like the same degree which a few days' distemper will cause. A dog with diarrhœa gets thin, but does not become a living skeleton, as he does when affected with distemper ; neither does he lie exhausted in his kennel, powerless to rise from his bed, and unable to relieve himself unless receiving support. The same applies to *simple* inflammation of the lungs, which may be treated with lowering medicine with good effect without reducing the dog too much ; while in chest distemper, even if the local symptoms are apparently as severe, a treatment half as energetic will be fatal from exhaustion following upon it.

The sequels of distemper are *chorea*, commonly called " the twich," and a kind of *palsy*, known as " the trembles." Both are produced by some mischief done the brain or spinal marrow in the course of the disease. They generally follow the kind described as head distemper. *Chorea* is known by a peculiar and idiotic-looking drop in one fore-quarter when the dog begins to move, causing him to bob his head in a helpless manner. At times the twitch is only partial, and at others almost universal, but disappears during sleep. Shaking palsy affects the whole body. It is more rare than chorea, which fact is fortunate, as it is considered incurable. All lowering measures should be avoided in the treatment of the various forms and sequels of distemper, as this is a most debilitating disease.

Inflammation is always to be feared, attacking either the brain, lungs, or bowels, and as bleeding and other remedies of a similar tendency form the most active means for getting rid of inflammation, there is left only a choice between two dangers. In the general treatment there are two things to be attended to: First, avoid lowering the system, and in severe cases, support it by good diet, consistent with the avoidance of encouragement to inflammation. Second, take particular care that inflammation does not go far enough to destroy life, or to leave such organic change in brain or lungs as shall render the dog useless for purposes for which he was designed. This, in theory, is simple, but requires some experience in practice. At times one is obliged to blow hot and cold at the same time, lowering the dog with one hand and propping him up with the other. Remember, always, that this disease has a natural tendency to recovery, the efforts of the powers of the system being to throw off a poison in the blood. Nature, therefore, requires to be aided, not opposed; the less interference with her operations the greater your success.

1. General Treatment—For the early stage give a mild dose of aperient medicine, such as castor oil and syrup of poppies in equal proportions. If the liver does not act give jalap and calomel. Avoid giving calomel if there is plenty of bile in the evacuations. After the early stage of the trouble is passed give no medicine. Keep the kennel clean, dry, airy and warm, changing the litter often. Avoid exercise till the running of the eyes and cough have ceased. Give nourishing broths, thickened with rice, flour, or arrowroot, when there is diarrhœa. If the bowels are confined give oat-meal. If there is very little water passed give as a drench five or six grains of nitre, with half-teaspoonful of spirits of nitre every night.

2. Head distemper requires energetic treatment in addition to the above. From four to eight leeches may be applied to the inside of the ears; bathe the part with milk and water first. Then put in a seton to the back of the neck, first smearing the tape with blistering ointment. Apply cold water to the head if it is very much affected, with a wet cloth or with a watering-pot. Give calomel and jalap to act on the bowels and liver, also a pill (one-half grain to one grain tartar emetic), twice a day. When the urgent symptoms have disappeared the dog will require supporting with beef tea and tonics.

3. Chest Distemper—Should there be inflammation, it sometimes becomes necessary to bleed, but it is better to avoid any such lowering measure, and use antimony or ipecacuanha. Mix one grain of either of these with half a grain of opium; give twice or three times a day. If the trouble is long continued apply a blister to the chest, or rub in mustard mixed with vinegar. Should the breathing be more rapid than the pulse, stimulants will be required, such as the bark and ammonia mixture in No. 5.

4. Distemper of the belly, attended with purging, requires the use of astringents. Opium is the best. The following has no equal: Prepared chalk, two drams; laudanum, one ounce; mucilage of acacia, one ounce; tincture of ginger, two drams; water, five and one-half ounces. Give a tablespoonful every time the bowels are relaxed. The diet should consist of boiled rice with milk or broth, and in case of much thirst give rice-water only.

If the bowels are confined, and, as generally the case, attended with "the yellows," take calomel, 3 grains to 5 grains; rhubarb and aloes, of each 5 grains to 10 grains. Mix and form into a ball with water, giving twice a day till it acts freely. Should bile begin to flow, there is still greater care required to avoid checking the diarrhœa on the one hand, while on the other the exhaustion caused by it is often very great. Broth, thickened with rice or flour, must be given often, by force if necessary. Where there is great exhaustion from diarrhœa, arrow-root and port wine will prove beneficial.

5. Malignant distemper is less difficult to control than that in the head. The great thing is to avoid reducing the system in the early stage. A mild dose of oil given as described in No. 1 will be beneficial. After this, the less done the better till the usual weakness shows itself. There is no chance of recovery unless by resorting to strong tonics and

good food. For this purpose there is no remedy like port wine or bark of ammonia. The former may be given, mixed with an equal part of water, and with the addition of a little spice, such as nutmeg or ginger. For the latter, take a decoction of bark, 1 oz.; aromatic spirit of ammonia, 1 dram; compound tincture of bark, 1 dram. Mix and give twice a day to a large dog, or half to a small one. If the bowels are relaxed, give the dog the astringent mixture, as in No. 4. Rest is absolutely necessary for the dog.

GENERALLY PRESCRIBED MEDICINES AND THEIR ACTION ON THE DOG.

Aperients.

To quicken or increase the evacuation from the bowels, aperients or purges are given. Their mode of operation vary a good deal. Some cause an immense watery discharge, which, as it were, washes out the bowels; others act merely by exciting the muscular coat of the bowels to contract; while a third set combine the action of the other two. Some purges act upon and stimulate the small intestines, while others pass through without affecting them and act upon the large bowels alone, and others again act upon the whole canal, showing that the various purges act also on different parts of the canal.

There is another point of difference in purges, depending on their influencing the liver, in addition, which mercurial purgatives surely do, as well as rhubarb and some others, which effect is partly due to their absorption into the circulation. They may be made to act by injecting into the veins, with the same effect and results as though swallowed and subsequently passed into the bowels. Purgatives are classed according to the degree of their effect—into drastic purges, that act severely, and laxatives, acting mildly.

1.   Purgative Injection—Castor oil, ½ oz.; spirit of turpentine, 2 drams ; gruel, 6 to 8 oz.   Mix.

2.   A Good Aperient Ball—Blue pill, ½ scruple ; compound extract of colocynth, 1 scruple ; powdered rhubarb, 5 grains ; oil of aniseed, 2 drops.   Mix.   Give to a large dog; but for a small one, give one-half or one-third.

3.   Strong Aperient Ball—Calomel, 4 grains ; jalap, 14 to 20 grains ; linseed meal and water, one or two boluses, according to size.

4.   Castor Oil Mixture—Castor oil, ½ pt.; laudanum, ½ oz.; oil of aniseed, 1 dram ; oil, 2 oz.   Mix, and give according to the size of dog, from one to three tablespoonfuls.

Anti-spasmodics.

Anti-spasmodics, as their name implies, are remedies which are intended to counteract excessive muscular action, called *spasm*, or when in the limbs, *cramp*.

1.   Anti-spasmodic Injection—Laudanum, sulphuric ether and spirit of turpentine, each 1 to 2 drams ; gruel, 3 to 6 oz.   Mix.

2.   Anti-spasmodic Mixture—Camphor mixture, 1 oz.; sulphuric ether and laudanum, of each ½ to 1 dram.   Mix. Give every two hours till spasms cease.

Alteratives.

To produce a fresh and healthy action in place of previous disordered functions, alteratives are given.   It is only by the results that the precise mode of action can be understood, and the utility of these medicines recognized.

1.   Plummer's pill, 2 to 5 grains ; extract of hemlock, 2 to 3 grains.   Mix, and give every night.

2.   Cod liver oil, from a teaspoonful to a tablespoonful, with one or two drops of wine of iron twice a day.

3.   Stinking hellebore, 5 to 8 grains ; powdered rhubarb,

2 to 4 grains. Mix, and form into a pill. Give every night.

4. Podophyllin, ⅛ grain; compound rhubarb pill, 3 grains. Mix, and give once or twice a week until the liver acts freely.

5. Liquor Arsenicalis—Dose, 7 drops to an average-size dog. Specially recommended for dogs rendered gross from want of work and over-feeding.

Anodynes.

To soothe the general nervous system, or stop diarrhœa, and sometimes to relieve spasm, as in colic or tetanus, anodyne medicines are given. Opium is the principal anodyne used in canine medicine, and may be used in quite large doses.

Anodyne Prescriptions.

1. For Long-continued Purging—Diluted sulphuric acid, 3 drams; tincture of opium, 2 drams; compound tincture of bark, 1 oz.; water, 6½ oz. Mix. Give tablespoonful every four hours.

2. For Slight Purging—Prepared chalk, 2 drams; aromatic confection, 1 dram; tincture of opium, 5 to 8 drams; rice-water, 7 oz. Mix. After every loose motion give two tablespoonfuls.

3. Castor oil, 2 oz.; tincture of opium, 1 oz. Mix by shaking. Give one tablespoonful night and morning while the bowels are loose.

Astringents.

Astringents, whether applied immediately or by absorption into the circulation, cause contraction in those living tissues with which they come in contact, whether in the interior or exterior of the body. They are divided into astringents applied locally to external, ulcerated or wounded surfaces, and those administered by the mouth.

1. Astringent Ball, useful in Diabetes or Hemorrhage—Powdered opium, 2 to 3 grains; gallic acid, 4 to 6 grains; alum, 5 to 10 grains; powdered bark, 10 grains; linseed-meal, enough to form a ball for a large dog, or divide in two for a small one.

2. Astringent Ointment for Piles — Gallic acid, 10 grains; goulard extract, 15 drops; lard, 1 oz. Mix.

3. Astringent Washes for the Eyes—Goulard extract, 1 dram; water, 1 oz. Mix. Or, nitrate of silver, 2 to 8 grains; water, 1 oz. Mix, and drop into the eyes with a quill; or wine of opium to be dropped into the eye.

4. Sulphate of zinc, 5 to 8 grains; water, 2 oz. Mix.

Blisters.

In the application of blisters to the skin of the dog, great care should be taken to muzzle him, and remove the muzzle only at feeding-time.

Before blistering cut the hair off with scissors from the part to be blistered.

Sweating Application for Enlarged Growths.

Lard, one ounce; red iodide of mercury, one drachm; mix. Rub in a little every day until producing a watery discharge, then desist for a few days, repeating when necessary; or paint with tincture of iodine every day until the desired effect is produced.

Emetics.

Sometimes emetics are required for dogs, but not often. Vomiting being a natural process with him, he seldom needs provoking. Emetics, if had recourse to too often, will cause his stomach to become so irritable that neither food nor medicine will remain on it. Their administration should be kept carefully within the bounds of absolute necessity.

1. Common Salt Emetic—Give a drench of one teaspoonful of salt to half the quantity of mustard dissolved in half a pint of warm water.

2. Strong Emetic—Powdered ipecacuanha, 4 to 5 grains; tartar emetic, one-half to one grain; mix; dissolve in a little warm water and give as a drench, to be followed by a half-pint of lukewarm water in a quarter of an hour.

Liniments or Embrocations.

This most beneficial remedy in use, when applied to the skin for the purpose of producing counter irritation, and specially useful in chronic rheumatism, colic, etc., is as follows: Liquid ammonia (strong), laudanum, spirits of turpentine, soap liniment, each one-half ounce; mix.

Caustics.

Substances which burn away the living tissues of the body, by the decomposition of their elements, are caustics, and are of two kinds: first, the actual cautery, consisting of the application of a burning iron, and known as firing; second, potential cautery, by means of mineral caustics, such as lunar caustic, corrosive sublimate, potash, etc.

Firing is seldom practiced on dogs, but it may sometimes be had recourse to with advantage. A very thin iron should be used. To stop bleeding from warts that have been cut from the mouth with the knife, or in a similar way for piles.

1. Lunar Caustic, or Nitrate of Silver—This should be kept handy in a wooden vessel made especially for it—valuable to the veterinary surgeon.

2. Blue Stone, or Sulphate of Copper—Should be rubbed freely into the parts affected. It is valuable for unhealthy sores, etc.

Corrosive Sublimate is used to remove warts, but should be left to the use of practiced surgeons.

Expectorants

Excite and promote a discharge of mucous from the lining membrane of the bronchial tubes, relieving inflammation and allaying cough.

1. Ipecacuanha Powder and Powdered Opium—Each one grain—confection enough to make a pill—give every six hours.

2. Expectorant Balls—Ipecacuanha powder, 1 to 1½ grains : powdered rhubarb, 1 to 3 grains ; compound squill pill, 1 to 2 grains ; powdered opium, ½ to 1 grain ; linseed meal and water enough to make a ball. Give night and morning.

3. An Expectorant for a Recent Cough—Almond emulsion, 1 oz.; tincture of lobelia, 10 to 15 drops ; ipecacuanha wine, 5 to 10 drops ; extract of conium, 2 to 3 grains. Mix. To be given two or three times a day.

4. An Expectorant Mixture for Chronic Cough—Syrup of poppies, 1 dram ; diluted sulphuric acid, 5 to 10 drops ; Friar's balsam, 10 to 15 drops ; mucilage, ½ oz.; water, ½ oz. Mix, and give two or three times a day.

Cordials.

Medicines acting as warm temporary stimulants, augmenting strength and spirits when depressed, are cordials. They often relieve an animal from the effects of over-exertion.

1. Cordial Drench—Sal volatile, 15 to 30 drops ; infusion of gentian, ½ to 1 dram ; tincture of cardamons, ½ to 1 dram ; camphor mixture, 1 oz. Mix.

2. Cordial Balls—Ginger, 20 to 40 grains ; powdered caraway seeds, ½ to 1½ drams ; oil of cloves, 3 to 8 drops. Mix, and give 10 grains for a dose.

Diuretics.

Diuretics are remedies which promote the secretion and

discharge of urine, the effect produced by each medicine being done in a different manner. Some act directly on the kidneys by sympathy with the stomach, while others are taken up by the blood-vessels, and, in their elimination from the blood, cause an extra secretion of urine. In either case their effect is to diminish the watery part of the blood, and thus promote the absorption of fluid effused into any of the cavities or into the cellular membrane, in the various forms of dropsy.

1. Diuretic and Alterative—Nitre, 4 grains; iodide of potassium, 3 grains; digitalis, ½ grain; extract of gentian, 5 grains. Mix, and give twice a day.

2. Diuretic Ball — Digitalis, ½ to 1 grain ; ginger, 4 grains; nitre, 6 grains; linseed-meal and water to form a ball. Give night and morning.

Worm Medicines.

1. Male fern-root, 1 to 3 drams; oil, 10 to 30 drops, in tape-worm.

2. Spirit of turpentine, 1 to 4 drams; tie up in a piece of bladder and give as a ball, for obstinate case of tape-worm.

3. Arica-nut powdered; give 2 grains for every pound of the dog's weight. Good for worms.

Febrifuges.

Fever medicines allay fever, by increasing the secretions of urine and sweat, and reducing the action of the heart.

1. Fever Mixture—Sweet spirits of nitre, 3 drams ; min-dererus spirit, 1 oz.; nitre, 1 dram ; camphor mixture, 6½ ozs. Mix. Dose—Give two tablespoonfuls every six hours.

2. Febrifuge Pill—Calomel, 1 to 3 grains ; nitre, 3 to 5 grains; digitalis, ½ grain—confection to form a pill. To be given every night.

3. Tartar emetic, ⅙ grain ; nitre, 3 to 5 grains—confection to form pill. Give night and morning.

Washes or Lotions.

Mange Wash—Calvert's carbolic was diluted with twenty times its bulk of water, and rubbed into the roots of the hair, in red mange.

Ointments

Are greasy applications, by which means certain substances are brought in contact with the vessels of the skin.

1. Digestive Ointment—Venice turpentine, $1\frac{1}{2}$ ozs.; beeswax, $\frac{3}{4}$ oz.; lard, 2 ozs.; red precipitate, 1 oz.   Mix.

2. Mange Ointment—Lard, 1 oz.; green iodide of mercury, 1 dram.   Mix.   Rub a small quantity every other day to the affected parts.

Be careful not to leave any superfluous ointment on the surface of the body.   Never dress more than one-fourth of the dog's body at one time.

Tonics.

Tonics increase the vigor of the whole body permanently, while stimulants only act for a short time.   They are useful after low fever.

1. Distemper Tonic—Compound tincture of bark, one dram; aromatic spirit of ammonia, one drachm; decoction of yellow bark, one ounce; mix.

2. Tonic Pills—Ginger, two to three grains; bisulphide of quinine, one to three grains; extract of gentian sufficient to make a bolus   give twice a day.

3. Tonic Mixture—Decoction of yellow bark, seven ounces; compound tincture of bark, one ounce; mix.

Dose—Two tablespoonfuls two or three times a day.

Stomachics

Are prescribed particularly to increase the tone of the stomach.

1. Stomachic Draught—Compound infusion of gentian,

one ounce; tincture of cardamons, one-half dram; tincture of ginger, five drops; mix. To be given twice during the day.

2. Stomachic Pill—Powdered rhubarb, two grains; extract of gentian, five grains; mix, and give twice a day.

Styptics.

Remedies having a tendency to stop the flow of blood from either internal or external surfaces, are known as styptics. They are made use of by either the mouth or by direct application to the part, in the shape of a lotion, and also by the actual cautery, which is the best for external bleeding.

Internal Styptics—For bloody urine, or bleeding from the lungs: Tincture of matico, $\frac{1}{2}$ to 1 oz.; superacetate of lead, 12 to 24 grains; vinegar, 2 drams; water, 7 to $7\frac{1}{2}$ oz. Mix. To a full-sized dog give two tablespoonfuls two or three times a day.

Administration of Remedies.

It is often very difficult to administer physic in any shape without some little patience and knowledge of the temper of the dog. Even the keeper of a large, powerful dog of a savage temper, can with difficulty control him. A resolute man with his hands properly guarded by gloves, can easily handle a dog of less than 40 or 50 pounds weight.

To give a pill or bolus to a small dog, place him gently into the lap of the operator, and laying hold of the space between the canine teeth and the molars on each side, with thumb and forefinger of the left hand, force the mouth open and drop the pill into the throat with the right hand, following it rapidly with the forefinger, and pushing it down as far as can be reached with the finger. Keep the mouth closed for a few seconds to give the pill time to reach the stomach. To treat a large dog, he must be backed into a corner, then straddle over him and put a thick cloth into his mouth;

bring the ends of this over his nose and hold with the left hand. An assistant then takes hold of the lower jaw with the aid of another cloth, if necessary, and wrenches the jaw apart; the right hand of the operator pushes the pill or bolus down the throat, being careful, as before, to keep the head up and the jaws closed for a few seconds. The manner of drenching is either to pour the fluid down, using the cheek as a funnel, or to open the mouth as for a pill or bolus, and pour it down the throat by means of a sauce-ladle or water-bottle. Keep the mouth closed directly the fluid is received, to force the dog to swallow it.

Mange—No. 1.

This disagreeable and loathsome disease, although very prevalent, is but imperfectly understood, from inattention and want of knowledge of location and treatment. The dog rapidly becomes weakened and debilitated, and is too often abandoned by his owner to his fate. By adhering to the following directions the disease will rapidly yield, your pet and companion will become again a sprightly creature, bounding before you in healthy, agile life.

The most common form of the mange is produced by the presence of a small parasite, invisible to the naked eye, and similar to the parasite which appears as the itch, on the human body; and can be conveyed to the healthy from the diseased dog by simple contact, the parasite readily leaving the emaciated victim to fasten upon a healthy subject. The dog, when perceived to be affected, by the fact of scratching, should be examined, and there will be seen small, red points, like flea-bites. These eventually pustulate, and ex-ude a thin, irritating liquid or matter. There are many recipes. The best and simplest is :

Take Ung. Hydrarg..................... ½ oz.
Oil of Tar........................... ½ oz.

Sulphur Sub........................ 8 oz.

Whale Oil, about.................... 8 oz.

Mix thoroughly, and after shaving the hair from the part affected, and washing well the entire body of the dog, apply carefully and well. After the expiration of three days, wash off and apply in the same manner, and again in less than a week, if it seems necessary.

This remedy is within the reach of every one, and I have found it absolutely efficacious.

Mange—No. 2.

This species of mange, being deeper in the skin, is not as contagious as the first form. Dogs infected may associate with healthy animals, yet not extend the disease. For this reason many persons have denied the contagiousness of the mange.

This feature in follicular scabies is accounted for by the habits and situation of the parasite. It only leaves the body of the dog when carried off by the fluid thrown out in the follicle. The slightest accidental contact suffices for its transference from the diseased to the healthy dog, and spreads with remarkable energy.

Symptoms—First, hot tumefactions of the skin take place and are usually patched with red, and blotchy. Soon small pimples show themselves, rapidly becoming pustular, break and exude serum, and (in extreme cases) pus, which forms in scabs or crusts. The skin becomes thick and chapped, as in common mange. The disease usually begins on the head, extending thence all over the body. It is very obstinate in yielding to treatment and is of long duration.

Treatment—The best results have been attained by the use of the following :

Acid Acetic...................... 2 drams

Oil of Terebinth................... 2 drams

Oil of Tar.............................. ½ oz
Ung. Hydrargi .... 1 oz
Sulphur .... 8 oz
Whale Oil........................10 oz

Mix the whole thoroughly and rub the affected parts for five minutes. In forty-eight hours wash off with soft soap and warm water. When dry apply to the surface whale oil; the following day repeat the ointment—dressing without washing. Repeat the operation in a week.

CONTENTS.